THE ORDER OF THE OWED
BOOK TWO

Inconvenient marriage

CARIN HART

For those who want to take a broken playboy and turn him into a man whimpering at your feet all while knowing that he can be as fierce as any wolf on the hunt—especially when you're the one he's chasing after...

PLEASE NOTE

Thank you for checking out *Inconvenient Marriage*!

The moment Bas showed up on page in *Bloody Wedding*, ready to help Adrian gun down Desmond, and then how he insisted on using himself as bait to piss off Jack Collins so that Adrian could rescue Loni, I couldn't wait to tell you his story—and this is it!

Inconvenient Marriage includes: a secret society that has its own laws and plays outside of any rules; explicit sex scenes without any protection (and no pregnancy or scares, though Plan B is referenced); liberal use of the 'my wife' trope; so many f-bombs because Sebastien reeeeally likes the word 'fuck'; on-page murder; off-page murder (including a staged suicide); DV/grooming (from the antagonist); blackmail; blood play; orgasm denial; dubcon; primal chase; minor choking/hand necklace; knives; smoking; drinking; allusions to sex work (approved mistresses for the Order's members); and mentions of stalking/tracking/breaking and entering by the hero.

I also want to let you know that I can be pretty cruel. Enjoy the spicy prologue because, after that, buckle up for a bit of a slow burn ;)

Happy reading!

xoxo,
Carin

Marriage Agreement Between
Sebastien Reynolds & Annaliese Crawford

Section I — Purpose of Agreement

The purpose of this contract is to establish a temporary marital union between the undersigned parties for the duration of one (1) year, beginning on the date of signing.

This agreement does not constitute a lifelong marital expectation unless mutually renegotiated at the end of the year.

Section II — Living Arrangements

- Each party may maintain separate living quarters, with no obligation to cohabitate.
- Shared residence may occur is necessary for public appearance.
- Neither party may enter the other's private residence without explicit permission.

Section III — Public Presentation

- Both parties agree to present as a unified, amicable married couple during all Order events.
- Any public conflict will be handled privately and delayed until after the event.
- Both parties agree to maintain discretion regarding former intimate partners.

Section IV — Financial Arrangements

- All current debts of Annaliese Crawford remain her responsibility unless otherwise negotiated.
- Household or event-related expenses shall be covered by Sebastien Reynolds for the duration of the contract.
- Neither party shall interfere with the other's financial autonomy without consent.

Section V — Intimacy Clause

- No sexual intimacy is required as a condition of marriage.
- Should either party request intimacy the other may decline freely without penalty.
- If intimacy is mutually desired, it must remain consensual, private, and free of obligation.
- No expectation of monogamy is required, though discretion is preferred.

Section VI — Termination

This contract shall terminate automatically at the end of one year unless both parties agree in writing to extend or convert the marriage into a permanent union.

"BAS"

Sebastien Reynolds   _Annaliese Crawford_

Sebastien Reynolds   **Annaliese Crawford**

PROLOGUE

THREE MONTHS AGO

SEBASTIEN

The Last Prayer isn't the kind of place you come to forget. The opposite, really. It's the kind of dive you hunker down in to fucking disappear so the world forgets *you*.

Dim lights. Peeling paint. Smoke in the air despite the 'no smoking' signs posted on the walls and in the bathroom. Some dented jukebox stands near the back, playing songs about heartbreak, homicide, or some haunting combination of both. No one looks like they want to be here. Shit, most men in the Order wouldn't even be caught dead in here.

Of course, that's one of its selling points for me. It's why I like it.

It's why, when I need a break from the eyes on me down at the Court, I take a ride about ten minutes out of Harmony Heights—firmly in Sackerville—and lean my bike up next to the others parked out front. The Last Prayer… guy named Jones owns the joint, and he'll serve you a beer with a glare, never pretending this seedy ass bar is anything but what it appears to be.

Good. Then I don't have to be anything different, either.

In the Last Prayer, no one cares who I am. Sebastien Reynolds, second son of a founding family, Order royalty, and consistent disappointment. I can be Bas, with my bike helmet parked on the stool next to me as a warning for other patrons to keep their distance, and my motorcycle gloves covering up the ruined skin on my palm.

Sackerville is too close to Harmony Heights for me to risk flashing my Order brand around. The first two bar fights I ever got into had something to do with a townie thinking I'm high and mighty because I'm one of the Owed, but I sure as fuck don't look like it. They expect slicked-back hair and a suit. Me? I have helmet hair and you'll never catch me without my road jacket.

I fit in here, and sometimes that's all I need. A break from being a Reynolds and all the expectations that carries—plus all the ways I've failed to live up to them. I wasn't looking for anything else tonight.

Doesn't mean it didn't find me, though.

I'm two beers in, pretending I'm not listening to the bartender talk to the owner about a leaking pipe somewhere in the back, when the air shifts. A shiver runs down my back, not because the door outside opened to mid-December weather, but because I can sense someone hovering a few steps behind me.

They hesitate, seeing the helmet on the stool next to me. Letting out a soft breath, they shift away from me, climbing on top of the empty one on the other side of my helmet.

I glance at her, then nearly snap my neck doing a double-take.

She's a beauty all right. Shiny brown hair falling in waves down her back, a delicate face with a sloped nose and pretty brown eyes. There's innocence in her expression, something pure that extends to the simple white fitted tee she's wearing over a pair of tight light blue jeans. She has a puffy black coat crumpled up on her lap. Realizing it's not very comfortable the way the stools are posted so close to the bar, she follows my lead, laying her coat on another empty stool.

My first impression is that she doesn't belong in this hellhole. There are plenty of women at the Last Prayer, but it was easy to ignore all of them... until her. Now I'm watching her closely out of the corner of my eye, picking up on some details I didn't notice at first.

Her eyes are brown, but they're also rimmed with red. Her hair is fluffed out, like she's run nervous fingers through the length a hundred times before she forced herself to walk into the bar. Her knee is bouncing. Her gaze darts over to me one, twice, and I can sense when she's gotten a good look at me, too.

I know what kind of face I have. One that, no matter how I mess it up, the fucking *prettiness* of it shines through. When I was younger, I used it to my advantage.

Now, only a year away from thirty, I'm a little choosier about who I smile for.

I smile at her.

She chokes on a breath before quickly turning her attention to the bartender. While I'd been scoping her out, he'd come by to take her order. She murmurs something—some kind of cocktail that I doubt they serve up in here—but the bartender nods anyway. Two minutes later, he's placed a drink in front of her.

She touches the side of her neck with unsteady fingers before lifting the glass, taking a sip. By the time she winces like the drink hurt, I can't bring myself to look away.

So, instead, I shift my position, turning toward her. I clear my throat. "Bad day?"

She doesn't glance up. "Please don't."

Interesting. "Don't what?"

"Talk to me. Flirt with me. Try to be the nice guy who sees a lonely girl at a bar and thinks she'll be an easy target."

My jaw flexes. I just wanted to check in with her, but… "I didn't say that."

"You didn't have to." She takes another sip, blinking too fast. Shit. Those aren't tears, are they? "I can't handle kindness tonight."

I hate to hear that. Especially since it's obviously what she needs. And I'm the sort of guy who could give it to her. Sure, I know my rep. I've had my fair share of women, but despite what half the town thinks, I'm not a user. I'm not a player. If you need a shoulder to cry on, I've got a leather-clad one to lend you. And if you need to lose yourself for a night… I'm excellent at doing that, too.

But she doesn't know me. I don't know her. I've never seen her at the Last Prayer before—I would've remembered—so she probably thinks I'm just another barhound hitting on her.

I should leave her alone. I should… but that's not who I am. "Then what are you here for?" I ask quietly.

She finally turns so I can look her dead in her face.

Holy shit.

Up close, she's beautiful in a way that feels way too dangerous. Like her beauty is the thing that got her hurt. Like she's been trying to put herself back together all evening and hasn't quite managed it, but someone *did* do some damage, and I have a sudden need to find out who and beat the shit out of him.

It gets even worse because her voice cracks when she whispers, "I don't want to remember his name anymore."

Ah. Now I get it. Now I understand.

I don't know who the bastard is, but I hate him instantly. I hate him, and I'm so fucking jealous that it burns the inside of my throat.

"Let me guess. You're here because you want distraction," I ask.

Her breath shakes even as she nods. "I do. Just for tonight, that's the only thing I want."

Then she came to the right damn place.

Ignoring my beer, I rise up from my stool and move so that I'm next to her. With an inviting twist to my grin,

I hold out a hand I don't expect her to take. Still, it's there if she wants it.

And so am I.

She stares at my glove, trembling. For a heartbeat, I think she's going to refuse. Just shake her head, mumble something under her breath as her cheeks go pink, then drown her sorrows in her cocktail.

Only that's not what happens. As though she's made her mind up about something, she slides her fingers into mine—and something in my chest pulls tight. It's a perfect fucking fit.

Before either of us can think twice about what we're doing, I guide her past the bar, down the hallway, toward the bathroom. It'll be dark and private, without meaning we have to leave. I don't know if she has a car. Me? I came here on my bike. We need somewhere warm to get acquainted. The bathroom will do.

Once inside, she takes her hand back, planting both palms against my chest. She pushes me near the first stall, following me in. While I marvel at the change that's come over her, she reaches behind her, engaging the lock.

And then she grabs my t-shirt with both hands, yanks me down toward her, and kisses me.

Hard. Desperate. Like she's drowning and I'm the air she craves.

My hands find her waist, her hips, her jaw. I don't touch her roughly. I don't take more than she gives. But she's giving me a hell of a lot. Enough that I have to brace her against the back door of the bathroom stall as she continues to fist both hands in my shirt, unable or unwilling to release me.

There's only one way this is ending. I know it, and I think she does, too.

Just in case, I have to make sure we're on the same page.

"Tell me to stop," I groan against her mouth.

She shakes her head, pulling away from me so I can see how serious she is. "Don't you dare."

Thank fucking God. "Okay. Then tell me what you need."

"You," she breathes. "Tonight? All that I need is *you*."

And that's the only answer that *I* need.

I press her gently back against the door, let her feel exactly how much I want her, how desperate my body is for hers as I squeeze a tit through her shirt. She whimpers; soft, broken, and so goddamn sweet it almost tears me apart.

I've been with women before. Too many to count. And yet… there's something about this one that has me ready to fuck through my jeans.

I stumble back, taking her with me. My upper calves slam into the toilet. As quickly as I can, I unbutton my jeans, yanking them down past my ass. My boxer briefs are next. I'm not surprised to see my erection spring free. I started getting hard the moment she put her hand in mine.

I stroke the heated flesh of my cock, the leather of my glove doing jackshit to cool me down. Not when she's biting her lip, brown eyes gleaming in the flickering fluorescents of the Last Prayer's bathroom. I can't tell what that look on her face means. Whether she's impressed by what I'm packing, or if she's having second thoughts.

Maybe she is. Maybe she's a good girl who isn't made for wild bathroom sex in a dirty bar. Maybe—

She shoves my chest again, stronger than I expect. I have no choice but to drop down on the toilet seat, cock pointing straight to the ceiling, I'm that fucking hard. She grips me, replacing my rough stroke with one so incredibly soft yet possessive, I've got to flex my ass cheeks to keep from spilling all over her hand.

"Yes," she whispers. "This is exactly what I need."

I reach up, fisting her hair. Staying seated because, damn it, that's where she put me, I yank her down to me, stealing another kiss from those luscious lips. I'm probably smudging her lipstick all over my face, but I could give a shit. She tastes too damn good not to enjoy her mouth.

I want to enjoy her *everywhere*.

She doesn't want to play, though. Oh, no. With my pants already down, she reaches for her own button.

Okay. Yeah. We're definitely doing this, and I can think of a hundred reasons why I shouldn't, but with my cock in control, the only thing I'm thinking about now is working it inside of… of…

I untangle my fingers from her hair, cupping the back of her neck for a second to catch her attention.

When I have it, I ask, "What's your name?"

It's a pant. A moan.

A *demand…* and one my pretty brunette outright refuses.

"Not tonight," she whimpers. "No names tonight… just this."

So tomorrow morning, then? I have no doubt in my mind that she has to know who I am. Everyone in Harmony Heights knows the train wreck that is Sebastien Reynolds, whether they're in the Order or not. Sackerville is different; then again, so is she. I've just got that certain kind of reputation; the same reputation that led this beauty to accept what I was offering her, confident that I'll bang her in this bathroom. I doubt she's Order-affiliated—not a Used or an Offering, either—but if all she wants is to fuck some other guy out of her head, well… I'd hate to disappoint.

No names. Fair enough.

"Then I'll call you 'love," I tease, tugging on her jeans, desperate to get them off of her, "and, for tonight, I'll be yours."

"Thank you," she whispers, and for the next few minutes, that's all either of us says.

Once I have her jeans down around her ankles, she kicks them, allowing her to climb up on top of my lap. Part of me expected her to ride me cowgirl-style, back to my front so that she could get all of the pleasure of fucking me without the intimacy of looking into my face.

Like I said, I know what I look like. Delicate boyish features that don't belong on a man my age, though they definitely work to attract women. Pouty lips. A sharp jaw and soft cheeks. Eyes that one of the Used told me reminded her of melted chocolate, and dark blond hair that looks pretty damn good even after a fifteen-mile ride.

But if you look closer, there are the marks I've worked hard to earn over the years. There's a divot missing in one cheek. When I was twenty, I broke my nose twice in the same year, and now it has a slight crook to it. Some wannabe Order member pulled a knife on me, nearly taking out one of my eyes after he found out I fucked his girl. She was a Used. That's what they're there for. To pleasure the Owed… it was his fault for getting into a relationship with one of the Used without giving her a ring. The only way out of that life is to get married—preferably to an Order member back in Jack Collins's days—and they were barely dating. Of course I fucked her. Hell, she requested me when I visited the backroom of the Court, so obviously I was in the right.

When I got him on his back and slit his throat during the fight, blood dripping into my eye because he missed, poor bastard learned that the hard way.

I'm not an Order enforcer, but I learned long ago to fight back. Half the time, I fight *first*. My lifestyle means that I'm used to women falling for my looks before they see the truth of who Bas Reynolds really is.

I expect her to keep that element of anonymity—and I'm wrong. Instead of just wanting a man to fuck the memory of another out of her head, she climbs on top of me, locking faces as she throws one arm around my neck.

The other hand goes to my erection. With her legs

straddling me, spread out over my lap, she guides me into her before sinking all the way down on top of me. I grit my teeth, eyes nearly rolling back into my skull as her tight pussy squeezes me.

She holds onto me like she's trying to crawl into my skin and outrun whatever memory she brought with her. And when she starts to move, slowly riding me once she adjusts to the way that I've filled her up, I have the sudden urge to clutch her to me and never let her go.

She's wonton. That's the only way to describe her. I'm grunting, she's panting, and she throws her second arm around my neck, burying my face in her chest.

I suck on her tit through the thin fabric of her t-shirt. I leave wet circles, turning the material see-through, as she tugs on my hair, gasping for breath. My hands go to her waist again. I don't want to move that much, afraid my bare ass will slip off the slick, porcelain toilet seat, but I use my strength to lift her, helping her bounce up and down on top of me.

I don't even need to. She fucks me like a woman possessed, as though she's searching for something she hopes she can find with me at the Last Prayer.

"Easy, love…" I murmur against her throat, even as she arches into me like she wants me to mark her with my tongue, my teeth. "Slow down. Even if anyone comes in here, they won't care about what we're doing. There's no rush."

For me, maybe.

"No," she breathes. "Don't slow down. Don't stop. Just keep… *yes*… just keep doing *that*."

I curse under my breath and grasp her chin, kissing

her again. It's harder this time, letting her know just how badly I crave her at this moment. She gasps into my mouth, digging her nails into my shoulders, through my jacket, and I have to force myself to keep a lid on the desperation clawing through me before I nut and end his for both of us.

"Oh, love. You feel fucking incredible," I growl, my voice lower than I've ever heard it.

Her whole body shivers on top of my cock.

"Say that again," she begs. "Please… say it again."

I brush my lips along her jaw. "You feel so fucking good. Like you were made for me."

Her breath stutters. She whines, eyes closing shut.

I curl a hand at her waist to hold her steady. "Look at me," I demand.

She snaps open her eyes, and I peer into them. They're wide, glassy, almost afraid of how much she wants this.

Wants *me*.

"That's it," I say, encouraging her, panting softly as she squeezes me again. "Just like that."

When she pulls me closer, a soft, desperate sound catching in her throat as she throws her head back, I nearly lose it. I cage her in my arms, not trapping her, simply keeping her upright, keeping her with me before she slides off my lap.

She grits her teeth, and I know exactly why she has.

"Uh-uh, love. You don't have to be quiet with me," I tell her. "You can let go."

She shakes her head, breathless. "You don't under-stand. This feels—" Her fingers tremble at the back of my neck. "*You* feel... I didn't know it could... fuck me."

"I'm happy to," I rasp. "You got me, love? You let me make you forget all about him."

Did she hear me? Maybe, or maybe her last bounce felt even better than the one before it because she tosses her head back again and, this time, she moans so loudly, it echoes around the stall.

At the same moment, she shudders on top of me, her body tightening in my hands before she slumps forward, clinging to me as her soft breaths hit my ear. The way her body clenched as she climaxed... I'm not that far behind her.

So I stand up. I don't even think she realized that I moved until I'm on my feet, jeans down by my knees, holding her ass cheeks as I buck into her. She gasps as I resume the fucking, giving her everything I have... and when my sac tightens, my body getting ready to blow, I give her that, too.

I should've pulled out. Coming inside of her like that... that was a mistake. I know better. The last thing I need is someone showing up at Maman and Dad's, telling my folks that I knocked them up. Of all the fucked-up things I've done, I've never had to deal with paying off the mother of my kid or bribing her to get an abortion. Oh, no. That's all Alexandre, and if there's one thing I managed not to screw up, it's that.

All of the Used I fuck are on birth control. I keep a condom in my wallet for occasions like this. I haven't forgotten to wrap up since I was eighteen and my girl at the time had a pregnancy scare. It was too risky for a

Reynolds, and I forgot that when this woman turned her sad brown eyes on me.

Great. Fucking great.

She seems to think the same thing. She scrabbles down, climbing out of my arms, dropping down to the floor. Her hand goes right between her legs, face paling when she dips her fingers inside, pulling out the evidence of just how bad I wanted her.

"Love—"

She shakes her head. "It's fine. I… don't worry about it. I'll take care of it."

I nod. Of course. If she's in the habit of banging strangers, she's probably very familiar with Plan B. "Sorry. I shouldn't have—"

"No. Don't apologize. Tonight… you gave me everything I needed. Thank you."

Huh. That 'thank you' sounds suspiciously like a goodbye.

Too bad I'm not ready to see her go just yet.

I wait until she's gathered up her jeans, stabbing her legs into one side, then the other. Mostly dressed, I follow her lead, pulling my own jeans up over my ass, tucking my spent cock back into my underwear.

Only then do I reach out, tilting her chin up. "Come home with me."

She freezes. Something… maybe fear… flashes across her face. "No. Please. I *can't.*"

Because of him. That's why. Because of the man she wanted to fuck me to forget… and I didn't do as good a job as I thought I did, huh?

That doesn't mean we have to part right away. "Then I'll walk you to your car."

"No." She steps back, shoving open the bathroom stall, putting space between us. With my jizz dripping out of her, she can't look at me anymore.

"I have to go," she whispers.

She has to go, and I let her. I don't want to spook her. I hang back as she dashes for the bathroom door, lingering long enough to notice that she left her panties on the floor. I scoop them up, shoving them in my jacket pocket like the trophy they are.

I stay exactly where I am until her panicked footsteps fade down the hall, then I drag a hand over my face, trying to do my best to forget her. I have to. A woman like that… she could make a man like me want things I can never have, but how, when she belongs to someone else?

I have to forget her—and I know I won't.

Because she did the one thing no one ever does to me.

She walked away, and if that isn't enough to snare my attention, I don't know *what* is.

ONE

SUMMONS

ANNALIESE

Three months after I ended things with him for good, Eric summons me back by text with the same number of words:

EW

Come to me.

No greeting. No explanation. No apology, as if a high-ranking member of the Order—and my hidden lover for more than two years—would ever lower himself enough to apologize to the woman he ruined.

Ruined.

He *ruined* me.

I believed him. When he told me he loved me, I believed him. When he told me I was special, I believed him. When he said that his wife was in hospice, unable to do her duties, and that when she eventually passed, I would be her replacement because we were meant to be… I believed him.

But Cicely Ward was never sick. Too naive… too enthralled… to question all of the inconsistencies, I let him keep me a secret, let him coddle me, let him turn me into the perfect mistress. I wore my hair the way he liked. I dressed in outfits that he paid for and approved. I lived in his house before I found an apartment of my own… and I ignored any sign of the woman who had been his Offering two decades before.

She didn't live with him. That much I know is true. She had her own residence; their marriage one of convenience these days, one of standing. There is no divorce in the Order of the Owed. It's 'til death do you part, and I thought her death would lead me to my happily-ever-after.

For four years, he was my client. My mentor. My friend. Then, slowly yet inevitably, he became *more*. My confidant. My boss.

My lover—until I pushed for a marriage that would never happen, and he became nothing more than the man responsible for taking an Offering and making it so that I could *never* marry a ranking member of the society.

He called me his 'good girl'. He promised me forever, but didn't hold up his end of the bargain. He *lied*, and now he thinks he can text me for the first time in months and I'll drop everything to go running to him?

I should've blocked him. Stupid Annaliese. I should've

blocked him, but when all he said as I grabbed my purse, abandoning everything else I owned behind me, was to make sure I left my keys behind on my way out, I didn't see why I should. Eric made his position clear. He would never leave Cicely, and all I could hope for was my place in his bed and whatever trinkets he thought would distract his young mistress. I refused, and he let me go as easily as if the last two years hadn't meant a thing to him.

As if *I* hadn't meant a thing to him.

Because old habits are hard to kill—even when the smarmy man who shaped them deserves to be dead and buried beneath them for his cruelty—I read the text and instantly have to resist the urge to obey. My body goes rigid, my breath tripping over itself as I stare at the three words.

For a moment, I can't breathe. It's like I'm twenty-three again, foolish enough to believe that an established member of Harmony Heights' secret society would love me for me, and not because I was twenty years his junior.

Come to me.

I delete the message without replying.

Two minutes later, another arrives.

Now.

I could leave him on read. Eric might get the hint then, or he might actually call me next. Sure, I could refuse to answer, but… damn it.

Panic mingled with perverse curiosity wins out.

I type out a two-letter message while biting down on my lip.

Ok

ERIC'S HOUSE LOOKS EXACTLY THE SAME: CLEAN WHITE stone, perfect hedges, and a gate out front that he left open since he would've known I couldn't resist before I sent my text. It's expensive without trying too hard, a house that whispers old money and even older power. The kind that only Order men from founding families can flaunt.

It's always belonged to the Wards. The house that Cicely lives in was gifted to her after their Order-arranged wedding. She kept it when their marriage turned into what it is now, and Eric returned to *his* family home.

He told me it would be ours.

I park in the circular drive, my racing heart hammering against my ribs. For two years, it *was* mine. So why doesn't it feel like I've come home to be back again?

I grab my purse; I don't want my phone or my keys out of my reach, just in case. Then, checking my lipstick and hair in the rearview mirror one last time—also out of habit—I climb out of the car. A quick brushing down of my skirt and I'm ready to go.

The front door opens before I even get the chance to knock, and there he is.

Eric Ward.

He has a staff, and I expected Jonathon to be the one to let me in. It would've given me a few more moments to compose myself before I was brought before Eric. Seeing him cast his icy blue gaze over me, smiling in approval at what he sees, I hate that a part of me preens to know that I've passed his inspection.

Of course I did. Eric spent a lot of time and effort turning me into the Annaliese I am today. All it took was one text, one summons, and I was able to slip right back into the same role.

He doesn't look any different, either. Standing in the doorway, backlit by the warm golden light of his front room, he looks every inch the polished gentleman I was fooled into believing he was. Cream-colored sweater, brown slacks, salt-and-pepper hair perfect as always. His smile is soft. Welcoming.

It's another lie.

"Please. Come in," he says.

My legs move on their own, heels *click-clack*ing against the hardwood floor as he leads me past the pristine foyer toward the den. In the entire house, it's the only one I considered to be Eric's room. It suits him, with the dark leather furniture, the heavy mahogany bookcase, the massive desk where he'd work after leaving the office, and a noticeable bar cart in one corner stocked with his preferred—and very expensive—whiskey.

I pause in the doorway. Eric sidles around me, hand swiping possessively over my ass as he lingers long enough to breathe me in. I shiver, but he's already gone.

Wearing a pleased smirk, he walks around his desk, taking the seat.

There is no seat for me. For anyone, really. After all, this is *Eric*'s space, and I was rarely invited in here. That he wants to have this discussion here makes my nerves even worse. I move to stand in front of his desk while he's sitting, but rather than feel as though my height gives me the advantage, it's more like I'm back in school, facing off against the principal.

"Annaliese." His tone is too, too familiar. "You've kept me waiting."

I swallow back the shakiness. "I left as soon as I received your text."

"I think we both know that that's not what I mean." He laughs, low and amused, only I'm not buying it. The look in his eyes… "You've been sulking, sweetheart. It's unseemly. This has gone on long enough. Come home."

"I don't live here anymore, Eric. I have my own place—"

He scoffs. "A hovel on the west side of town. Please. You know it doesn't compare."

He's not wrong. It doesn't compare, but it's not a hovel. I have a one-bedroom apartment on the third floor of a decent building full of middle-class families and bachelors trying to break into the Order's stranglehold on Harmony Heights. It's nicer than I could afford without my parents' help, but it's mine. That's the important part. It's *mine*.

"You broke up with me," I remind him. I gave him an ultimatum: marry me or lose me forever. He can't marry me, and that meant he had to end things. Sure, I fool myself into believing that I broke up with him, but I don't have any power when it comes to Eric Ward. I never have. "I loved you. I wanted to stay. But you? You pushed me away."

His practiced smile turns brittle. "You're upset. Understandable." He leans forward in his seat, resting his elbows on the top of his desk. "But I've decided I'm ready to forgive you."

I freeze. You have got to be fucking kidding me.

"And," he continues smoothly, "I'm willing to take you back."

As his mistress?

"No," I say. Quiet. *Firm.*

He cocks his head.

I shake mine.

Eric sucks in a breath. His cheeks sharpen. His jaw goes tight. "What did you say?"

He heard me. I know he did. It's just that, as a part-nered lawyer at Ward, St. James, and Marshall's firm, he's not used to anyone saying 'no' to him. Especially not me. I was his companion, his lover, his goddamn personal secretary after he convinced me to leave Mom's event planning company three years ago so I could work for him instead as some kind of glorified note-taker… I wasn't allowed to say 'no'.

It feels pretty damn good to be able to do so now.

"I'm not coming back to you."

His eyes turn frosty. "You forget who you belong to."

No. I don't. "It's not you, Eric."

Not anymore.

"You will do what you're told. Come back to me, and I'll make it all up to you."

Do what I'm told?

I *won't.*

I chose obedience over love—and made the worst fucking mistake of my life. Before Eric seduced me into sleeping with him the first time, I lived for the moments when I'd earned his approval. There wasn't anything he could tell me that I wouldn't do. I was his from the moment he first complimented an event I'd helped my mother plan, and eventually he had a piece of every part of me: heart, body, and soul.

I obeyed, and then I loved him, believing that one would lead to the other. But there's no love anymore. Not from the moment he tossed me aside like I was garbage and I licked my wounds by doing the most impulsive, reckless thing I could think of: stopping at the first dive bar I found outside of Harmony Heights, trying my first cocktail, then picking the most gorgeous guy in the bar to fuck the memory of Eric Ward's cold blue eyes out of my brain if only for the moment.

It worked. I replaced Eric's with a pair of soft brown ones, a charming smile, a dimpled cheek, and an inch-long scar over his eye that didn't detract from his prettiness. Oh, no. In the smoky haze of the Last Prayer, it only highlighted how attractive my stranger was. Three months later, I still kick myself for not taking him up on his offer to go home with him, but I'd promised myself when I left Eric for the last time, I would never willingly obey a man again.

Not the man with the dark blond hair and a body

made for sin—and not the man who is waiting expectantly behind his desk for me to give in.

Again.

No.

"You can't fix something you broke. Not like this. Not with a snap of your fingers or one of your backroom deals. I'm a person, Eric—"

"You're mine."

I was. "If this is all you wanted to talk to me about, I should be leaving."

"Talk? Sweetheart, I didn't ask you here to *talk*." He snorts softly. "Talk… no. This is my attempt to negotiate."

Always the lawyer, I think. "Negotiate what? I made my terms very clear."

"I know. You wanted me to Claim you as my Offering, forgetting the fact that I'm well past thirty, my dear, and I already have one. And you… you're not an Offering, are you?"

Bastard. He knows that I'm not. Not really. I can't be.

"That's what I thought. Return to me, Annaliese. Or would you rather be one of the Used?"

"That's what you made me," I spit out, a hint of venom finding its way into my tone.

TWO
A PLAN

ANNALIESE

Eric frowns, his sudden disapproval stinging as much as his earlier approval lifted me up. He doesn't deny it, though. The first time he took my hand, led me to his bedroom, and fucked me, he changed my life forever.

This man took everything from me. So I gave him my love. I gave him my virginity. By allowing him to choose me without Claiming me, I gave up any chance of being an Offering. No one else in the Order would settle for me as their bride, and I didn't care. I would have Eric.

Cicely has Eric.

I only ever met her once. I found out too late that part of their agreement said that she had to give him advance notice if she wanted to meet with him at his house. Cicely had their former family home, while the one I lived in with Eric was specifically his, allowing him to play house with *me*. They had an arrangement. She lived her life, he lived his, and neither interfered with the other. She had lovers of her own. Eric planned on keeping me.

Of course his wife knew about me. In the Order, it's almost expected for an Owed to have a mistress. I bet most women in my position believed that they would eventually replace their lover's wife, but I *really* did. If Cicely was on her deathbed, I just had to wait out the clock—and I held onto that silly belief until she showed up at the house while Eric was at work because she got the dates wrong and thought he'd be there.

He wasn't. *I* was. And though Cicely wasn't surprised to find me at the house, it was a shock to see the beautiful woman in her late thirties, wearing a dress not too dissimilar to mine, her blonde hair arranged in a similar style, wagging her fingers at me, saying I must be her husband's new toy.

Toy. I thought we were building a life together, and Eric referred to me as his fucking *toy*.

I confronted him that day. Begged him to tell me the truth. Pleaded with him to end things with Cicely so that we could be married. I wasn't after his money. It wasn't even about my status in the Order changing, going from an Offering to a wife. I just loved him so damn much, I wanted to be tied to him legally.

But he told me he couldn't marry me then, and as though I haven't replayed the cold way he rejected me a million times over the last three months, he has the nerve to say the same exact words again now:

"I can't marry you."

His tone is softer. Gentler. He's lost the cruel edge, but the message is the same. All I can ever be is his side piece.

I knew that. Divorce isn't a thing in the Order, but marrying again as a widow is almost expected. If Cicely died tomorrow, I'd have a chance. As long as she's alive, she'll be his wife. It's just how things are done in the Order.

"I know."

"But you still insist on pretending that I haven't claimed you in every way that counts?"

There's claimed and then there's Claimed, and I know exactly which one Eric means—and it's not the one that will help me survive Harmony Heights.

"I'm not yours. I can't be."

"Is that why you gave yourself to another man?"

Ice slithers through my veins. I'm frozen solid, his off-handed comment turning me too damn cold. "What?"

Eric's crystal blue eyes sharpen, even icier, voice dropping to something hard enough to bruise. "You think I don't know where you've been? What you've done?" Rising up from his seat, he stalks over to me. Still too stunned to move, he snatches my arm, gives me a rough shake. "The Last Prayer? Really? A *bathroom*? Classy." He shoves me away from him. "I thought I trained you better. You want to act like a whore? Maybe that's where you belong. My fellow Owed will sure as hell enjoy themselves with you when you work the back-rooms at the Court."

I stumble away from him, the force of his shove nearly knocking me off my three-inch heels. I recover—I've had the practice—but by the time I'm standing straight again, he's returned to smirking at me.

"Look at you. You didn't even deny it," he points out. "Still, I put too much time… too much money into you. So I'll be generous. Come back to me, and I won't hold your… indiscretion against you."

Indiscretion? If that's what he wants to call it. Me? I think of it as the first time I let the real Annaliese out in ages, and I had some of the best sex of my life in that crowded bathroom stall.

I never thought I'd let anyone but Eric touch me like that. Oh, how it must piss him off to know that I did—and that my motorcycle-riding stranger was *better*.

I don't tell him so. He's teetering on the edge of losing his temper, and if Jonathon isn't here, I doubt any of the help is, either. It's just him and me, and I don't know this man anymore.

I don't know if I ever did.

So, staying calm, I simply say, "No, thank you."

Another crack in his well-bred mask. Another shift in the level of tension in the den.

Without saying a word, Eric moves past me and heads to the bar cart. Bristling in ill-concealed fury, he pours himself a drink the way he always used to, as if my refusal didn't happen because he doesn't want it to.

With the glass in his hand, he sighs. "You're making this more difficult than it needs to be."

"I can't put it any plainer, Eric. We're done," I say.

He stirs the whiskey lazily, ice clinking against the glass. "No. We're not."

Eric turns toward me, leaning back against the bar, still swirling his whiskey. "I'll give you one more chance to show some loyalty. Don't make me remind you what you owe me."

Owe him? "I don't owe you anything."

"Wrong." His voice drops to a dangerous softness. "You owe me *everything*. Your reputation. Your place in the Order. Your future." He takes a small sip. "And I'll destroy all of it if you continue to defy me."

Oh, no… "You can't."

A slow, satisfied smile curves his mouth. "Silly girl. You still don't understand how this works, do you?" He sets his barely-touched glass down on the bar cart. "You think I ruined you, and maybe I have. By August, you won't have to worry about skipping another Claiming ceremony where… whoops… none of the Owed will Claim the woman that I chose as mine at your first one. You're not an Offering, Annaliese. You're mine, but if you continue to play these games, I'll up the ante. There won't be *any* Crawfords at the Claiming ceremony this year. And you know why? Because I'll get the King to send you *both* to the Court." I gasp, and he looks at me smugly. "That's right. You'll be demoted to the Used, and so will your pretty little sister."

Miranda.

No!

Miranda is only seventeen. While my dad didn't get inducted into the Order until I was twelve and in middle school, she was four and ended up being raised as the perfect Offering for a future Owed. She got lucky. She fell for Colton Dawes during their first year of high school. Now, with graduation looming in a few months, he has every intention of Claiming her when the Order holds the annual Claiming ceremony in August.

But if she gets demoted before then because Eric arranges it—because the Order is so misogynistic that, if one Crawford daughter slept around, the council would assume that the other did, too, and penalize Miranda—then my sister will lose her sweetheart *and* her future.

My heart stops.

Eric watches with obvious relish as the horror settles on my face. Then, while I gape at him, he steps closer to me, gently tucking a loose strand behind my ear like he used to. It must've fallen free from my updo when I stumbled, giving him the excuse to get even closer to me.

"Miranda's Claiming is soon, isn't it?" he reminds me. "Such a lovely girl. So excited. It would be… tragic if her reputation were compromised. If she were reassigned." His breath warms my cheek. "If she were forced to serve as a Used."

I whisper, "Eric—"

"You don't want that," he says conversationally, like we're discussing weekend plans instead of my former lover threatening me. "So behave. Come back to me. Before I make your sister pay for your stubbornness."

My legs go weak beneath me, but I don't fall. I pride

myself on that. I don't fall, though I do take a few steps away from Eric.

"I think I should go," I gasp out.

"You'll be back." He returns to the bar cart, saluting me with his drink. "You always come back."

I turn to leave, pausing only when Eric calls out, "Oh? Annaliese?"

I glance at him over my shoulder.

His expression has shadowed. "If I hear that you're fucking some random guy again? I won't text you next time I find out. I'll kill him so you understand that this… what we have? It will never be over."

That's what he thinks.

I don't know how he found out about the stranger in the first place. I purposely went as far away from Harmony Heights as I dared, hoping that anyone I met in the bar would never have heard of the Order of the Owed. I should've known better. Harmony Heights is bought and paid for by the secret society, but the King and his council's power extends further than I thought— and the Order has eyes everywhere.

I'm not surprised I was seen. I'm not really surprised that it took three months for it to get back to Eric. Knowing him, he must've only gotten the report today; otherwise I would've been summoned back to his house well before now. Whoever caught me must've decided to hold onto that little nugget until it meant something, which makes it even worse since only four people in this world know how intimately I was involved with Eric Ward: me, Eric, Cicely, and Miranda.

Miranda…

It doesn't matter how Eric found out. I doubt the man I had sex with told, since he was as far from a member of the Order as I could find—on purpose—and it's not like he's really in danger. For one, he looked like he could take care of himself. For another, if I don't know who he is, odds are Eric's informant doesn't, either. Sure, Eric's threat means that another one-night stand is off the table for the moment, but I don't care.

I only care about Miranda—and what I'm going to do next.

Before he can find another way to stop me, I walk out of the den, through the house, out the front door, and into the cold night. It's the middle of March, frigid when the sun goes down, and my light sweater isn't doing anything to fight off the chill.

That's okay. The fury running through me now that I've made my escape is doing a bang-up job.

My hands are shaking as I start the car. I force them to still so that I can make the twenty-minute drive across town without causing an accident. Somehow I manage, and by the time I'm letting myself into my apartment, my angry tears have turned into helpless sobs.

I slide down the wood and press my fists against my mouth so no sound escapes. Last thing I need right now is one of my neighbors checking to make sure that I'm okay.

But I'm not. I'm totally not.

He'll ruin Miranda.

He'll ruin both of us.

Unless—

It's a stupid plan. A reckless plan. One that someone

like me—with my need to people please added to my Type-A personality and undeniable naiveté—would only think of if she was absolutely desperate.

Now that? That's something I *am*.

Hope. I cling to it as I force myself up and into my bathroom. After splashing some cold water on my face, wiping away the remnants of the makeup I applied to meet with Eric, I stare at my reflection. I'm pale. Red-eyed. Lost, but definitely not broken.

Not yet.

There's one way out. A single loophole that the Order will honor if I can pull this off.

A husband. If I 'legally' belong to someone else, Eric can't touch me. He can't threaten my husband for touching me, either. If I'm married, my reputation secured by my husband's ranking, no one—not even the King—can demote Miranda unless she makes her own mistakes.

If one man can damn me, another can save me. It's as simple as that. It doesn't have to be a high-ranking member. In fact, since most Offerings are reserved for those at the top, I need to find a junior member, a new member, someone who's been barely inducted into the Order and doesn't rate an arranged marriage.

But if he's interested in a marriage of convenience, letting me share his name and his status until Miranda has Colton's, then I'll be the best fucking wife he can ask for.

I need an Owed to call my own. I'm not looking for someone to love. Been there, done that. In fact, I'd prefer it be someone who will be happy to act like Eric does with Cicely. A marriage in name only, though I'll do anything he requires if that's what it takes.

A man like that… there's only one place to find him. And while it might be even more dangerous with Eric's threats still echoing in my ears, I'm willing to risk it.

Tonight? I'm not going to the Last Prayer.

I'm going to the King's Court.

THREE
THE KING'S COURT

SEBASTIEN

t's good to be the King.

Whenever I go down to the King's Court—Harmony Heights' premier bar and gentleman's club—I usually sit near the bartender, nursing my drink, watching the women work the floor like sharks swimming circles around their prey. Everyone here is affiliated with the Order. The Owed sip their top shelf Scotch and choose the woman they'll follow into the backrooms, while the Used entertain the men, hoping to hook one long enough that they can become a kept woman instead of a communal mistress.

I don't have one of my own. I rotate between the Used whenever I'm feeling horny; I take a ride out of Harmony Heights when I'm looking for a little more variety and discretion.

Tonight? I'm not interested in pussy. I'm here

because Dallas asked if I wanted to go out for a drink, and even if he wasn't the King, I'd drop anything to spend time with one of my bros. These days, Connor is still busy with Haven, and it'll take a crowbar to pry Adrian off of his new wife, but Dallas… if he needs to vent, I've got an ear. If he wants to pretend he's not the most powerful man in Harmony Heights, I'll happily knock him down a peg or two. If he just wants to throw back a beer and reminisce about the old days, I can do that, too.

But he *is* the King. Most of the Owed are pointedly avoiding him; during Jack Collins' reign, it became understood that keeping under the King's radar is a smart move. That's why he's given a private booth, tucked off the side of the dance floor, with a dedicated manager to make sure the drinks keep flowing and the pick of the Used are available if he feels like fucking.

Good luck. Dallas doesn't go for the Used. Adrian didn't, either. I know they wondered why I do, especially when I don't hide how much I hate the Order… and that right there is the answer. If the Order exists to class our women into virgins and whores, I'm going to show them how the Used are just as important. Keep the Offerings. I want a woman who knows what she's doing, and I'll be the man who will treat them as more than a vessel to get off. I take the time to know them. Talk to them. It's never just about sex for me—which is why, three months later, I can't get over how the mysterious brunette from the Last Prayer used *me*.

But I'm over it. Really. I'm not obsessing over who

she was, what she was doing there, why I can't fucking get her out of my head…

I'm over it, and I've spent half the night trying to convince myself of that again, only to admit that I'm full of shit. I know better. When Hilary came by, trailing her hand over her hips, a questioning look in her big brown eyes, I flicked her off. I wasn't in the mood for any of my usual lovers.

She paused, making eyes at Dallas next. She's a bold one. When Jack was the King, he had at least four or five girls that he fucked regularly, but he had them all come to him. Most of the council take their sex out of the club. It's another reason why I purposely go to the Used. To me, they're worth it, and I especially like the upper echelon of Order society looking down on me for slumming.

That's how they see it. They made the Used, but when the women only exist to service the Owed, if they're not handpicked by a powerful member of the secret society to be their mistress, they're basically glorified whores.

In so many ways, Jack fucked Dallas up. If Hilary tried to invite Dallas to join her, he would only insult her. He wouldn't do it on purpose. He doesn't give a shit that she wears the brand on her neck which means she's Order property. Nope. Her only crime is that she isn't Lucy Wright, but tell Dallas that. Like me, he pretends that he's over her.

Like me, he's a shit liar.

Besides, he may be the all-powerful King, but sometimes he just wants to be Dal, no crown required. He'll scare all the girls off, even if his rep—as an Order enforcer, as Jack Collins' son, as the new fucking King— didn't already. Me? I'm just not into casual sex these days, though I'm sure that'll change sooner or later. Tonight, though? I'm only in the mood for one particular woman, and if I've been in a dry spell since the night I met her, I remind myself that at least the Harley-Davidson Road Glide bike I've been working on for months is halfway built.

It's stalled lately. I need a bespoke part that I ordered from a specialist I know. I should have it by the end of next week, couriered right to my front door, but if my brain is torn between imagining what my ride will look like with the new part and reliving the moment the Last Prayer temptress wrapped her arms around my neck and came all over my lap, at least I know Dallas well enough that I can carry on a mindless conversation while ignoring the way my balls ache.

I could easily take Hilary into the back, bang her on one of the chaise's set up for the Used and their lovers, and try to fuck the brunette out of my head. Or I could drink enough to get whiskey dick, sleeping it off in one of the rooms meant for the Owed.

I nudge Dallas. "Another round?"

He looks down at the bottom of his glass. He was on his second whiskey neat, but I know he can handle more than that when he's in the spirit. It isn't often that he wants to lose himself in a bottle, and if I know that yesterday was Lucy's birthday, I keep my damn mouth shut.

That's what Dallas needs from his bro, and I'm happy to give it to him.

He picks up his glass, swirling the last mouthful before downing it. "Yeah. I think I could use another."

I lift my hand, ready to signal Brucie, the manager.

Dallas shakes his head. "Nah. I'll go to the bar and get a refill. I'm fucking sick of people thinking they can serve me."

That comes with being the King. Comes with being a Reynolds in Harmony Heights, too, not that I'm going to point that out.

Why, when Dallas and I have both spent nearly thirty years trying to outrun our fates?

We've been friends since diapers, the five of us— well, *four* now—and we've all grown up in the Order. We didn't have the same childhoods, though. Adrian's parents neglected him, leaving the housekeeper in charge. My folks did the best for my brother and me before eventually giving up. Desmond's dad planned for him to be a mini-me. Connor was the only one of us who wasn't fucked up, but hell if he doesn't have his hands full with Haven now.

Dallas got the worst of it. Me and Adrian were basically born with a silver spoon in our mouths. If it wasn't for Dallas's mom being a sweetheart who protected her boy, Jack would've shoved one up Dal's ass. He hated his son. Hated that he would one day succeed him. He did everything he could to break him. Just because he's dead now, that doesn't mean that Dallas is fixed.

I know because the Order broke me, too.

So I scoff at the advantages it gave me, Adrian's

worked behind the scenes for a decade to control it, Connor ignores it, and Dallas would run from it if he thought he could get away with it.

Then there's Des. He's dead now. Sometimes I'm jealous of him. He's the only one who made it out. Sure, Adrian shot him, but that's why you don't break the bro code.

Dallas wants to go get the drinks? You got it, buddy.

"I'll take another beer."

Dallas leans over, ruffling the top of my hair as he slides out of the booth. "I saw a couple of the Used eye-fucking you. If you wanna take a few minutes in the back, I can make sure the bartender doesn't fill the order right away."

I shake my head. "Not feeling it tonight."

The look Dallas gives me says that that was the last thing he expected me to tell him. He shrugs, though, and adds, "If you change your mind, I won't be pissed if you ditch me."

I grin up at him. "Shut the fuck up and go get the drinks. I'm here with you tonight."

"Yeah, well, don't expect me to put out."

Dick, I think with affection. If he can make jokes like that with me, I've done something right tonight. If only for an hour or two, I've pulled him out of that dark place that no Collins wants to go.

When Adrian goes there, he plans. When Dallas goes there, people die.

I flip him off, biting back my smile as he chuckles. He slips into the crowd, heading toward the bar, pointedly ignoring the way it parts to let the King through.

Here's hoping he doesn't come back with a stick up his ass.

He doesn't. Less than five minutes later, Dallas returns carrying his glass and my beer. Knowing how I like it, he left the cap on.

I take out my pocket knife. With a practiced motion that has gotten me laid more times than I can count, I use the tip of the blade to pop off the cap, catching it before it hits the table top.

Dallas snorts. "Show off."

Damn right.

He sips at his booze, guarded eyes still watching the crowd. "Be careful. We've got Bait tonight."

Bait. A term for a woman who is willing to put it all on the line to catch the attention—and the wallet—of one of the Owed. In Harmony Heights, a wedding ring will do wonders to get them into the Order. It's protection. It's power.

It's obnoxious.

"What are you telling me to be careful for?" I tip my beer back, take a gulp. "Shouldn't you be worried? You're the King and all."

"Fuck you."

Yeah. I should've known better than to say that. My smart mouth has gotten me into more fights than I want to admit, and even my friends aren't immune to wanting to slug me.

Even worse, I don't know when to stop myself from pushing my luck.

"Sorry, Dal. I'll fuck anything, but I need a pair of tits and a pussy first."

Dallas snorts. "Classy as always."

Well? It's the truth.

Ever since Caroline Wilson, way back in tenth grade, I've realized that I can lose myself in a willing body and forget that I'm the black sheep of the Reynolds family. So it's been just me and my hand these last few months. Nearly fifteen years of experience tells me that it won't last.

Huh. I'm not in the mood for any of my regular lovers. Maybe some fresh meat is just what I need to get over *her*.

"Okay. I'll bite. What kind of Bait are we talking about?"

"I saw her making her rounds while I was waiting at the bar. Jim Finch said she's not even hiding it. She wants a husband, and she's going up to anyone she sees with the Order's brand to see if they'd be interested in taking her as a wife." Dallas leans back into the booth. "I should probably find her, put a stop to this. The Court is for the Used, not some Bait."

"You sure? What if she sets her sights on you?"

Since taking over the Order, Dallas has become the most eligible bachelor in Harmony Heights.

Maybe if he ever gets over Lucy, the women will have a chance. Since there's a better chance of pigs sprouting wings and flying over the Fortress, I doubt it.

My friends don't understand how to be chill when it comes to the woman they decide is theirs. Connor is a rabid guard dog who will bare his fangs and snap his teeth at anyone who even tries to get within a few feet of

Haven. Adrian… woof. Adrian spent a *decade* obsessing over Loni from two states away, interfering with every relationship she ever had from the shadows, and the second he thought he might actually lose her to Desmond St. James, he crashed their Order-arranged wedding and shot the sorry bastard right in front of the altar.

And I can't forget about Dallas. I feel the worst for him, though I know I'd have his knife to my throat if I ever let him figure that out. Because while Connor and Adrian always knew that, one day, they'd have the woman they wanted—no matter what—poor Dallas had to watch as his Lucy was Offered to another Owed only for him to whisk her out of Harmony Heights, out of his reach for good.

He was the heir. Next in line to be the King, he couldn't go after her. If he did? His old man made it clear. Just like Dallas's mom, Lucy would have an 'accident'. The only way to keep her safe was to let her go, which might've seemed like his only choice while Jack Collins was still alive. And while he might be dead now, Lucy's been married to another man for five years, and Dallas… there's not a damn fucking thing he can do about it.

Sometimes it's good to be the King. Other times? It sucks so bad, I don't blame him and Adrian for threatening to overthrow the Order instead of updating it.

Dallas lifts his glass. A sly look my way before he says, "You know, if my dad didn't fuck up the succession, you could be King."

No the fuck I couldn't.

I shake my head. "That would be Alex, mon ami."

Dallas snorts. "Your mom is French. How can you still have the shittiest accent ever?"

"Easy. Because I'm a constant disappointment to my folks."

FOUR
HER

SEBASTIEN

have no intention of ever Claiming a bride. That's
Alexandre's job, and if my older brother needs to
shit or get off the pot, that's not my problem. With
our dear leader's untimely—and well-deserved—demise
last summer, Alex got a small reprieve. He didn't have to
lock down an Offering by thirty, but even my being tight
with Dallas won't save his position in the Order if he's
not saying 'I do' by August.

I don't have to get married. That doesn't mean that
there aren't hungry social climbers in the secret society
who think it'll be a coup to get Bas Reynolds wrapped
around their finger—a fact that Dallas knows as well as
I do.

"Anyway, I told you to be careful because she's not
just some outsider trying to find her way in. The Bait, I
mean. She's got Order connections."

I peek out into the crowd. I have no idea what she

looks like, so I can't find her. Still, I'm curious enough to ask. "You know who she is?"

"Yeah. Jim gave me her name. Something Crawford. She's Claudia Crawford's oldest daughter. Twenty-five, maybe twenty-six. She never got Claimed, and I guess she's feeling the time crunch because she's working the floor like she's auditioning to either be an Offering or a Used."

Crawford... the name's familiar, but... "Order family? Or she works for us?"

Dallas gives me a look of pure exasperation. Even before his 'ascension', the Order was his life. His old man insisted on it. I've avoided it just as long. How the hell am I supposed to know all this shit?

I don't, but he does.

"There's two daughters. Both were raised to be Offerings, I think. The younger one should be having her Claiming ceremony this August. But the older one... I get the feeling she was already marked by one of the old guard. It didn't make sense why she went through more than a couple of Claiming ceremonies without a bite otherwise."

Got it. And yeah. That would definitely explain her desperation now.

It happens. More Order politics that I'll never approve of. It usually involves members who got branded-in years ago, but every time a new crop of Offerings comes of age, they handpick a few that they want to keep. Some of the fresh-faced eighteen-year-old girls are groomed, then seduced, turned into one of the Used before they ever have the chance to be Claimed.

Then there are those who are basically blacklisted. A married Owed will unofficially 'Claim' a second Offering as his, making her untouchable until she gives in because no one else will have her. Just like in the first case, she eventually ends up with a Used brand on her throat, and the companion to an Owed until he tosses her aside for another mistress.

An Offering can become one of the Used; all it takes is getting caught fucking before the Claiming ceremony, since being 'virginal' is a ridiculous part of being an Owed's bride. It's rare, but a Used can marry a single Order member and be elevated to a protected member. It's the same as an Owed marrying outside of the Order. It happens more often in the lower ranks —someone like Dallas or Adrian or, well, *me* could never marry anything other than an Offering when Jack ruled Harmony Heights—so I guess it makes sense. If the poor Bait was tossed to the side by her Owed lover, finding someone to marry her is the only way out of her current position before she ends up in the backrooms of the Court instead of working the dance floor.

I get it, but making the rounds at the King's Court isn't smart. Sure, it's where half the Order goes to drink and fuck, but that's my point. The Used don't like competition, and the Owed aren't looking for a bride here. They're looking for a quick nut, not forever.

Dallas is right. We should shut that shit down.

And if she might be the right sort of Bait to get me out of this rut...

I place my beer bottle down. The *clink* disappears

into the hum of the crowd, the music of the club. "I got this," I tell Dallas.

"Bas—"

"It'll be better coming from me," I point out.

Dallas thinks about it for a second. "Yeah. You're right. She's wearing a white dress. Trust me, Bas. You won't be able to miss her."

White in a club full of the Order's whores? A wannabe bride? Dallas is spot-on. No way I'll miss that. Just like how, as the one member wearing black jeans, a white tee, and my road jacket, I'm probably the only member here who looks like he got lost on his way to a biker bar.

The King's Court is made up of varying shades of blacks, browns, golds, and reds. Moving into the crowd, viscerally aware that no one is stepping aside for me, I meander my way around, searching for a white dress.

And then I see her.

I see *her*.

My cock twitches. My mouth dries. My ears replay her moans, and I'm suddenly thrown back to the Last Prayer, watching her button up her jeans before she left me alone in the bathroom, too weak-legged—and, fuck it, *proud*—to chase after her.

I know the name of every single partner I've ever fucked. They've never been just a body to me, not just a good time. I made sure I got their name so I could grunt it… except for one.

Except for the mystery woman I called 'love' and haven't been able to forget in months.

Her hair is pulled up and out of her face, pinned

back in a fancy twist instead of the waves spilling down her back. She's wearing a simple white dress that hits her knees. A white sweater is hiding her shoulders. For fuck's sake, she's wearing pumps.

Pumps.

White pumps that will look amazing dangling off her feet as she wraps those long legs around my waist…

Cool it, Bas. She's not here to get laid.

She's here to get *married.*

Why? I think back to what Dallas said. How the elder Crawford daughter went through plenty of Claiming ceremonies without finding a husband until she was forced to go on the hunt as though that was her only chance to survive in Harmony Heights.

It could be. It might even explain why an Offering was willing to let a stranger in a leather jacket rail her in a seedy bar bathroom.

Unless… unless she didn't grab that Plan B, after all. Unless she has a bun in the oven and she needs a daddy.

I glance at her, taking her in again. Three months… she would be showing now, right?

How the fuck would I know?

Does it matter? Well, yeah, if she's pregnant with my kid, it matters. I never wanted kids; I never wanted them to have to grow up a Reynolds like I did. A wife, I can handle, so long as we're on the same page. But if one night of me being a reckless idiot means she's in trouble…

Well, if she is, I'm here. I walked out to break up a Bait looking to hook an Owed, but if that's why she's really here? She's already done the job.

One thing for sure: she's not an Offering, is she? She's not a Used, either. She's something else, and whatever it is, I *want* it.

I push through the crowd, not caring who I shove. I watch as she speaks earnestly to some recent recruit, barely nineteen. What would a kid like that do with a woman like her? That dress doesn't fool me. The fancy hairdo… nope. And those pumps… hell. A woman wearing fuck-me shoes like that needs a man to answer her call.

She needs *me*.

I tap the kid's shoulder. He turns, glancing up at me. I jerk my thumb over my shoulder, the universal sign for scram.

It takes a second for his pissed-off expression to switch to one that's a clear 'oh shit'. Yeah. I get that a lot. I smile, but that doesn't seem to put him at ease. Without even an excuse to the lady he was talking to, he vamooses.

She tilts her head up to look at me.

My smile widens.

So do her eyes.

I instantly recognized her. It takes her a second to place my face, but I know the second that she does. She swallows roughly, her cheeks heating up, though she doesn't scatter like the kid did.

Instead, with a royal shake of her head, she says, "Will you marry me?"

I blink. Okay. Not what I was expecting. I don't lose my grin, though, as I say, "Hello again to you, too."

I wait for her to react to the 'again' part of my comment. She doesn't.

Good.

"I heard there was someone going around the Court, looking for a husband. Couldn't believe it… definitely didn't expect it to be you, love."

She doesn't react to the same name I called her in that bathroom, either.

Interesting.

"Is it not allowed? Men propose all the time. Maybe it's my turn."

I can see that. "Most people date before marriage comes up."

And a good amount date before they fuck the first time, unless they met like we did.

I don't add that. I don't have to. She knows exactly what I'm thinking. I'd bet on it.

"Most people aren't interested in a marriage of convenience," is her prim retort. "And that's what I'm proposing."

I cross my arms over my chest, suddenly amused. Aroused, too, because she looks fucking gorgeous in that dress… but amused, too. She proposed to me. *Me*. I'm sure I'm just another target, and I hate to think she might've banged her way through the Order, so that doesn't make me special, but I won't deny the way my heart jumped the same time my cock twitched just to hear her husky voice again.

"And you think I'm a good choice?"

Come on, love. Give me something to work with.

Admit you remember me, let me know if there's a good reason why you'll choose *me*—

"I just need a husband."

I glance at her lower belly. "Because you're in the family way?"

Her mouth works for a moment. She blinks. "In the… did you just ask me if I'm pregnant?"

I shrug because… yeah. I did.

She gives me a quelling look. "Not that it's any of your business—"

"It isn't?"

"No," she says firmly. "And I'm not. Like I said, I just need a husband. If I can't find one, my sister… let's just say, I *have* to find one. Not forever. Give me a year, and I'll be the most perfect wife you'll ever ask for. I will be for whoever marries me. I'm not picky."

Ouch. That shouldn't sting as much as it does, especially since she already proved that at the Last Prayer. She wanted a man that night, too, and I was there.

I'm here now.

She wants a husband. I can see the determination written on every inch of her stunning face. The first guy who says *sure* will get to call her his. Not because she's knocked up with a Reynolds baby, but because she's trying to get around the Order's rules.

As if I couldn't be any more attracted to her, I have to admit: she's a woman after my own heart. I live to mess with the Order.

And I'd kill nearly every bastard in the Court to be the one she chooses to marry.

She's desperate, but face to face with the woman who's haunted me for months, so am I.

I can't let her know it. Easy, Bas. You got this.

Leaning back on the heels of my boots, I ask, "How do you know I'm not already married?"

She's undeterred. "I don't. If you're one of the Owed, you very well could be."

Freeing my right arm, I flash her my palm.

Every Owed gets branded in. The Order was founded in August, some two hundred years ago by my great, great, I don't know how many greats, great-grand-father, Samuel E. Reynolds. In case I can't forget that he was the first King, all I have to do is drive downtown and visit the Fortress, the Order's headquarters. My ancestor's name is written in big brass letters on the front.

She nods slowly. Obviously, I'm one of the Owed. You can't get into the King's Court without a brand. It should be the same for the women, too; the Used have a smaller, daintier version of the Order's emblem burned onto their neck to mark them the same way a wedding ring does for a Claimed Offering.

No mark for my beauty. No ring, either.

Not yet.

Her gaze returns to my easy grin. "Is that why you wore the gloves? To hide that?"

Gotcha. I knew you remembered me, love. "I really do ride. My bike's out back if you want to see."

"Thanks, but I'll have to pass. I'm actually quite busy."

"No time to reminisce about the past?" I ask, concealing my desire with a lighthearted tease.

"None," is her flat response. "So if you'll excuse me——"

Fuck, no. I'm not letting her get away so soon. I match her step, blocking her before she can detour around me, continuing on her hunt.

She bites the corner of her mouth.

I nearly cream my pants.

That should've been the warning sign. I was already in too deep, just from one night that left me addicted to the promise of a woman I couldn't have. Now you're telling me that I can? I'm not some horny teen who can't control myself. I'm a grown man who's used to women throwing themselves at him.

And then there's *her*. The woman who didn't offer me shit, but took it——and now she asked me to marry her... *marry* her... and she's ready to move on before I even have the chance to answer her.

She flashes me an annoyed grimace, then moves quickly again, her heels clacking against the shiny wood floor.

I block her again, running my fingers through my hair, giving her a rakish look that's won me hundreds of hearts. "By the way, I'm not."

Her grimace becomes a frown. "Not going to marry me?"

"Not married already."

She nods.

I reach down, taking her hand in mine before she

can snatch it back. Bringing it to my lips, I kiss the top of her hand. "Yet."

She sucks in a breath. "Oh. Okay."

"What do you say, love? We at the point for names yet?"

Her pretty brown eyes glaze over. For a moment, she's stunned in the center of the Court, the overhead light shining down on her. I've blocked out the Owed. Blocked out the Used. Right now, it's just me and—

"Annaliese," she says breathlessly. "My name is Annaliese Crawford."

"Sebastien Reynolds," I answer, emphasizing the French pronunciation of my first name in a way I usually don't bother doing unless I'm trying to impress a chick. "But you can call me Bas. All my friends do."

"We're not friends."

Not quite the reaction I expected. Most everybody in town, if they don't already know who I am, have at least heard of me. I don't know if Annaliese has or not, but there's no recognition past looking at me and seeing the man who fucked her.

Just in case, why not a little reminder?

I lean toward Annaliese, whispering straight in her ear. "I'm glad. I don't fuck my friends."

She gulps. I'm close enough to notice, and I take advantage of rattling her by doing it again. I kissed her hand before. Now I brush a kiss against the top shell of her ear.

She shudders.

I pull away. "Yes."

"Yes?"

"Yes, I'll marry you."

Her lips part, mouth falling open just enough to give me a sudden fantasy of guiding my brunette beauty to the floor before feeding my cock past those puffy pink lips. I bet it would feel *amazing*.

If she's my wife, I might find out.

I already know she's attracted to me. I know she's not poisoned against the black sheep of Harmony Heights otherwise she would've heard my name and bolted. I know that there isn't anything I won't do to fuck her again and see if it was as magical as the first time.

And I know that, if she's desperate enough to agree, she must be in such a shitty situation, she needs my help.

Call me a soft touch. Call me a manipulative bastard. I'm both, and I lift my hand, rubbing my thumb along the edge of her jaw.

"What do you say, love? You and me... we doing this?"

"Just for a year," she says. "That's all I need. After that..." Her eyes clear. She jerks her head away from my hand. "You do understand that I just want a marriage of convenience? I'll do whatever it is you require of a wife, but this is more of a, like, business arrangement?"

If that's what she wants to call it. "You need a husband. I don't have a wife. You obviously need help. And me... what can I say? I'm a helpful guy."

I'm going to burn in Hell, too, but I've already resigned myself to that.

"What do you think, Annaliese?" I try not to let my sudden eagerness show as I repeat the same four words that I said to her the first night we met: *"Come home with me."*

"I don't think that's a good idea."

"Funny, I think it's an excellent idea. Unless you're backing out?"

She shakes her head. "No. I… if you'll do it, I accept. We'll have to make an agreement… lay out the rules, the expectations… but I won't mind marrying you."

"Gee, thanks."

Annaliese disregards my wry response. "There's so much I have to do. I… okay. I didn't expect this to be as easy as it was. Sorry. I'm a little shell-shocked."

"I have a tendency to cause that reaction. That's something you'll have to get used to as my wife."

She disregards that tease, too. "Tomorrow," she blurts out. "We can meet tomorrow."

And give her a chance to chicken out? I don't think I like *that* idea.

However, when the alternative is picking her up, carrying her out of the Court, plopping her on my bike and whisking her away to my place, I can't see what else I can do but hope like hell that she actually goes through with it.

Even if she doesn't, I have a name now. I know that she's from Harmony Heights, too.

She won't escape me again.

Just in case, I hold out my hand to her. When she looks puzzled, I say, "Give me your phone. I'll put my number in it. You call me, and we make this thing happen. You got that, Annaliese?"

"Um. Yeah. Yes, of course. That's a good idea. Thank you." She reaches into the small clutch purse she has tucked under her arm. The club's too dim to activate facial recognition to unlock her screen. Flustered, she enters in the six numbers to her passcode—3-4-0-1-2-6 because I'm a bastard and I sure as fuck commit that to memory instantly despite my minor buzz—before holding it out to me.

I enter my number and my name just like this: **HUBBY**🤍. I show it to her, smirking when her pink cheeks go a little pale. She doesn't say anything at first, simply slipping it back into her purse.

Only then does she tell me in a much softer, subdued tone, "I'll call you tomorrow."

"I'll be waiting, love."

For a moment, she stands there, adorably awkward, almost like she doesn't know what to do. That's easy. I duck my head, stealing a quick kiss before I run my hand possessively over her shoulder.

That breaks the spell. With another royal shake and a straight back, she turns on her heel before walking away from me.

This time, I feel a whole lot better about letting her.

Now, if only I can say the same about how to explain what just happened to Dallas.

FIVE

MIRANDA ON THE LINE

ANNALIESE

So… I think I'm getting married.

Opening the door to my car, shaky fingers struggling with the key fob, then the door handle… I finally get it open, tossing my purse onto the passenger seat before flinging myself into the driver's side.

Three hours ago, I panicked. I know Eric well enough that his are no idle threats. If I don't do what he says, he won't just go after me. He'll target my sister, and I can't let that happen.

So what did I do? I hatched a plan. If I could find a husband, Eric would have to leave me the fuck alone. Preferably an Order member for that level of protection, but the moment I started to get dressed to head out again, I admitted to myself that I wasn't really picky. I just needed *someone*.

However, if I wanted to convince one of the Owed

to take a chance on me, my best shot was at the King's Court. An Order gentleman's club, I had to flutter my lashes at the doorman to get in, then I spent a half an hour sizing up the men. I was looking for those who seemed on the younger side—but obviously still legal—because the odds of them being new members without a formal wife were a lot higher than the middle-aged men.

I thought I had one. He said his name was Kyle, he was twenty, and he didn't have the connections to Claim an Offering. He was still interested in getting to know me, though, and when I mentioned that I was looking to enter into a year-long marriage of convenience with an Owed, his only concern was whether or not he'd get to fuck me.

I was prepared for that. I doubted that I'd be so fortunate as to find a husband who didn't want to have sex with his wife, and after Eric, then my stranger at the Last Prayer, I felt confident that, so long as he treated me well, I could stomach fucking *anyone* if that's what he required of his wife.

So, yeah, I was prepared to go that far once our marriage was finalized, and I told him so.

What I wasn't prepared for?

Was my one-night stand walking up to me as though he owned the place.

One look. One gesture. He got rid of Kyle, sidling into his place, completely oblivious to the effect he has on me. I wanted to throw myself at him. Worse, I wanted to snag his hand, drag him to the nearest bathroom, and have a re-run of the night I haven't been able to forget.

I knew who he was, and then he gave me his name, and I think he expected me to *know who he was.* Sebastien Reynolds. It sounded familiar, and it took a second for me to remember that the big building downtown—the Order's headquarters down the street from Eric's law firm—is the Reynolds building. That means he must be super high up in the Order, and though I knew I shouldn't bother, I asked him anyway.

I asked him to marry me.

I thought he'd laugh. I definitely thought he'd admit that, like Eric, he's married and just wanted a little strange on the side. I… yeah, I didn't think he'd jump to the conclusion that I was pregnant, though when I remember that we didn't use any protection that night in the bar, it makes sense that he'd be concerned.

He doesn't have to be. When I lived with Eric, he insisted on birth control. Not condoms, of course; he was too good for them. But I was on the pill since he— at his grand age of forty-six—wasn't ready for kids. I've stopped since I left him, but I'm not an idiot. Even though it was only a day or two after I took my last pill when I went to the Last Prayer, I'm not the type of woman to take risks. I swallowed a morning-after pill the, well, morning after, plus I had a panel done a month later to make sure that my stranger—and my former lover—didn't pass anything else along to me.

I was all clear. Like I told him, I'd be the perfect wife. I can cook. Clean. *Fuck.* I'm a pro at organizing, and if he wants me out of his sight, I can disappear, too. I just figured that he already had one.

He doesn't. At least, he told me that he didn't. I

want to believe him… but I believed Eric once upon a time, too.

Which is why, despite the way he smiled at me, asking me to come home with him, I had to refuse. There's so much I have to do, and as I start my car, heading out of the Court's parking lot, I start by texting my sister one-handed.

> Hey. Do you know a Sebastien Reynolds?

It's late, Miranda has school in the morning, but she's a teen. That phone is glued to her hand 24/7, and I'm not surprised when she answers me right away.

> sounds familiar… Order?

> Yes.

> cool

> I can ask around, get back to you later?

> That would be awesome. Thanks!

> np

I toss my phone back to the passenger seat.

Sebastien Reynolds. *Sebastien.*

"Sebastien."

I try out the sound of his name on my tongue. I don't think I said it half as well as he did, but the way he whispered in my ear how he doesn't fuck his friends…

yeah. I don't think I can bring myself to call him Bas if that's all I am.

He's Sebastien, and if this actually happens, he'll be my husband.

Yikes.

<hr>

I WAKE UP THE NEXT MORNING WITH A GASP, HEART pounding, sheets twisted around my legs as if I spent the whole night fighting them.

Know what? I might have.

My sleep was a mess of half-dreams—Sebastien's voice, Eric's threats, my sister's face—everything blurred together like a warning I don't understand. And that's a lie. I know exactly why they haunted my consciousness, just like I know what I'll have to do to make them go away…

Sitting up, I reach around my messy bed for my phone. I find the charging cord first, yanking it toward me. Tugging my phone off of it, I peer down at the screen.

I shudder out a breath.

Okay. It could've been worse. Six missed calls—all from Miranda, all before eight—as well as four texts. Three are from Eric, one from Miranda.

I look at hers first.

RANDA

Are you awake? Call me.

I glance at the time. It's ten o'clock, later than I

usually sleep. It's also Thursday. Miranda will be in school. I could call her, and she'd totally answer, but I don't want to get her in trouble. She has lunch at eleven-forty. I'll just wait to call her then.

Without the excuse to avoid the other three texts, I brace myself and tap on Eric's name.

> EW
>
> We need to talk.
>
> Don't ignore me.
>
> You owe me a response, Annaliese. Stop this.

No, thanks.

My hands are shaking as I go through the motions that finally block him. If I really do get married, he'll probably be one of the first to hear about it. I just need to get this done as soon as possible so that Eric doesn't interfere.

I know him. He'll expect me to ignore him, get pissed that I am, doing exactly what he accused me of doing—namely, *sulk*—and then reach out again when he feels like it. Sure, there's a chance someone saw me at the Court and ran right to him, but here's hoping that I'm lucky enough that my half an hour visit was missed by Eric's spies.

That's the best part of a marriage of convenience. All I have to do is spend an hour or so getting a marriage license with my husband-to-be, sign it, and Eric can fuck off. There's no need for a wedding. No big to-do. I just want the protection that comes with marrying one of the Owed, and if Sebastien honestly will go along with it, we can be married by tomorrow.

It could be today, but even I'm not that hasty. I spent three years working with Eric. I'd be a fool to marry a stranger—even one as sexy and good-looking and, well, *blessed* as Sebastien Reynolds—without some sort of protection.

And I don't mean condoms this time.

I want a contract. A marriage agreement. A set of rules that we can both live by, including the one-year time limit that I'm insisting on. After that, we can go our separate ways. He can be Eric, I can be Cicely, and as long as we stay discreet, we can have our own lives while Miranda and Colton start out theirs.

Of course, that's assuming that Sebastien *will* marry me. That I want to marry *him.*

That depends on what Miranda found out from her friends in the Order. Me... I never had any. By the time I was eighteen, I'd already caught Eric's eye. I had no idea that he'd basically Claimed me without Claiming me. He was just always there, being sweet, being kind, helping me with Mom's event planning business before he swooped me away, getting me to work for him.

And once I did? That wasn't all he wanted from me.

I was his in every way that counted except for in the eyes of the Order. But because he coddled me, protected me, kept me hidden... *groomed* me, I don't have the same contacts that my sister does. Something tells me I should know who Sebastien Reynolds is, but I don't, and I only hope she does.

While I wait for Miranda to reach her lunch break, I

get up. Because there's another phone call I'm avoiding, I go and have breakfast, then shower. I'll change later, but for now, I throw on a pair of sweatpants I bought after I left Eric. I add a t-shirt, only realizing after I tug it on that it's the same one I was wearing when I took that fateful trip to the Last Prayer.

If that's not a sign, I don't know what is.

By the time I'm done drying my hair, my phone alarm's going off, letting me know that I can call Miranda.

Sitting down on the edge of my bed, nibbling on my bottom lip, I wait for her to answer.

My sister picks up on the second ring, breathless and audibly excited. "Are you okay? Annie? Did something happen?"

I hadn't expected her to sound so alert during the school day. "Hey, Randa. Yeah. I'm fine. Why?"

"Because you asked me about Sebastien Reynolds, and when I got the scoop, you didn't answer."

Because I was sleeping. Because I had erotic dreams about my maybe-husband, and nightmares about what Eric would do to him if he found out that the man I slept with in Sackerville is actually a member of the Order.

They must know each other. It's something I tried not to think about last night. If Sebastien ranks as high as I suspect, my husband and my former lover will have some kind of connection—and Eric threatened to kill any man I fucked while he considers me his.

No wonder I could barely sleep. On the plus side, if I *do* marry Sebastien, I won't be Eric's. Besides, I'm pretty sure he can handle himself, and what Miranda has to tell me only confirms it…

"Sorry. I was still in bed."

"Alone?"

What? "Yes! Of course I was alone. Why wouldn't I be?"

"Because you were asking me about Sebastien Reynolds."

She says it like it's the most obvious thing in the world. "I don't understand."

"Okay. This all comes from Deirdre." Colt's older sister. She's twenty-two and was Claimed her first year. She's promised to marry a mid-level Owed, but they're putting it off until he's closer to thirty for some reason… "But if you actually talked to him, odds are you'll end up sleeping with him."

Uh-oh. "Why's that?"

"Maybe because nearly every woman in the Order has? Well, not me. Not you. Not Deirdre, but that's because she's an Offering, too, and if she banged anyone, Henry will break their engagement. But, like, the Used and some of the wives? Yeah. He's had them all."

I stay quiet.

Too quiet.

Miranda squeals. "Holy shit. You *did* fuck him!"

Heat shoots up my neck. "Miranda."

"Oh my god, you so did."

I'm going to crawl under my bed and die. "I didn't say that."

"You didn't deny it," she sing-songs.

I press two fingers to my temple. "It doesn't matter. I need information about him. Good information. Not… whatever this is."

Hearing the aggravation—and the brewing headache—in my voice, she calms down. "Fine. What do you want to know?"

"Everything."

A soft humming sound comes through the phone. "Okay. So… Sebastien Reynolds. Bas. First of all? He's the hot mess brother."

"What does that mean?"

"He has an older brother. Some guy in finance. I don't know what Bas does, but Deirdre says that he's some kind of, I don't know, trouble-maker. But, then again, he's also, like, sweet."

I blink. "Sweet?"

"Yeah. Like… really sweet, Annie. He's reckless, but he treats people well. Especially women."

My chest tightens unexpectedly. I remember the man at the bar, sitting by himself with his motorcycle helmet and his beer, locking in on how distraught I was, even when I told him not to be kind to me. He was anyway. Sure, his kindness ended with me fucking him in a bathroom stall, but that's because *I* needed it.

I needed *him*.

"So, get this. He hangs out with the Used all the time, but not for the reasons people think," Miranda continues. "I mean—yes, he sleeps with them. But everyone says, despite his rep, he's respectful. He listens. He pays tabs. He fixes things. He's not a dick even if he thinks with his."

Not a dick… that's definitely a point in his favor. Sleeping with the Used… I don't have to like it. It's how things are done in Harmony Heights, and how can I be that much of a hypocrite? Isn't that what I am? Eric made me his Used, but while he was good to me for a while, he's a dick now.

At least I'm not going into this in love with Sebastien. I don't want love. I want protection.

Besides, I met him at the Court last night. Even more notably, our first meeting ended with me on his lap. So he's a playboy. I'm not looking for loyalty.

I can handle this.

Miranda drops her voice. "Colton says he's a good man who doesn't know he's allowed to be one."

I close my eyes, remembering how he held me in that bathroom like I wasn't broken. Like he didn't need anything from me except me in his arms for as long as I wanted to be there.

"Look, Annie… he's trouble, but he's not scary. And he's definitely not like Eric. So if, you know, you did bang him… you could've picked worse."

She has no idea how much that helps steel me toward going through with my plan. "Thanks, Randa. You were a big help."

"I try. Besides, you'd do the same thing for me."

She's right about that, too. Everything I'm about to do… I'm doing it for my sister.

"Love you."

"Love you, too, Annie."

Once Miranda is gone, I return to my contacts. I look at the most recent entry, heart thumping a little bit wilder when I see how Sebastien entered the number in under **HUBBY**🩶. I know he's teasing. I know he's not taking this seriously.

Still, my heart skips a beat as I press down on it.

One ring.

Two rings.

Three—

"Bas here."

I close my eyes. "Hello? It's me. It's Annaliese."

"Hello, love," he says, the nickname he gave me that night in the Last Prayer turning my stomach into knots. "I was waiting for your call."

Oh, God. "Right. Anyway, if you're still agreeable to my proposal, I'd like to meet with you this evening and talk it over. Would that be all right?"

"Sure. Now that I have your number… it is your number, isn't it?"

"Um. Yes."

"Good. I'll text you the address. Whenever you're ready, I'll be here."

And I think I'm going to hurl from nerves. "Thank you. I… I'll see you later."

"I look forward to it… Annaliese."

As the phone disconnects, I shudder in place. Annaliese… the way he said my name, so warmly, so possessively… oh, this is a bad idea. A really fucking bad idea.

But you know what? I'm going to do it anyway.

Once I have a draft for our marital agreement ready for him to go over, that is.

SIX

MARRIAGE AGREEMENT

SEBASTIEN

spent the entire day at home, halfway convinced that Annaliese talked herself out of choosing me to be her 'fake' husband. That she would've done some kind of recon, taken my name, and asked around Harmony Heights before being like *nope* and backing out.

That's what I did—minus the backing out part, of course.

I didn't even have to try that hard. One call to Adrian and, twenty minutes later, I had the deets. Annaliese Crawford. Twenty-five as of February 21st so she's four years younger than me. She graduated from Harmony Heights High that many years after I did which meant that we never crossed paths in school since I was done the year before she started.

She has a younger sister. Miranda Jane Crawford. Seventeen. That caught my interest. Seventeen and an

Offering… she'll be eighteen in July, and due up for her first Claiming ceremony in August, just like Dallas said. No wonder Annaliese said she was looking for a husband for her sister's sake. She probably didn't want the fact that she went unClaimed to affect her sister's future in the Order.

The one thing that Adrian couldn't find out? Was why no one has already Claimed Annaliese. Dallas mentioned that there were rumors that a member of the old guard had his eye on her, but if they did, they fucked up by not making her theirs when they had the chance.

I already fucked her. In the Order, that's enough to earn her a brand on her neck if she's an Offering. Marrying her is the least I can do when my carelessness means that one night with this woman was enough to make her one of the Used.

There's some confusion about that, too. According to Adrian, rumors run that she's been blacklisted. While she hasn't been moved to the Court formally—and, staring at her neck, I can still see she hasn't been branded—it's clear that she won't be attending August's Claiming ceremony. If she wants an Owed for a husband, being Bait was her only shot.

Thank fucking God I went out for drinks with Dallas last night so I could be the lucky prick to swoop her up before some other bastard did…

I didn't know she had once been an Offering. I've met my fair share of the pristine princesses that are groomed to end up as a Stepford wife to the men who sell their souls to the Order of the Owed. Virginal and obedient, meek and quiet… none of that describes the woman who took my hand, joining me in that bathroom, fucking me in a stall.

But it was her. The moment I looked into her face, the flash of recognition telling me that she knew who I was—her nameless lover, not Sebastien Reynolds—I was sure she was the one who walked away from me. The woman I haven't been able to get out of my head for months now, and she was desperate enough to come crawling to the Court to do what so many women in Harmony Heights do: offer herself up to the men who rule it.

I would've killed any of them to be the one she chose. I didn't even give my would-be rivals the chance to take her for themselves. She went from Bait in my mind to *bride* the second our eyes met, and though she refused to come home with me last night—*again*—she called my number earlier today, shaky voice requesting a time when we could meet to lay out our terms later on.

Terms? Fuck that. She can tell me what she wants, I'll say whatever I have to to have a second chance with the ghost who's haunted me since that night in the Last Prayer, and nothing will stop this marriage from happening.

Oh, I'm sure there are plenty of those who would insist I slam the brakes if they knew about it. Alexandre, for one. My folks. Dallas would shit a brick if he heard I'd shut down the Bait last night by being the one who got caught by the pretty lure, snagged on her hook. Adrian... okay. Adrian would probably find it highly amusing that the one of us who swore up and down he'd never give in to the Order's pressures was entering into a secret society-arranged marriage like so many others.

But that's the thing. It wasn't arranged by the old guard, the council... even if Dallas tried to force me to get hitched, I'd slap the King upside the back of his head, then tell him to suck my dick first if he wanted to fuck me over. I'd have my fun with the Used, maybe settle down with a townie who was kept out of the Order, or just take my bike up to the mountains and become a hermit before I took a Barbie doll bride and started popping out Reynoldses to grow up into the same insanity that I did.

And then a woman with a determined glint in her eyes and the lushest lips I ever stole a kiss from walked into the King's Court with an offer I couldn't refuse and, well, here we are.

Annaliese sits stiffly on the edge of my couch, her arms wrapped tightly around the binder she's clutching to her chest; the matching one is perched on my thigh. Her legs are crossed demurely at the ankle, a far cry from the woman I fucked in a seedy bar bathroom. Today, she's wearing another dress that screams Offering: soft pink, fitted waist, clean lines. She looks like everything I shouldn't touch.

I want nothing more in this moment than to touch her anyway. To muss up her perfect updo, to trail my finger down the slender column of her throat, to pluck the pristine fabric to the side and press a kiss to the top of her tit before working my way south...

Down, Bas. Control yourself. If she had any idea how bad I want this... how bad I want *her*... she'd take that binder and her offer and run for the door. I have to lock her down first, then do whatever it takes to keep her.

I lean back into my chair across from her, spreading my knees wide, watching her in a way that's not half as predatory as I feel. I smile, she gulps, and I lazily glance down at the open binder in my lap.

Thank fuck it's not in legalese. My parents have a lawyer that they assigned to me for whenever I screw up, but the thought of going to old Jerry with this… nah. This is between my future wife and me, just the way I like it. Besides, I'd put money down that this isn't a legit contract so much as a list of rules and conditions that Annaliese is laying out so that we both know what we're getting into.

I tap the top page with my fingertip. "So. Marriage agreement. One year."

"Yes," she says firmly. She wears an icy expression like armor, swallowing her nerves, her binder a shield as she forces herself to meet my obvious stare. "Then you can walk away. I know the Order doesn't do divorce, not really, but there are plenty of couples who live separate lives. I just need to have it appear like I'm under your protection until after my sister is Claimed and established. After that, I can take care of myself."

It still amazes me that she's willing to offer herself up to the highest bidder for her *sister*.

Adrian's intel told me as much, and Annaliese herself confirmed it. After I invited her into the house, leading her to the living room where I spend most of my time when I'm home, she quieted any attempts at small talk on my part by handing me the binder—the 'contract', she called it—and explained that she was doing all of this to keep her family's standing in the Order exactly where it is.

I don't know why she is convinced that the Order will turn on Miranda Crawford just because Annaliese believes she won't be Claimed herself. These days, there are more Owed than Offerings, and though Dallas is gunning to shut all that shit down, even he can't stop the next Claiming ceremony from coming without a total revolt. If Miranda wants to be Claimed, she'll be Claimed; I have no doubt about that. But if Annaliese is willing to hook up with me to make it so that her sister does what she's going to do anyway, that works, too.

I'm not above using her fears against her. Does that make me an asshole? A prick? A piece of shit? Probably, but it also makes me her husband.

One year. Oh, love. If she really thinks I'm going through all of this for only one year, she's adorably naive. I'm a Reynolds. If there's one family trait that I've inherited, it's a sense of entitlement.

I want Annaliese. Not for a night. Not for a year.

I want her for as long as I can have her, and that begins with today.

I'm sold. Nothing she has typed on any of these pages… and *fuck*… there's gotta be like twenty thick ones making this sheaf up… none of these sections and clauses and lines will do a fucking thing to change my mind.

Oh, no. That's just Annaliese who, despite this being

her idea, is doing her best to talk me out of it without realizing it.

"I'll do whatever you want me to. Be the perfect wife. Like I told you, if you prefer to sign this and forget about me once the marriage license is filed, that's fine. I just need the Order to consider me your wife."

I couldn't fucking care less what the Order thinks. "You think I'd marry you, then pretend we didn't already consummate this union before we ever knew each other's names?"

Her cheeks turn pink, though there's steel in her pretty brown eyes as she meets mine purposely. "I assumed your memory of that night is the reason you agreed so easily to this. If that's what you want from me, you can have it."

How nice. My wife is doing everything she can to avoid dropping from an Offering to a Used, and that includes her whoring herself out to *me*. Not because there was a spark, a *connection* between two people who happened to meet one night, but because she thinks promising to fuck me is the only way to get me to sign this contract.

Look. There. She even has a whole section devoted to it in her contract.

No sexual intimacy is required as a condition of marriage... should either party request intimacy, the other may decline freely without penalty... if intimacy is mutually desired, it must remain consensual, private, and free of obligation... no expectation of monogamy is required, though discretion is preferred.

If I had any doubt that Annaliese is what she appears to be—a fallen Offering—then that would've smashed it. All the Offerings are raising with the idea that their husband will have a woman who sleeps at his side, and at least one who sleeps with him whenever he wants. It's rarely the same woman, but while I won't deny that my sexual history is… extensive, the one thing I've never done is fuck around when I'm in a committed relationship.

And what's a bigger commitment than holy matrimony?

I underline the section with my fingertip. "I see. You got a whole section about fucking in here."

Her flush deepens. I wonder if, like me, she's remembering the way she threw back her head and moaned as she rode me. "I like to be very clear."

"Very organized, too."

A single crisp nod and a slight pursing of those lips.

Fuck. Who knew I had a hard-on for the prissy, prim act she's got going on?

Especially when she says, "If there's any addendum you'd like to, well, *add*, please do. This contract is to protect us. So we know what we can both expect. It is, after all, a marriage of convenience. Nothing more. If you keep flipping through the pages, I even outlined an initial prenup that makes it clear that, what we enter this marriage with, we leave it with."

I swallow my scoff. Does she think that I'd sign this thing if I was worried she was only marrying me for money? I have too much of it. She can fucking take it. I just want her, and it's getting a little tiring how much she is really pushing this fake marriage thing.

"If that's what you want."

Something in my flippant tone has Annaliese frowning. "If you've changed your mind—"

Why do I get the feeling that she'd like that if I did? As if she's having second thoughts?

It's possible. Shit, it's more than likely. But if she learned anything about Bas Reynolds, it's that I never do what's expected of someone with my fucking pedigree.

Then again, my old man is Guy Reynolds. He gave up being King because he was so obsessed with Maman that he trapped her in Harmony Heights, then baby-trapped her by getting her knocked up with Alexandre first, and me immediately after. To him, his wife was worth more than the promise of power.

My left sock is worth more to me than what being a Reynolds in Harmony Heights means. But the promise of keeping this woman as mine… it's worth the fucking Order thinking that I'm finally falling in line at last.

Because that's what I'm doing. Taking the weight off of Alex's shoulders, getting married to an Offering—former or not, I don't give a shit—so that he doesn't have to. To protect Annaliese, I'll have to play along with Order politics, something I swore I would never do… until she fought back her obvious surprise at seeing me approach her before boldly asking if I would marry her, and if that's what the price of having her is, I'll pay it.

"Fuck, no, I haven't changed my mind. You?"

SEVEN
WHATEVER IT TAKES

SEBASTIEN

Annaliese goes still. She swallows, and with my gaze locked on her, I watch the motion of her throat.

It's *intoxicating*—and so is she.

"Sebastien."

It's the first time she's used my name. She already had my complete attention, but now I'm letting her see a hint of the real me through my easy-going grin, and I think it's making her more than a little nervous.

Okay, then. "Yes?"

"I need you to take this seriously. To understand. This isn't about love. This isn't romance. In Harmony Heights, a wedding band is akin to protection. This is survival. For me... for Miranda. I'm doing this so they don't steal my sister's future because I stupidly ruined mine."

Annaliese says it so matter-of-factly, I know that she

must've spent ages coming to this conclusion. Whatever she did to get booted from her class of Offerings, she's sure it's so bad that her sister will be tossed to the Court instead of getting the chance to be Claimed.

And I get that. The Order is so fucked up with its rules and its bylaws and its expectations. Annaliese could make a mistake that leads to her family's standings tanking with her. Jack Collins would've delighted in punishing the entire Crawford family if one of the precious Offerings stepped out of line.

But Jack isn't the King anymore. Dallas is. I know my buddy. My bro. He might not be able to save Annaliese from her fate, but he wouldn't go after Miranda the same way his vindictive father would've.

Hell, if I ask Dallas to erase whatever black mark is next to Annaliese's name, he would, no questions asked. Of course, then she wouldn't feel compelled to marry me, and… yeah.

Before that night in the Last Prayer, I would've helped her, would've let her walk away. But now? Hey. Turnabout is fair play. She walked away once. No fucking way I'll let that happen again.

She has a point, though. This contract spells out everything for this fake marriage she's insisting on… including a section on living arrangements.

"I see you added a part about us keeping separate residences. I get that you might want to hang on to your place, but when an Owed takes an Offering for a wife, she has to spend at least one night in his bed a week. No getting around that."

Not when I'm dying to have Annaliese in *mine*…

Her body jerks. It's a quick shudder, but I saw it.

I arch an eyebrow.

"I know, but that doesn't apply to this marriage." She exhales softly. "Because I'm not an Offering. Not really."

Ah. There it is. Confirmation. "I thought you were."

Beneath her renewed icy composure, I can tell she's wagering whether or not she wants to answer me. For a moment, I think she's going to brush past it, but she surprises me by tilting her head up just enough to come across as defiant as she admits, "I was. I'm not anymore."

Fuck, she's so damn sexy. "Why's that?"

"Why do you think? You keep reminding me of that night… if you Claim me, no one ever has to know that I was meant to be demoted to one of the Used during the next ceremony."

More Order fuckery that I can't stand. It happened to Loni Dougherty when we were in high school. She slept with Adrian and got caught when Desmond St. James started running his mouth, and what happened? She got kicked out of being an Offering, too. Even if Adrian wasn't related to the former King, nothing would've happened to him. Nope. It's the women in the Order who need to be held to some ridiculous standard.

The second she had penetrative sex for the first time, she lost any worth she had as an Offering. I don't agree with it, but it's how the Order is. If I'd known she was an Offering, I never would've followed her into that bathroom. She sure as hell wasn't acting like an unpracticed virgin that night, but—

My tongue darts out, moistening the corner of my suddenly dry mouth. "Real quick. I wasn't the one who" —shit… how did she put it?—"ruined you, was I?"

I don't want to be. It wouldn't change a damn thing if I was, since I have every intention of keeping Annaliese, but when she slowly shakes her head and my gut feels like someone kicked it, I realize something: I hate the idea that someone else got to her first more than that I could be responsible for her being desperate enough to marry a man like me.

Of course. Why else was she at the Last Prayer? Some prick hurt her, and she found solace in my arms. That was heartbreak that chased her into the dive bar, onto my cock, and I still see echoes of it as I look in her eyes.

I hate the fucker. I don't know who he is, but I will, and it doesn't matter. I hate him.

I shove it down just like I do everything else that has the old anger crawling up my spine. "And you can't marry him?"

"No."

It's obvious that that's all the answer I'll get out of her on that topic—and it's enough.

He's history.

She's *mine*.

"*Good.*"

I reach inside of my leather jacket.

If she thinks it's weird that I wear it in my house, get in line. I'm pushing thirty myself, my birthday next November, but my road jacket is like some little kid's blankie.

When I wear it, I *am* Bas Reynolds.

I'm the black sheep. The outcast. The rebel who's stuck his middle finger up at the Order his entire life, but whose last name keeps him from being kicked out despite Jack's best attempts over the years.

I need that reminder more than most. So does half of Harmony Heights.

Plus, the inner pocket is pretty handy for storage. When Annaliese handed me the binder before she eased herself down on the edge of my couch, she gave me a pen, too. I shoved it in my jacket. Now, I grab the pen, uncapping it with my teeth before flipping back to the front page.

At the bottom, there's a pair of lines with two different names printed beneath it: Sebastien Reynolds and Annaliese Crawford.

We look damn good next to each other.

I scrawl my signature over the first line. Then, meeting the relief in her eyes as I recap the pen and close the binder, I tell her the truth: "You don't think I figured most of that out? I know exactly what I'm signing."

A contract that says that she's my wife for one year. But, more than that, I noticed a simple clause right near the top that's going to be my new best friend.

This agreement does not constitute a lifelong marital expectation unless mutually renegotiated.

Understood, love. Under-fucking-stood.

"Then why—"

I shrug. "Because you asked me to marry you."

Annaliese blinks, stunned.

My lips quirk in another one of my trademark grins. "And, if we're being honest here, you gave me a night I haven't been able to forget."

Her breath catches. Good. If it affected her half as much as it did me, it's going to be a hell of a lot easier than I expect to satisfy the bullshit 'mutually renegotiated' part of that line.

Rising up from my seat, I move to her side of the room, holding out the binder and the pen. "Your turn."

Annaliese sets down her copy of the contract. She accepts mine, opening it to the front page with my signature on it.

She hesitates for only a moment before adding her signature to the next line. That done, she closes my binder, handing it back to me. I guess this is my copy of the contract to keep. Considering she grabs hers, signing that one before standing up and holding it out so that I can do the same, I figure she wants us both to keep a copy.

Tucking hers under her arm, she picks her purse up from where it was waiting for her on the couch. "Thank you. It doesn't seem adequate, but—"

"Then don't bother. Besides, I don't know where you're going. We're not done here."

She blinks. "I don't know what you mean."

That's what she says. The way she braces herself, it's like she expects me to invoke one of the intimacy clauses then and there, telling her to strip so I can fuck her here and now.

And, sure, that sounds pretty fucking amazing, but that's only if I want to enjoy my new wife for a year.

Fuck, no. Like Adrian, I looked at this woman and saw the promise of forever—and that's what I'm playing for now.

"'Course you do. You proposed to me, love. I don't know about you, but I'm expecting a wedding." Giving in to my desire to touch her at last, I grip her chin between my thumb and my pointer finger. "The sooner the better. I need your input before I can hire someone to put it together for us."

Her lips part. I nearly dip my head, kissing her, but as though she can sense my hunger, she uses the excuse to drop her purse back to the couch before sitting demurely down again to put some distance between us.

"No need to hire anyone," Annaliese says primly. "I used to be an event planner. Though I don't see any reason why we need to have a wedding for a marriage of convenience—"

I flash her a grin. "Humor me. I never planned on getting married at all. If I'm going to do it now, I might as well do it right."

She clears her throat. "Yes. Well… if you think we should—"

"I insist. Nothing fancy if that's not your style. We book St. Catherine's so that no one can deny we had an Order wedding, then have a small reception somewhere. You'll need a dress, of course. Flowers. Whatever you want for your wedding—"

"Fake wedding," Annaliese cuts in.

"I don't do fake," I toss back. This time, I reach into the back pocket of my jeans. Taking out my wallet, I rifle through my cards while she stands there, trying to understand just what I mean by that. You'd think it would be pretty clear. I say what I mean, mean what I say, and if I'm getting hitched, it'll be for real.

I pull out my black Amex. "Here. Take this. Whatever you want for our 'I do's, you get it."

She takes it with trembling fingers, her expression a mix between surprise and suspicion.

I wordlessly dare her to say something to me about the card.

Yes, my family is loaded. Yes, my parents have used money to bail me out a thousand times. They pay for my mistakes, and I've let them because I never asked to be born into the secret society that's turned me into the man that I am. I'm not as bad as I used to be—becoming even more of an outcast when half the town blames you for one of their own taking a swan dive off a building because of you has a tendency to straighten even the biggest assholes out—and I only use their money to survive these days… but if Annaliese was willing to open up about what being in the Order means for her, I might as well start by doing the same.

She reads my name on the card. Glancing around, I see her taking in my living room with a different eye. Earlier, she was too nervous to really focus on her surroundings. Now? She sees the expensive furniture, the huge ass television, the knick-knacks that Maman bought for me to add some 'personality' to my home after I left hers.

"I used to be an event planner," Annaliese murmurs. "What is it you do?"

I smirk. It's a defense mechanism that I've used for

so long, I barely notice that I'm doing it. If I'm not being charming Bas, I'm being Sebastien Reynolds the cocky prick—and that's infinitely better than the scrappy bastard who will throw a punch first, ask questions later.

"Me? I'm a trust fund baby. Why? That turn you off?"

It sure as fuck does me. I'm the world's biggest hypocrite. I rail against the constraints of the Order while relying on what it's done for my family and its wealth over the last two hundred years to live my life.

She's quiet for a moment, then she shakes her head. "I don't want your money, but if you have a card like this, you won't miss what it'll cost to host a small, intimate wedding. After all, you want one."

Her unsaid *I don't* hangs between us.

I don't care. My smirk softens into an honest smile regardless. I don't know what I would've done if she tried to refuse or tell me that she would pay, but I won't have to worry about that. She's right. I won't miss it, and neither will my folks. Hell, once they figure out that the charges are because one of their sons is getting married, they won't say a damn word about me using it for more than gas and my tab down at the Court. And when I let Annaliese keep it in case she needs it—despite her ridiculous idea that what's mine is mine and what's hers is hers—they won't stop me.

If giving my new wife whatever she wants is all that makes me a worthwhile husband, at least I can do that.

I'm not above using her fears against her—or buying her if that's what it takes.

EIGHT
BLOOD OATH

SEBASTIEN

When Dallas took over as the King, he did it because there was no one else better for the job. He had his father to thank for that. Jack Collins spent more than two decades beating every last thing there was to know about the Order of the Owed into his boy. When Jack died, the Order succession meant that Dallas was his heir. It didn't matter that he wasn't married, or that he still isn't thirty until next year. He was next in line, and the Order's bylaws were clear: unless he stepped down, the title was his.

The title, and the responsibility.

He wanted to refuse. It was Adrian who pointed out that, as King, Dallas had the power to make changes. They're slow-going, but he already shut down the basement, put an end to the auctions that eventually cost Jack his life, and he even gave my brother a year's reprieve when he put a hold on last year's Claiming ceremony due to the fallout from Jack's death.

Death. Ha. Only a handful of people know the truth about what happened. After Jack tried to auction off Adrian's wife, Loni, Adrian hired an assassin to poison his uncle. He died, good fucking riddance, and because no one could trace the poisoned booze back to Adrian, the self-proclaimed kingmaker got away with toppling Jack from his throne.

He deserved what he got. After what he did to Dallas's mom… Jack got what was coming to him, and I'm glad he's gone. Dallas might not have wanted to be King, but he'll be a hell of a lot better at it than his old man.

Of course, that means he's the one I have to talk to about my wedding. I spent another hour with Annaliese, looking for any way to keep her from leaving. Somehow I found myself helping her build our guest list and planning what sort of wedding would work for us as she took meticulous notes on some spare paper that I found for her in the office I never use.

The more we planned it, the more I was determined to see this through. And since I didn't want to spring this on my best bros when they received the invitation to *my* wedding, I decided to talk to the three of them in person.

So I sent a text to each of them, asking them if they were free to meet with me. I got lucky. Dallas and Adrian were working late at the Fortress, and while Connor couldn't make it, the other two said they'd hang out in Dallas's office until I got there.

The penthouse apartment on the top floor of the Fortress, plus the one below it, belongs to the King. Dallas refused to take over the penthouse where his parents used to live before they were both murdered. He has his own place, just like Adrian and me, and he stubbornly insists on staying there.

His office, on the other hand, had belonged to Jack for more than two decades. Jack kept an enforcer at his door and an ever-changing secretary sitting at a desk in the lobby. If you wanted to see the King, you had to get through them.

Dallas put a bullet through the skull of Jack's last enforcer. He fired the secretary, then had Adrian hire a new one for him.

With my helmet tucked under my arm, I salute the woman seated behind the desk. She's tapping away at her laptop, waving back as I make my way toward the door that leads to Dallas's office. Her strawberry-blonde hair is pulled up in a high ponytail, a smattering of freckles dotting her nose.

The big rock on the ring finger of her left hand is a gift from her husband; the slender golden band tucked under it is a sign that she's married to one of the Owed. The easy way she smiles at me as though I didn't help Adrian torment her for most of her childhood makes me feel like a fucking ass.

Growing up, it was me, Dallas, Adrian, Connor, and Desmond. We were tight, basically brothers, and Adrian was our ringleader. When we were kids and he teased Loni Dougherty, I went along with it because I was a fucking idiot. Later, when I realized that he was desperately in love with her, I took a back seat, figuring Adrian would get his head on straight eventually.

Love makes a man reckless. One of my oldest friends taught me that lesson, but when I see how happy he and his wife have been lately… shit. It almost makes you forget that Loni escaped Harmony Heights more than a decade ago, got dragged back by Dallas so that she could marry Desmond, then ended up being hitched to Adrian after he used his blood oath to kill the man that betrayed him.

His blood oath… I can tell myself that I'm here to fill Adrian and Dallas in on what went down at my place this afternoon, but I'm still a shit liar. Always have been. I can't even lie to myself.

I know exactly why I'm here.

"Hey, Bas," Loni says warmly. "Adrian's in there with Dallas. They're waiting for you. But don't take long, okay? I was just finishing up when my husband said you were on the way. I'm ready to go home."

Loni isn't just another nepotism hire. In the Order, you see plenty of them, and though Adrian could've convinced Dallas to hire Loni so he could spend time with his wife at home *and* at the Fortress, there's more to it than that. Adrian is the head of finances for the Order —both legit and not. His wife does something with numbers. An auditor of some sort. Hell if I know what that means, but in between nooners with Adrian and telling Order members that Dallas is too busy to meet with them, she's helping Adrian figure out just how far Jack's embezzling went, plus how much he made sex trafficking women to outsiders before Dallas put a stop to that shit.

Good thing, too. Loni was almost one of them. I did my part, distracting Jack while Adrian and Dallas rescued her from the basement. I'm not sure how Adrian detailed the three of us running to save her to his wife, but in the more than half a year since, she's seemed to have forgiven the rest of us for how we treated her back in school.

Except for Desmond. Fuck Des. He got what he deserved, too. Going against the bro code… trying to Claim Loni when he knew how much Adrian needed that woman? Yeah. He got three bullets to the chest courtesy of Adrian's Tomcat while I stood guard outside of St. Catherine's, sitting on my bike. Because I had my bro's back, and I only hope that he'll have mine.

I flash her a charming grin. "Don't worry, Loni. I won't be long."

Pushing open the door, I let myself into Dallas's office.

Maybe it's because I know what happened to its last occupant, but the room smells like old leather, sour booze, and a hint of something rotten that's stuck in the carpet. Honestly? It's probably the essence of Jack Collins, haunting his only son for daring to sit behind his desk after he helped his cousin plan the old King's death.

I blow the stink out through my nose. "Shit. Crack a window or something, Dal."

"And give one of the old guard ideas?" is his wry

response. "No, thanks. I don't feel like taking a dive today."

I wince, hiding it with a nod at Dallas, then Adrian. I should've known better than to make a crack like that. If there's one thing that Dallas doesn't like to be reminded of, it's how his mother died.

Oh, they say that Therese Collins jumped out of the penthouse apartment of the Fortress. We know better. Her husband was the one to give her a push, and Dallas spent the last five years scheming to make Jack pay for what happened to his mom and Lucy.

Poor Lucy. If what happened to Loni was bad, what Jack did to Lucy was a hundred times worse. It was another way to show Dallas how much he owned his son, and I think he sealed his fate that day.

Dallas will eventually blow up the Order to spite his father, and I'm all fucking for it.

Adrian will help him do it, too. With his ledgers upon ledgers, he has the keys to the Order's destruction, and if he doesn't like the way the new guard is going, he'll do it with a smile.

God, I love these fuckers.

Adrian is currently leaning back in the chair opposite Dallas, ankle resting on the other knee, an unlit cigarette tucked behind his ear, nestled in his messy curls. The warm light from overhead winks off of the pair of golden hoops in his left ear as he turns just enough to watch me cross the room, plopping my helmet on top of Dallas's desk before I drop down into the leather seat next to Adrian's.

"Hey, fellas."

Adrian shakes his head, a half-smile tugging his lips. "Dal, you owe me a hundred bucks."

Dallas reaches up, absently scratching the spade tattooed on the side of his neck as his pale green eyes— the same as his cousin's—narrow on me. "What did you do?"

I widen my own eyes, going for innocent. That's one of the perks that come with being born with a face like mine. If you don't look too closely, don't pay attention to the imperfections I worked hard to achieve, you'd think I was harmless. So I ride a motorcycle. So I'm never without my leather jacket. I'm a pretty boy who wouldn't hurt a fly…

Dallas curses under his breath. Lifting his ass off of his seat, he pulls out a wad of cash from his back pocket. He peels off a hundred-dollar bill, slaps it onto the desk, sliding it over to Adrian.

He leans out of his seat, picking it up with two fingers. "Thank you."

"I should know better than to bet against you."

"No, you should know better than to underestimate Bas's tendency to get himself into trouble."

"Me?" I ask, momentarily forgetting why I'm here. "What about me? What was the bet?"

Adrian disappears the money into his suit jacket. "I bet Dallas that you'd be a sucker for that Bait you met last night. He told me that you sent her home without an Owed of her own. Then you asked me to look into her. When you texted us, I bet him a Benjamin that you came down here to tell us that you're going to Claim this Annaliese Crawford."

I cross my arms over my chest. "Give him his money back."

"Oh?" Adrian makes no move to do that. "So you're *not* going to Claim her?"

"Nope. No point. I'm not waiting until August to make her mine. We're already engaged." I glance at Dallas. "So, technically, you won."

"No the fuck I didn't. I told Adrian that there isn't a woman in Harmony Heights that would ever convince you to settle down. You've had most of them already—"

Can't deny that. "Guilty as charged."

"Right. So why would you marry an Offering?"

"She's not an Offering," I tell them. "Not anymore. She's convinced she's been demoted."

Dallas frowns. "My dad did the same shit to her that he did to Loni?"

Adrian's jaw goes tight, though he doesn't say anything. He was only able to arrange to kill Jack Collins once, but whenever he remembers that he spent ten years separated from Loni because of the former King, you just know he's imagining resurrecting him if only to watch him suffer and die again.

I shrug. "Don't know. Someone did, and I know it wasn't you. It doesn't matter. She thinks a marriage of convenience is her only way out of it."

Dallas gives me a pointed look. "And you didn't tell her that she doesn't need to go through that?"

I grin, and Dallas groans.

Adrian shakes his head. "I knew it. You agreed to marry her without thinking it through."

Maybe, but the way he says that... it's like he thinks

this is just another way for me to rebel, to take the Order's traditions and ideals and wipe my ass with them. And while that's normally something I would do, I've been on my best behavior since Dallas took over for his dead dad.

I hate the Order, but I really do love these guys; Connor, too, even if he has to stay home with Haven. I wouldn't do anything to fuck up Dallas's reign now that he's reluctantly the head of the Order. I know only too well how vindictive and cruel some of the other Owed can be. If he shows any weakness at all, he's a target, and I would never do something to fuck with him.

This isn't about the Order. This is about Annaliese and me, and I need my friends to understand that.

"Screw you, Adrian," I say, though there's not any heat to my words. "I promise, I thought enough."

"Sure you did." Adrian arches an eyebrow. "The question is: with which head?"

That's easy enough to answer. "If it was just about sex, I already banged her in the bathroom of the Last Prayer."

Dallas groans again to hear the name of the bar where I first met Annaliese, and Adrian chuckles softly under his breath. "Fuck me, Bas. You're such a sap."

"Why's that?"

"She's the one who got away, isn't she? The one that got stuck in your head. That's what this noble, knight-in-shining armor bullshit is about. Annaliese Crawford is the mysterious woman who walked away from you, and now you're going to… what? Marry her because she's the first woman who ever got a taste of you and wasn't immediately begging you to fuck her again?"

I flip Adrian the bird. "Sorry. We can't all lurk in the shadows and wait a decade before taking the woman we want."

"I had a *plan*—"

"A plan that had Loni almost ending up as Des's wife," I remind him. "Sure, you made those hours at the shooting range count. You're happy. She's happy. Now, I might be reckless, but I'm not stupid. If Annaliese is willing to marry me, I'm snapping that woman up before someone else Claims her."

As usual, Dallas watches our back and forth with interest. "You're serious."

"As a fucking heart attack." I lean forward. "Listen. It makes sense. She wants a husband. I want *her*. Alexandre's off the hook since at least one of us Reynolds will marry and satisfy the Order's ridiculous requirement that members of the founding families have to get hitched. When the old guard comes down on you, tell 'em to fuck off. You got Bas Reynolds in line. Even if we didn't go way back, that should be enough to earn you a little wiggle room."

I hate that Dal needs it. He's been a kickass King so far, but the Order fucking sucks. One wrong decision, one wrong step, and there will be someone ready to try him for his figurative crown.

He does have some of the old guard in his corner, like Stephen and Oliver. The young guys all worship him, and his fellow enforcers know what he's capable of.

At the very least, he's a Collins. You don't want to fuck with him, and if they try, I'll always have his back.

I just… I also want him to be cool with me marrying Annaliese.

Dallas sighs. "Okay. I know you're not asking me for permission, Bas, but it's fine. Go ahead. It's… what? A year, right? That's what you said. This marriage of convenience thing she's after was only for a year."

Right. "Yeah. About that… she thinks it's for a year."

"And what do you think?" asks Adrian.

In answer, I yank my pocket knife out of my jeans pocket. I flip it open. One quick slash over the brand on my palm, blood welling up instantly along the slice, and I show it to my friends.

"Got a piece of paper? And, Dal… I'm going to need you to seal this." I pause, the blood beginning to drip down my wrist. "And, fuck, I owe you a hundred bucks, bro, because Adrian's right. I…I'm gonna Claim Annaliese Crawford."

After all, that's how you make a blood oath in the Order of the Owed—and with one of those, no one can ever take her away from me.

NINE

THE WEDDING

Most Order weddings come together quickly. When Desmond fucked up and tried to marry Loni, she received an invitation to her own wedding in two weeks' time.

Annaliese had ours planned to be held in eight days.

I know she's rushing it. I've done my best, trying to figure out who 'he' is—the fucker that convinced her she was ruined—but despite my efforts... and Dallas's... and *Adrian*'s, who is taking it as a personal challenge to figure out his identity... I still don't know. Eventually, I'll earn enough of Annaliese's trust that she'll tell me. For now, I'm happy to see the whole wedding come together quickly because, well, that just means that I have her, and no one else can.

It's a simple affair. That was fine with me. I didn't want a huge shindig. None of those weddings with three hundred guests. Still, to prove to my new bride that I didn't consider this a 'fake' marriage, we needed to have a real wedding. So, eight days after I signed the marriage agreement she drew up, the two of us stood in front of Father Francis as the Order's priest married us.

We held the ceremony at St. Catherine's, like nearly every other Order wedding. Instead of allowing it open to any and all guests, ours was a closed service. On Annaliese's side, she had her mother, her father, and her younger sister, Miranda. That was all.

On my side, Maman and Dad sat with Dallas and Adrian. In the last pew, Connor was holding Haven's hand. Seated on Haven's other side was Loni.

I was so glad to see that Connor and Haven had shown up. That Loni was sitting with her childhood best friend, the two slowly resuming the friendship after what happened to Haven and Loni's decade-long disappearance from Harmony Heights… that just made it all the more special. All of the people who are important to me were there.

Except one.

Except Alexandre.

My brother was invited. Of course he was. Because we kept the wedding small, we didn't bother with bridesmaids or groomsmen, maids of honor or a best man. Still, I figured that my older brother would at least come to meet my bride.

He didn't, and by the time Annaliese came walking down the aisle to the chords of 'Here Comes the Bride', I was struck so damn speechless, I forgot all about my brother. It was easy when everything I am was completely consumed by the vision of my new wife.

I already knew that Annaliese is gorgeous. My attraction to her is undeniable. But seeing her float toward me, wearing the understated wedding gown that, despite being off-the-rack, fit her like a fucking glove… I understood why Adrian was willing to gun Desmond down to take Loni, calling her his princess. That's what Annaliese looked like to me in her dress, her hair pinned up, showing off her face… she's a princess.

She's *mine*.

The ceremony was simple. Because we both want this so badly—for our own reasons, yeah, but still—there were no objections. We did the Order standard vows, and when Father Francis told me I could kiss my bride, I did so with as much enthusiasm as I did when I had her up against that bathroom door.

The one thing I suggested during her planning was where we would hold the reception. Since Annaliese wasn't too big on the whole 'let's throw a wedding' thing, she said she'd try to get it for me. I told her just to give the owner my name, and we should be good.

That's how we ended up renting half of Martino's out for our after-wedding meal. My favorite café has outdoor seating and a beautiful interior. Since our wedding was taking place during the evening at the end of March, we figured the inside would be best.

I wanted privacy. No surprise that Annaliese jumped at the suggestion. The restaurant could have seated plenty of others. It's a Friday night, too. Oh, well. I liked having the inside space just for our party, if only for the relief coming off of my new wife as she realized that no uninvited guests could join us here, either.

If only the servers that agreed to work our meal helped make her feel just as at ease…

The moment I told Annaliese that I would marry her, I knew that was the end of my whoring around. How can I expect her to want to stick around if I'm not loyal? And I sure as hell will get rid of anyone who thinks they can try to take her from me. There will be no 'discretion'. So long as we're wearing the matching Order wedding bands, we're it for each other.

The staff at Martino's knew that this was a Reynolds wedding. It was the name that Annaliese gave them when she booked it, and I'm pretty sure that the waitress who offered to lead the service took the job because she expected me to be here.

The way Polly shoots Annaliese a nasty look as I guide my wife in, her hand resting lightly on the arm of my suit jacket, tells me that she never expected me to be the *groom*.

I knew she was into me. Apart from tipping her well after I had my usual salad lunch, I didn't give her any sign that I thought of her as anything more than the sweet server who always got my order right and delivered it quickly. She has no reason to be jealous of my new wife, but she is, and Annaliese gets a puzzled pinch to her features as she notices Polly's sneer.

Shit. This is something I don't want to deal with, especially on my wedding night. I went from a bachelor to a married man in less than ten days. It'll be a shock to the way things have been in Harmony Heights, but that doesn't mean that any of my previous lovers—or wannabe lovers—can treat Annaliese with anything less than respect.

Especially since I'd prefer that she didn't know just how extensive my history is. It's bad enough that I'm jealous of *one* guy that she used to be with. If she grows to be attached to me in any way at all, it'll make things difficult if she's the jealous type who runs into my past partners.

I don't think she's jealous. We were engaged for nine days, and she hasn't given me a single hint that she's regarding this as anything other than what she proposed: a marriage of convenience. That's when we're alone, though. In public, surrounded by our friends and family, she really is the perfect bride. I can almost fool myself into believing that she's as happy to be formally married as I am.

I kiss her cheek, wiping away her look of confusion while also making it clear to Polly to back the fuck off. Then, guiding Annaliese to the table set up for us, I position her opposite of her sister, sitting her next to Loni. Loni leaves a seat beside her for her suddenly missing husband. I, of course, sit on the other side of my wife.

The rest of our guests settle down. Dallas grabs the chair next to me before turning to engage my dad in conversation after he chucks my shoulder, offering me another round of congratulations.

Annaliese stiffens whenever Dallas comes close. That's also my fault. I don't think she realized that the King of the Order was actually the Dallas I wanted at my wedding until he showed up and she paled.

He noticed, too. My bro refuses to start any drama at my wedding—especially since he was such a vital part of the drama that went down during Adrian's bloody wedding—so he's been careful to not startle my bride. I appreciate it, just like I have to thank Loni for being so welcoming to Annaliese.

Connor and Haven came to the wedding, though I expected them to cut out before the reception like they did. Getting her out of the house for the hour in the church was damn near a miracle. I couldn't ask any more from Haven, though I did thank Connor for the wedding gift he slipped me before they left. Without Haven to watch over, and Adrian still weirdly missing, it was easy for me to distract Annaliese long enough for Polly to take our drink order by pointing out the fact that my wife planned the whole wedding to Adrian's.

"Aren't you thinking about your reception with Adrian?" I ask, taking my seat, slinging my arm around Annaliese's shoulder.

She goes ramrod straight at the familiar contact, but I ignore it. She'll have to get used to it. I'm a touchy-feely guy, and I'm happy to show her off. That she doesn't scoot away from my arm is hopeful. She even leaves my arm where it is as she turns to look at Loni.

"Oh. Are you getting married, too?"

Loni flashes her rock. "Already did. But our wedding was… different than yours. We had a church ceremony. We keep meaning to have a reception, but we haven't done it yet. But you… you planned this in a couple of weeks?"

"Eight days," I say proudly.

"It helps when you have a client who gives you an open budget," she counters. "Sebastien told me to get it done, and I did."

I laugh. "Hey. You wanted to get married as quickly as I did. Don't deny it." I make sure the entire table can see my charming grin as I say, "You couldn't wait to make us official."

Annaliese doesn't deny that, either. I didn't think she would. I don't know what, exactly, she told her parents and her sister about our sudden wedding, but since the Crawford family is here, supporting the eldest daughter instead of snatching her way from Sebastien Reynolds' clutches, I can guess she made it sound like she really did want to do this.

Whether a love match or in the name of the Order, it doesn't matter. She said 'I do' and meant it—and everyone here knows it.

Polly returns, along with a male waiter I don't recognize. He trails behind her, carrying a second tray of drinks. She mutters to him, telling him where to place them, then the two vanish back to the kitchen to bring out the salad course.

Adrian returns just as the two servers are clearing up the empty salad plates. He waves away his untouched dish, choosing instead to take a sip from the cooled coffee that his wife ordered for him before he mimics my pose, wrapping an arm around Loni.

I shoot him a look, trying to figure out where he's been. He gives me an enigmatic smile before using his other hand to reach up, checking to see if the unlit cigarette is where he left it. It's been almost a year since he's quit. I know he didn't sneak out to bum a smoke—not unless he wants to disappoint himself *and* Loni—so where was he?

Before I can ask, Polly and her partner come back, serving our main courses. Only after we started making a dent in our meals does Loni nudge her husband with her elbow.

"Hey. Did you know that Annaliese is an event planner?"

She clears her throat. "I used to be."

Adrian ignores her, all of his attention on his wife… like usual. "Of course I did, princess. So's her mother." Adrian glances across the table, nodding at Claudia Crawford. "You threw my mother's fiftieth bash. A Hawaiian-themed luau about a year ago. It was excellent work."

Claudia smiles warmly. "I did. Thank you, Adrian. How is she?"

Adrian covers up his snort with a wry grin. "She loved it so much, she's spent half her time in Hawaii ever since. Dad, too. We saw them at Christmas. They're alive and happy. That's about all I know."

"Alive and happy." Claudia lifts her glass of red wine, a toast in mine and Annaliese's direction. "If only that's something we could all strive for."

Murmurs of agreement break out through the table. Maman echoes the same sentiment in French before taking Dad's hand, interlocking her fingers in his, pressing a kiss to his knuckles. For as far back as I can remember, they've had a contentious marriage; based on the way it began, and especially how young they were, it's to be expected. Still, there's no denying that they love each other.

Fuck. I want a love like that.

That's what I want. To be sitting with Annaliese, twenty-five years down the line, smiling together and holding hands like newlyweds…

If Annaliese's mother's appearance is any hint to what my wife will look like in twenty-five years, I'm one lucky bastard. Her hair is short, cut to her chin, showing off her delicate features. Her eyes are the same shade as her daughter's, and her skin is unlined. She's an Order wife with a front-facing job. She probably is very friendly with the local medspas, but I couldn't care less. She takes care of herself. Annaliese obviously does, too.

Yeah. I'm super fucking lucky—and I manage to hold onto that thought until we've finished our main course, waiting for the dessert Annaliese arranged in lieu of a cake, when Adrian clears his throat and gestures over his shoulder.

He'd been in the middle of talking to Annaliese and Loni about possibly hiring my wife to give Loni and Adrian the big wedding reception they never had. It wouldn't be too soon. They seem to be thinking that it could be a big bash that celebrates their union *and* Loni's thirtieth birthday. That means it would be next June— not this one, but the one after it—which Annaliese agrees would be plenty of time for her to plan something outrageous.

Adrian controlled the conversation, but as though he was expecting this, he noticed the other man first. I follow the gesture, swallowing a curse when I see a last-minute guest standing anxiously in the doorway.

He's in a suit. I guess I should be glad that he at least made *some* effort.

Too bad he's, like, two hours late.

I tap Annaliese's shoulder, getting her attention. "Hey. Stay here. I'll be right back."

"Um. Yeah. Of course."

I trail my fingers down the sleeve of her dress. "Save me something sweet, would you?"

She flushes, just like I'd hoped she would. Then, regretfully climbing out of my seat, I walk away from her, heading toward our guest instead.

I grab his arm, jerking him to the far corner of the room. This way, I can still see the table behind me, but we have some semblance of privacy in case I need to kill him.

"Sorry. I know I'm late. Adrian called…" Adrian. Of course he did. "He told me to get my ass to Martino's so I can at least congratulate you guys." He glances around me, searching for something… or someone. "So, which one is she? Which lucky girl decided to join our fucked-up family?"

Don't kill Alexandre, I tell myself. Maman and Dad won't be happy, and I don't want to ruin Annaliese's hard work. So no murder, even if he really, really deserves it right now…

Look at him. His eyes are bloodshot. His tie crooked. He reeks of whiskey and smoke.

If he wasn't my brother and this wasn't my wedding reception, I'd at least slug him—and he'd deserve *that*.

Fisting my hands at my side so that I resist the urge to swing, I grit through my teeth, "You got wasted instead of going to my wedding?"

Alexandre was always the golden child. He never did anything wrong. Even when he *did*, it was somehow my fault. No wonder I ended up doing everything I could to earn my rep.

But even I wouldn't show up late to Alex's wedding like this.

A hurt expression twists his features. He looks puppy dog awful, like I kicked him when he was down, and he doesn't understand why I would. I'm used to it. Like me, he knows how to use his pretty face to his advantage, and even looking like he hasn't slept in two days, he's pulling on my heartstrings.

Damn it.

"Alex—"

He frowns. "I'm not wasted, Bas. I just… needed a little liquid courage."

"For what?"

"For the same reason that I couldn't bring myself to meet the family at St. Catherine's." Alex lets out a wry laugh. "What if I got there and the whole wedding was in place, but instead of you getting hitched, I got shoved up to the altar?"

"Shit, Alex. You *are* wasted. Why the hell would you think something like that?

"Because of Desmond and Adrian."

Oh. Fair point, I guess. Alexandre wasn't at the wedding last June—he never attended any of them, as though he's allergic to the idea of holy matrimony—but, like the rest of the Order, he heard about what went down.

"Yeah, but Desmond planned on marrying Loni. It was Adrian who showed up with a gun so that he could take his place. Unless you planned on shooting me to take my bride, you had nothing to worry about."

"I know. I *know*. But with you having this wedding so soon without any of us even knowing you were serious with this girl… you gotta admit it's kind of fishy." He lowers his voice. No. He *thinks* he lowered his voice, but that just means that he's talking at a normal, if slightly slurred, volume. "If you did this because you felt like you had to… like one of us needed to take a wife, we can stop this. I… I still have time."

Technically, Alex's time ran out last August. He got lucky that Jack was killed when he was because Dallas was able to push back the Claiming ceremony. But now that I'm married…

"Don't worry about it, bro. I wanted to get married."

He raises both his eyebrows at me, an expression of disbelief obvious.

I nod. "I'm not shitting you. Maybe I didn't before, but then I met Annaliese. Trust me. I'm right where I want to be. But, hey, that's me. If you don't want to settle down, take a wife, pop out some babies… fucking don't. You're only thirty. You have your whole life ahead of you. Don't sweat it."

"But the Order—"

"Fuck the Order," I say simply. "I mean, look at Maman and Dad. He could've been King, but he wanted *her*." Just like I need Annaliese in a way I wouldn't have thought possible before that December night. "So you don't play along with the Order bullshit. What really happens? Dallas won't give a shit, and I'm sure you don't care what he thinks, King or not. As for Dad… you think the man who gave up everything for love would penalize you for not marrying someone you don't?"

Alex's blurry eyes seem to clear a little, almost as if I'm making sense. His brow furrows. "But you… you did."

I give my older brother a smile, clapping my hand on his shoulder. " I'll tell you a secret, big bro. Remember how Dad said he knew Maman was the one the instant they met? He looked in her eyes and knew he wouldn't let her go?"

He nods. "Yeah."

Annaliese was desperate enough to marry me. She promised a year, but now that we've done it, I know one thing for sure: that woman isn't going anywhere. I'll make her love me, and as for me…

Alex's eyes go wide, a look of horror on his face. "Holy shit, Bas. You actually love this chick?"

Only in the Order would a man get such a terrified expression when he talks about love like that. Ditto for how it's completely acceptable to have a shotgun wedding when love is an afterthought, and duty—plus a makeshift contract—is all that matters.

Do I love Annaliese?

I pat his shoulder, then step back. "Worse," I admit. "I think I'm *obsessed*."

To a man like Alexandre Reynolds, that is somehow worse. "Oh, Bas—"

My brother's obvious drunken pity is interrupted by a gasp, a squeal, and the sound of chairs moving.

I snap my head, looking at the table. Annaliese is on her feet, staring down at the front of her wedding gown. Loni has joined her, bending slightly, dabbing at it with a napkin. Adrian is saying something to the waitress holding a tray down at her side. His expression is ruthless. Hers would be contrite if it wasn't for the gleam of satisfaction in her gaze.

It doesn't take a genius to figure out what happened. Just in case, I push past Alex, making my way back to the table.

"—it'll be okay. Adrian's housekeeper is a miracle worker. She can get blood out of anything. I'm sure she'll be able to get this stain out, too."

Annaliese gives Loni a thin-lipped smile. "I appreciate it. Thank you. You know what they say: accidents happen."

I look at Adrian, then Polly.

Yeah. This was no accident.

Firming my jaw, I glare at the waitress. Her face falls. No wonder. All those times I came to Martino's, chatting it up with the girls, tipping them handsomely because they were always so sweet to me… and this is what I get? I have our wedding reception here, and the moment I step away from Annaliese's side, Polly 'spills' a glass of red wine all over her wedding dress?

Too late, she stutters out an apology.

Gracious and well-mannered as always, Annaliese brushes it off.

Of course she does.

Me?

I move to her side, placing my arm over the back of her shoulders. Then, coldly turning away from the waitress, I address the rest of our wedding party.

"Thank you for coming. For sharing our special day with us. But I think it's time I bring my wife home."

And if I enunciate 'my wife' a little more strongly than necessary before giving a side-eye to Polly?

Well, I'm sure that was an accident, too.

TEN
EXTRA PROVISION

ANNALIESE

As far as I know, Sebastien has two main vehicles: a shiny motorcycle and a bright red Porsche that is as flashy as it was probably super expensive. I'd shut down the idea of renting a limo for our wedding. I was trying to keep it on the down low as much as I could. A big stretch limo bringing us all to St. Catherine's, then the café that Sebastien insisted we all eat at? No, thank you. We could all find our way to and from the church and the restaurant.

He thought I was being frugal. After jokingly telling me to hold on to his card, he reminded me that I could spend whatever I wanted to plan our wedding. I didn't have a problem with that. Hey, my folks do pretty well for themselves, too. We don't have Reynolds money, no, but I'm not the sort of woman who will refuse someone else's generosity.

If I was, I never would've ended up with Eric as long as I did…

My new husband insisted on driving us to the church. I almost pointed out the old adage about it being bad luck for the groom to see the bride in her dress before the wedding, but then I remembered that this isn't a real wedding. For all intents and purposes, this is basically fake. So when he said he'd drive me, I agreed. Besides, it wasn't really a wedding dress. It's a simple white gown that I picked up from Felicia's, one of my favorite shops on the north end of Harmony Heights.

A white gown that is currently covered in sticky, half-way-dried red wine courtesy of the clumsy waitress who was in charge of serving our wedding reception at Sebastien's restaurant of choice.

I don't want to think poorly of anyone, but I'm not so sure how much of that was an accident. She returned with a single glass of wine, though no one asked for a refill, and she just so happened to stumble in time to drop it on my lap. And maybe I could excuse it for a slip if it wasn't for the way I saw her watching Sebastien so closely, jealousy pinching her features, as though she wished that *she* was his bride…

But she's not. I am. 'Til death do us part—or, you know, next March when the one-year term of our contract is up—I'm now Annaliese Reynolds. It was a stipulation he added off-handedly during the last hectic days of wedding planning, and I agreed because it was such a small concession. Besides, if I kept my name, it would only be obvious that I'm not truly his wife. And if

I'm not protected by an Order member, I can only imagine how far Eric will go to make me pay for my disobedience.

He threatened Miranda. I have no doubt in my mind that he'll go through with it, taking Colton and her future as his wife away from her. The Dawes family is too enmeshed into the Order of the Owed for me to believe that Colton—for all the love that he has for my sister—would ever choose her over the secret society. His parents wouldn't let him, and neither would Miranda.

But that's not all. Mom has slowed down with her event planning business over the last year. She claims she's preparing to retire, but she's barely fifty. She could work if she chose to, but I have the feeling that her jobs started drying up, oh, about three months ago—right around the time I ended things with Eric.

And Dad… he's an engineer. That's how he ended up getting inducted into the Order. Some project he did a decade ago earned quite a few Owed a pretty penny, and they repaid him by sponsoring him into the society. His job changed our lives, and I know he'll work until he's on his deathbed… but not if Eric interferes.

Fucking *Eric*.

As Sebastien pulls up outside my building, he kills the engine to his Porsche, though he doesn't get out right away. His hands rest loosely on the steering wheel instead, a picture of relaxed confidence.

He glances my way. "You alright?"

"I'm—" My voice cracks. I quickly clear my throat. "I'm fine. Just tired. It was a long day."

"But a good one?"

I nod, and he flashes me a grin that has my heart stuttering in my chest.

So I'm married to a man I barely know.

To *him*.

In this car, just the two of us… I feel like I've known Sebastien Reynolds my entire life. I could pick out the slight imperfection on his cheek with my eyes closed, trail my finger down the pale slash over his left eye, trace the curve of his nose and his jaw… but before I can do any of that, he pops open his door. He circles around the front of the car, opening my door for me, helping me and my stained wedding dress climb out of the Porsche.

"Come on, love. Let's get you home."

Home. Right. This is my apartment because, despite us just having our wedding, I'm living in my apartment, he's living in his mansion, and there will be no wedding night for us.

Not when it was a fake wedding.

This is the first time he's been to my place. Any planning we did was over the phone or after he invited me to return to his house. As we take the elevator up together, I'm suddenly nervous. It's nothing like what a Reynolds would be used to, but I want him to like what I've done with my space.

It's not much. I have a living room, a bedroom, a bathroom, and a small kitchen. It's more than enough for just one person, and as I use my keys to open my front door, I suck in a breath before shoving it in.

I almost expect Sebastien to leave now that he's

followed me up to the third floor and has seen me safely to my door. If so, I don't know him at all. Of course he follows me in, his dark gaze sweeping over the entryway.

He sidles past me, hands momentarily bracing my shoulders—my skin tingling upon the slight contact—before he moves further into the apartment.

"You got good security here, love?"

Why would he want to know? "Um. Yeah." I toss my keys in my purse, put my purse on my couch as I pass it, joining him in the living room. "A sturdy lock. Window latches. A chain when I remember to engage it."

"No cameras?"

I give him a curious look. "No. Why?"

Sebastien turns to me, chucking my chin. "We'll have to get you some. You may insist on staying here, but I need to know my wife is safe."

My wife.

My wiiiiiffe.

Oh, boy.

That shouldn't warm me up the way it does. Or how he cares about my safety like that… "I'll look into it."

"Don't worry, love. I'll take care of it. After all, I am your husband now."

The way he says that is like he's daring me to tell him that he isn't. How can I? Especially when I'm still standing here in the dress I wore to marry him…

I nod, and he chuckles under his breath, visibly pleased with himself for winning that minor battle so easily.

I open my mouth to say something—*anything*—but

before I can find the words, Sebastien walks over to me, moving until he's behind me. He hooks a finger somewhere in the back of my dress.

"Long day, remember?" he murmurs. "Let me help you get out of this, then I'll go."

I almost argue—but I don't. For one, if my husband wants to see me in my underwear, that's his right, isn't it? I promised him intimacy if he wanted it, and this *is* our wedding night. For another, he's not wrong. I'd needed Miranda to help me zip up into this after she came by to get ready with me before Sebastien picked me up. Miranda went home with our parents. How did I expect to get *out* of this dress?

Sebastien handles that part. He slides the zipper down, slow enough to make every nerve in my body light up with undeniable want as he reveals my back to him.

The dress loosens around my shoulders. However, before I can climb out of it, Sebastien backs away.

"All done," he says softly. "Goodnight, Annaliese."

Oh. Okay. "Goodnight."

It's for the best. Emotions are running high tonight, and if I'm not careful, I could get myself into even more trouble. Besides, this is what I wanted, isn't it? A marriage of convenience? A *fake* husband?

I wait for him to head for the front door, looking at the floor instead of at his pretty face. Then, dress clutched to my chest, I hurry into my bedroom and close the door.

I have to take my hair out. I have to wash the makeup from my face. I have to figure out a way to get the red wine stain out before it sets and my 'wedding' dress is ruined. First, though, I shimmy out of it. After I lay it out on my bed, seeing how much damage that klutzy waitress did, I throw on a pair of pajamas I would've never dared wear in Eric's house: an oversized t-shirt for just this purpose, plus a pair of cozy sleep pants almost as silky as my dress.

Phone, I think. I left my purse on the couch, and if I want to look up how to get that stain out, I need my phone. So, still made-up, my hair still done, I pad out in my bare feet to my living room—and let out a muffled shriek when I find someone sitting on my couch. I clap my hands over my mouth faster than I'm able to recognize him.

Heart racing, I throw my hands down at my side. "Sebastien? I thought you left!"

He holds up my phone. "Sorry, love. I found this on the floor of my car. It must've fallen out of your purse or off your lap during the car ride over. I thought you'd might want it."

Oh. "Thank you. I'm sorry for screaming. You… you startled me."

"I didn't mean to—"

"No. No, I know that. But thanks." I go over to him, holding out my hand. He drops my phone against my waiting palm, though he doesn't get up from my two-seater couch.

Well, that's not totally awkward, is it?

"That's not all you forgot, either, love."

My brows knit. My purse, my keys, my phone… "I… what else did I forget?"

My new husband stands up from the couch, slowly and deliberately, before he moves until he's standing right in front of me.

I let out a shaky breath as he tilts my chin up with a knuckle. And then he kisses me.

One hand slides to my jaw, the other to my waist, anchoring me to him like he can't bear the idea of any kind of space between us. His mouth is warm and slow, devastatingly tender, but underneath it is pure *want*. It's the kind that tells me he's been starving for me since our last kiss, back at St. Catherine's.

He pulls back just enough to breathe against my lips.

"God," he whispers. "You have no idea how long I've wanted to do that again. And that peck at the church didn't count, Annaliese. *That* is the kind of kiss I expect."

My fingers curl into his shirt. I don't even realize I'm doing it as I ask, "What do you mean?"

"I'm your husband," he reminds me, eyes dark and lazy, but undeniably possessive. "I expect a kiss 'hello' and a kiss 'goodbye'."

Breaking away from me, my hands untangling from the fabric of his dress shirt, he reaches inside of his jacket. With a crooked grin, he pulls out a pen.

He holds it out to me. "You can put that provision in your copy of the contract." The grin develops a wicked edge that makes my knees go weaker than they were during our kiss. "I'm sure as hell adding it to mine."

I WAKE UP THE NEXT MORNING, HALFWAY CONVINCED that yesterday was one hell of a dream. I didn't really marry Sebastien Reynolds, did I?

Two things assure me that I did: the whisper of his cologne lingering in my apartment, somehow seeping into my room, plus the weight of the gold band on the fourth finger of my left hand.

After our kiss, he left, and listening to his comments about keeping 'his wife' safe, I double-checked that I locked the door and the windows. Then I took one cold-ass shower, trying to keep from begging him to take me again. Instead I touched myself to the memory of that night in the Last Prayer before curling up alone in my bed.

I'm there now, still stunned that this... this happened. This is my life now. And, sure, nothing's really changed except my last name and my marital status in the eyes of the Order, but I can't help but think that my life as I know it will never be the same.

And I get confirmation of that about an hour later when my phone buzzes and I pick it up, reading the text message that just came in:

HUBBY🤍

Good morning, Mrs. Reynolds. I have reservations for dinner tonight at Giuseppe's. I'll pick you up at seven.

My mouth falls open. Dinner? What does that mean? Is Sebastien... is my fake husband asking me out?

Well, no, he's not asking me anything. He's telling

me that we're going out to dinner, and I can't think of any reason to refuse him.

He'll expect a kiss, too. That's what he said. A kiss 'hello', a kiss 'goodbye', and who knows what else.

And I don't know what I think about *that*, either.

ELEVEN
HIRED

SEBASTIEN

I f there's one thing you need to know about a Reynolds, it's when we fall, we fall hard.

I already knew from the moment I was reunited with Annaliese that she was mine. What started as obsession has quickly turned into something more, and I now wear evidence on my skin so that I never forget—and I don't just mean the wedding band that I'm proud to wear beneath my motorcycle gloves.

I used to tease Adrian for how whipped Loni made him. If he had any clue what I was doing, he'd give me the biggest 'I told you so'. Good thing no one else knows... except for Connor, but considering the trouble he had convincing Haven that he worshipped her, he's probably the only one of my bros who understands. At least Adrian and Loni had history. The history that I have with Annaliese revolves around me being a manwhore and her trying me on for size just because she was trying to forget another man.

There's no other women for me. No men for her. It's just the two of us, even if my wife… she doesn't quite know that yet.

You see, according to the Order's bylaws, once a week, the Owed and the Offering he married are supposed to sleep in the same bed. Even though she keeps insisting she's not necessarily an Offering because she was supposedly dropped down to a Used, that's not the reason why I don't enforce that clause in the Order's manifest.

Nope. The reason I don't enforce it is because we've been spending the night in the same bed *every* night since our wedding.

That's on me. I told her that I wanted her to be safe. I wasn't lying. I'll kill anyone who tries to hurt her, but when I looked around her apartment, trying to figure out what sort of security measures she had, it's because I was already trying to figure out how I could get back in.

When she made the comment that she has a chain lock when she remembers to engage it, I can tell you that Annaliese… she doesn't. I brought a pair of wire-cutters with me if that's what it took, but I never even needed them. A simple lock-pick kit to break in through the shitty lock was all it took to let me inside.

I didn't touch her. I'm not that kind of perv. When I have my wife again, it'll be because she panted my name, begging me to fuck her. It'll be when I know she's ready to fully be mine. But ever since she proposed marriage and, fuck me, I really, really liked the idea of being able to call Annaliese Crawford *mine*, I haven't been able to sleep that well.

So I thought: what if I stretch out next to Annaliese in her bed? I'll know she's safe… I'll know she hasn't returned to the man who had her running to my arms in the first place… and I'll see if I could find some semblance of peace that I've been missing for a long ass time.

It helps that she's a super deep sleeper, and I wake up at the drop of a pin. Any time she shifts, I'm up, and by the time she stirs enough to get up, stumble to the bathroom in the dark, I'm already crawling under her bed.

Hey. I dress in black, I'm stealthy as fuck, and a good girl like Annaliese never expects to have a man sneaking into her bedroom to sleep next to her, so she never looks. Instead, she rubs her eyes, shuffling out of the room, oblivious to the fact that the only way I can sleep at all is beside her.

I have an internal alarm clock. I'm up by dawn every day, slipping out of her apartment. It's easier now. I borrowed her keys that first dinner at Giuseppe's, then went to get a copy made. Since then, I don't have to break in. I unlock the door, locking it again by the time I leave, and if any of her neighbors notice… well, I *am* her husband.

That's not all my sudden obsessiveness has led me to do—or the only thing I borrowed. As organized as Annaliese is, she's too damn trusting. As soon as she left her phone out, I installed a tracker app so that I always know where she'll be. I stuck another tracker to the underside of her car.

I'm going to burn in hell for it, but as far as I'm concerned, she gave me permission to protect her when she stood in front of Father Francis and said 'I do'.

She said 'I do'. So did I.

And now I *will*.

I'M SO FUCKING DESPERATE TO HAVE THE REAL Annaliese let me in.

Oh, there are glimpses. The woman I can't stop fantasizing about, who sat by me at the Last Prayer, and followed me to the bathroom. The no-nonsense woman who walked into the King's Court, proposing marriage to whoever would listen. The determined woman who walked into my living room with a pair of binders and a plan.

But, more often than not, I'm treated to the ice queen. Prim and proper and perfect… the way she does her makeup whenever I see her, not a single strand of hair out of place, the dresses that flatter yet do so much to hide her mouthwatering figure… for someone who insists they're not an Offering, she does a good job of pretending to be one.

And that's not fair. I know it's not. Someone did this. Someone took a firecracker and broke her until she was just another woman in the Order. At least, they *tried* to. Knowing there's something under that carefully cultivated facade… it's why I'm so obsessed. It's why I'm so hungry.

It's why I want her so badly.

I want to be the one she opens up to. The one she shows her real self to.

No matter what it takes.

It isn't long before I notice that the only time I really see Annaliese come alive—when I'm sure I'm witnessing the real Annaliese, not the Offering she once was—is when she's doing something that has to do with a binder. Our marriage agreement… the wedding plans… when she gets to organize and plan and make shit happen, she's fucking *radiant*.

It's after another dinner. Another date that, if you asked her, she would staunchly deny that that was what it was. I just tell her where I want to take her, and she goes, as though she's following one of the clauses in her contract.

She has to have that sucker memorized. Considering I stole it from her apartment about a week after our wedding, the way she keeps casually dropping clauses and sections into conversation… yup. She either has another copy or has it memorized, but she hasn't said anything about the signed copy being missing yet.

She hasn't said anything about the scent of my cologne in her bed, either, so maybe my dear wife is just that oblivious.

Could be. She's sure as hell doing everything she can to convince herself that she *isn't* my wife.

Of course, that's why I'm doing everything to prove her wrong. Including taking her out for dinner, and before I drive her back to her place—then wait until she's sleeping to let myself in—inviting her into my living room so that I could talk to her about something.

I don't beat around the bush. Once we're back in my living room, I wait for Annaliese to fold her skirt under her and sit down before I metaphorically pounce.

"So… why don't you work as an event planner anymore?" I ask casually, leaning into my seat.

Her shoulders tense like I slapped her. Whoops. She definitely wasn't expecting me to ask her that.

I wait, hoping that I made the right decision by bringing this up.

"I loved my job, but I had to leave it," she says softly. "And then when I was told that I would be demoted to one of the Used, it made no sense to return to the field. I mean, who would hire me then?"

I would. And I plan to. But first… this is the moment I've been waiting for. The opening I would be a fool not to take.

"Annaliese… who hurt you?"

I just want the fucker's name. That's all.

But she shakes her head, looking anywhere but at me. "I can't. Sebastien… please. I don't want to talk about that."

No. She doesn't want to talk about *him*.

Smart. If I ever find out who broke Annaliese before I ever met her, I'd borrow Adrian's Tomcat and pump a pair of bullets into his skull.

I plan on it. One day, I'll get the chance. For now, I let it go.

She needs me to.

"Okay, but you're not one of the Used now. You're the wife of an Owed. I don't see any reason why you shouldn't start your own event planning service now."

"What… really?"

"Yeah. You did an amazing job when it came to our wedding. Look, I want to throw a party for my brother."

Interested in spite of herself, Annaliese asks, "When's his birthday?"

"September," I answer. "He turned thirty last year, but I want this party to be soon, like a belated celebration."

Alexandre didn't want to throw a party last year because of what that age means in the Order. He can still Claim someone—especially since Dallas gave him a year reprieve due to canceling last August's Claiming ceremony—but now that I'm married, he doesn't have to if he doesn't want to.

I love Alex. Despite him being the golden boy in the Reynolds family, he's my brother, too, and I think celebrating him… showing him that he doesn't have to fear being thirty… would be good for him. Plus, it gives my wife something to do.

Way I see it, it's a win-win all around.

"What do you think? Throw Alex a party, then I bet everyone in Harmony Heights will want to hire you for their next shindig. But, please, block off the June after this one for Adrian. He'll have my head if you can't help him celebrate his wife when *she* turns thirty."

Annalise offers me a small, almost shy smile. "I liked Loni. She was very nice to me… and Adrian is—"

I decide to throw her a bone. "Devoted to his wife," I supply for mine.

Her expression turns wistful.

"I used to want a marriage like that," Annaliese says under her breath, more to herself than to me.

Too bad. "What happened?"

She lifts her head, looking at me. "Life did." A small shake of it, as though she's trying to convince herself when she says, "A marriage of convenience is best. A fake husband…" She gulps. "It's better this way."

Not this shit again. "Fake? No, love. I told you before. I don't do fake."

Panic flashes over her features. It's there and gone again, but I know what I saw. She banishes it quickly, and for the next moment, I almost think she's going to argue with me over my statement. Nope. Instead, she folds her hands in her lap, the gesture obvious as hell that she's done with the topic of conversation.

Feeling generous, I give her an out. "So, about Alexandre's birthday…"

Her face screws up into an adorably puzzled expression. "You're really just going to blow past that? I know we don't know each other well yet, but that doesn't seem like you, Sebastien."

See? That's where my wife is wrong. Because she can claim we don't know each other all she wants, but she's right: I didn't want to blow past it. I want to make myself as clear as possible when it comes to this marriage. I didn't think she was ready, so I didn't push it. But if she needs me to push her a little…

I lean back into the couch, propping my ankle on my

knee, amused despite myself. "When I saw the look of fear on your face? Yeah. I didn't think you were ready to continue that conversation."

Annaliese juts out her chin, showing off the slender column of her throat. Fuck me. If this wasn't so goddamn important, I'd have her flat on her back beneath me in an instant just so that I can swipe my tongue up the length of her neck, finding out just how good she tastes there before—

"I'm not afraid."

If she had any idea the sort of dark, twisted, perverted thoughts racing around my head right now, she would be. "Good, because this ain't no marriage of convenience. If anything," I add, "I'd consider it an inconvenient marriage because my wife acts like we're strangers."

"Because we are—"

I tap my fingers on my knee, working hard to keep my easy grin. Don't scare her, Bas. Not when you want to keep her... "I had my cock inside of you, your legs wrapped around my waist. We're not strangers, Annaliese. Not anymore."

She gulps. I follow the motion of her throat and, damn it, I still want to lick her up and down. Fucking *everywhere*. "You called me 'love'."

I shift, trying to get comfortable even as my growing erection screams for relief. Not even this lazy pose is helping, but at least I won't frighten Annaliese with how much I want her with my legs spread like this, tamping down the bulge in my jeans.

"I did," I tell her, "and now you're my wife."

She blushes. God, she's so fucking beautiful. And the way her cheeks go pink like that? It just reminds me of the blood rushing to my junk…

Annaliese clears her throat. "So when exactly are you thinking about hosting this party?"

I laugh under my breath. "Looks like I'm not the only one who changes the subject when it gets too real."

"How about May 1st?"

Okay. I guess we're forging ahead. I think about it. May 1st. That would give her a month to plan it. If she was able to pull off getting everything ready in eight days for our wedding, she can do this. Especially when my family's name, wealth, and status in the Order will make a lot of vendors pretty damn agreeable.

"Mayday. I like it."

She purses her lips. "So am I hired?"

"I don't know if you realized it, but I slipped my card into the back pocket of your tiny purse on our wedding night." I shrug as her lips part, stunned at my admission. If only she knew what else I've done… "Of course you're hired. And do me a favor, love. Make sure you pay yourself whatever you think you're worth."

"Sebastien—"

I'm not done. "Then go ahead and double it because that's what you're worth to me."

And, sooner or later, she'll figure that out.

TWELVE
SORT-OF DATE

ANNALIESE

'm the one who wrote out the marital agreement, plus the prenup, using everything I picked up working at Eric's law firm. All it needs to be formalized is to have a notary stamp it with their seal, but for all intents and purposes, it's a contract that sets out the terms for our marriage of convenience.

Our fake marriage.

About three weeks into being Mrs. Sebastien Reynolds, I realize that I forgot the most important clause.

I never agreed that I wouldn't fall in love with him.

Oh, I promised myself that I wouldn't. I fucking *swore*. After everything that happened with Eric, I never wanted to fall in love again. I could do cooking. Cleaning. *Fucking*. I could be a pretty face on his arm, no personality, doing exactly what my husband wanted, just like my former lover trained me to do.

But that was when I expected my fake husband would be treating this arrangement just like that. And, true, I should've suspected something was off when Sebastien insisted on us going through a real wedding with witnesses, but I couldn't deny that our fake marriage would have more standing in the Order if, you know, we actually *had* one.

Anything for Miranda. That's what I told myself. Anything for my sister.

I haven't heard from Eric. The fact that he's still blocked helps, but he knows where I live. He pointed it out the last time he summoned me to his house. He could come here if he wanted to, and I'm so damn glad that he doesn't want to. So far, my plan is working.

Except for the teensy tiny hitch in it.

I'm falling for my husband.

I don't want to. I keep trying to stop. I don't even know when it started. When that charming grin of his had me going breathless. When I looked at him poured into his black jeans, muscle tee, and leather jacket and couldn't stop endlessly reliving that night we shared at the Last Prayer. When his touches—as casual and careful as they were at the beginning of our 'marriage'—started to feel like promises against my skin.

When he called me 'love' almost as though he meant it, knowing that he can't...

It's stupid. No. It's *dangerous*.

Eric will kill him. If he finds out that I really did marry for love—no matter why I proposed to Sebastien Reynolds in the first place—he won't take it well. I honestly think he might be able to forgive an Order-approved marriage of convenience. But for me to love someone that isn't him? I don't even want to think about how he'll react.

Especially since there's no way that Sebastien will ever love *me*.

I promised I'd be the best fake wife possible. So far, he's been the best fake husband I could hope for.

He knows about the intimacy clause in the contract; he pointed it out himself. And yet... he hasn't pushed for any sort of it despite what happened between us at the Last Prayer. His touches can be possessive, but never disrespectful.

I know why. Of course I do. I might not have grown up in the Order, but I've been part of the secret society's way of life long enough to understand. Miranda only confirmed it. My husband is a regular at the Court. That means that he's known to sleep around, both with the Used and whoever will have him... like I did when I was looking for a distraction.

Sleeping with the Used isn't considered cheating in his world. Even if this marriage isn't fake, I know who I married. A high-ranking Order member, no matter how much Sebastien seems to want to distance himself from it... I'd have no right to expect fidelity from him. He *was* raised as an Owed. I doubt the idea of being loyal to his wife is anything those men know how to do.

Eric is a prime example of that.

And yet... when I'm alone at night, wondering where Sebastien is and what he's doing... *who* he's doing... I replay what he told me the evening after he signed the contract.

I don't do fake.

So what is this then?

We have dinner multiple nights a week. He makes an excuse to stop by my apartment at least every few days. He says it's to make sure everyone knows I'm his, but I saw him chatting with my next-door neighbors the other day. Kimmie and Paul aren't involved in the Order, so why did it matter if they knew I was in a relationship?

That I was *married*?

I mean, the ring on my finger gives it away, but for Kimmie to congratulate me and gush that my husband is adorably sexy… I hate that I was jealous. Kimmie is more than a decade older than me, happily married to Paul, and they have four kids. I shouldn't be jealous.

Damn it, I'm jealous.

But I can't be. And just like I told myself that I won't fall in love with Sebastien, I insist that I'll prove that I'm *not* jealous. I'll follow the contract to the best of my ability, sticking to the same 'marriage of convenience' refrain.

This is a professional partnership, nothing more.

And I manage to believe that until one Friday night, three weeks after our wedding, when I haven't heard from Sebastien in two days, and I let the bubbling jealousy erupt like a volcano.

I don't even know what triggers it. I'm used to being in my apartment alone. Sebastien hasn't asked me to come home with him since I proposed to him, and even when we have dinner, he drops me off at my door, the perfect gentleman. It shouldn't bother me that it's eight o'clock, my dinner is sitting heavily in my stomach, and my mind is providing unnecessary images of my husband kissing some faceless woman before offering her his hand, then leading her to a quiet spot so that he could fuck her the same way he fucked me once.

I shouldn't. I know better. I should grab a glass of wine, dull my jealous ache, and go to bed early—

I grab my phone. Taking a deep breath, I scroll down to H in my contacts and press the only one there.

It rings once.

"Love." His voice is warm, and my stomach flip-flops. "Was just thinking about you."

I called him. I proposed to him. This is my idea… and hearing him call me 'love' like that hurts more than it should. Not when he can't ever really mean it. "You shouldn't call me that."

Or tell me you're thinking about me when all I've been doing lately is obsessing over *you.*

"Shouldn't," he echoes cheerfully. "Still going to."

Damn it, Annaliese. Why does the way he say that soothe something jagged inside your chest? I shake my head, then find myself blurting out: "Just thought I'd call to say 'hi'. I mean, if that's okay."

"Of course it is. It made my day, hearing your voice. What's up? Is something wrong?"

I'm not surprised that he asked me that. After all, I only badgered him into this marriage for protection. "No. I was bored. Though I'd see what you're doing."

Instead of telling me it's none of my business, Sebastien actually answers me. "About to head out. I was supposed to meet with Dallas, but he bailed on me, so I figured I'd go get a drink by myself."

A drink.

With who?

How many Used women will throw themselves at him tonight?

"Where?" I ask. It comes out before I can think better of it.

There's a beat. "Why? Planning to join me?"

Holy shit. I wasn't expecting *that* answer, but if he's offering… "If you'd like the company, I wouldn't mind getting a drink."

He exhales softly, and unless I'm imagining it, he sounds *pleased*. "Great. I'll come pick you up. Twenty minutes okay?"

I glance down at myself, my heart already thudding at the idea of going on a sort of date with my husband —even if it's one I basically invited myself on. "Yeah. That's okay."

"See you then, love," Sebastien says, hanging up before I can chide him for using his pet name for me again.

The moment the line goes dead, I toss my phone and hop up from the couch. This isn't just dinner with Sebastien at an Order-run restaurant. I'm good at those; my relationship with Eric made me a pro, even if all of our dinners were kept to the shadowy corners and back-rooms where he kept me hidden. But drinks? There's no way not to compare this to the night we first met, and if I suddenly want to relive that night more than anything, I can't help it.

I walk over to my closet, tug the door open, and freeze.

Looking inside, I see rows and rows of dresses. Soft colors, pinks and creams and lavenders. All of their necklines high, the hemlines low, none of them climbing higher than my knees. I see silks and chiffons and purposely curated elegance.

The outfits that Eric bought for me are probably still at his house; if not there, then a landfill. Even so, when I moved out, I built a wardrobe that he would've been proud of. Not on purpose. Totally subconsciously. That's what so many years of being trained by your much older lover gets you, I guess.

He wanted the perfect Offering.

The perfect mistress.

That's what I became, but now I'm neither. I'm Sebastien Reynolds' wife, and as I reach for one of the dresses out of habit, I stop halfway as a memory rushes back to me.

It's Sebastien. Either the first night he picked me up for dinner or the second… he'd knocked at my door, and when I let him in, he cast his gaze over my clutch, my proper dress, my chignon, and my understated makeup. He smiled, but then he said in a soft voice, "You don't have to try so hard for me, love."

It was at that moment that I realized just how hard I tried for Eric.

My hand drops. I frown, disregarding the dresses in my closet. Then, with a spark of inspiration, I slam shut the closet door, dropping to my knees to grab the under-the-bed storage tote I shoved under there.

When I left Eric, my parents wanted me to move back home. I had a room there, right next to Miranda.

Everything I abandoned when I became *his* was still there. It could be like I never lost those years to him… but I couldn't do it. As though I needed to prove to myself that I could stand on my own two feet—with my parents' help, that is—I rented this apartment. I did go home and bring some of my old treasured belongings with me, including some of my favorite outfits that Eric used to sneer at if I tried wearing them around him.

Opening up the tote, I sift through the cotton and denim that smells faintly of another life. That belonged to a different Annaliese.

Soft t-shirts. Cut-off shorts. Blue jeans and leggings. Perfectly valid clothing for a woman in her early-to-mid twenties, and outfits I haven't worn in years.

I grab a white tee, plus a pair of shorts. I don't care that it's the middle of April. Sebastien might ride around Harmony Heights on his bike, but every time he takes me out, he uses his flashy Porsche. There are seat warmers, so I'll be fine, and wherever we go, I'm sure he'll be wearing his leather jacket and devil-may-care grin.

Maybe it's time I match my new husband instead of dressing for the man who never liked the real me.

I'm trembling a little as I get dressed. Instead of pinning my hair up, I brush it out, letting carelessly tousled waves fall down my back. I put on lip gloss and mascara, just enough to make my eyes pop. A spritz of perfume and some lotion to highlight my long, bare legs.

There.

For the first time in years, I actually look like *me*. I feel like me, too. And not a moment too soon since, just as I shove the storage tote back under my bed, there's a knock at my front door.

I hurry to open it, to let Sebastien in. When I do, I find him leaning against the wall between my door and my neighbor's. With his hands in his pockets, a soft half-smirk stunning on his features, it looks like he's settled down, ready to wait.

But I'm ready, and I notice the instant he sees that I am.

That same half-smirk slowly disappears. His eyes drag from my bare legs to my short shorts, my t-shirt to the hesitant expression on my face, and he nods.

"Jesus Christ," he grates out, wiping his mouth with the back of his hand.

Crap.

Heat suddenly floods my cheeks. "I... sorry. I didn't know what you had in mind, but I shouldn't have dressed down like—"

"No," he says firmly, stepping into my apartment, cupping my elbows to stop me from turning and bolting to my bedroom so that I can change. "This is perfect."

I blink, biting down on my bottom lip. "Are you sure?"

An honest grin splits his gorgeous face. "You're perfect."

Well. If he says so.

HE SAID 'DRINKS'. FOR SOME REASON, I GOT IT IN MY head that he'd be taking me to the King's Court.

However, once I'm settled in his front seat, it doesn't take long for me to realize that he's going in the opposite direction—or that I've gone this way before myself.

Just in case, I ask, "Where are we going?"

"The Last Prayer."

Oh.

When I don't say anything in response to that, Sebastien glances over at me. "Problem?"

"No."

Yes.

I'm being ridiculous. I should've known better. Taking me to the King's Court would mean public acknowledgement in front of half the Owed. I shouldn't even want that. It'll get back to Eric in no time, and my three-week reprieve from his commands will be over like that. Even so… it would've been nice if Sebastien didn't want to hide me like Eric did.

"I just thought you'd want to go somewhere more… familiar," I say carefully.

His brows lift, seeing right through my care. "You mean the Court?"

I stare straight ahead. "That bar is fine. At least I already know they make a good Manhattan."

Sebastien makes a small noise in the back of his throat, continuing to drive until we reach the parking lot. He kills the engine, the pink neon flickering on the window of his car just like it would've the night we met if we'd driven here together instead of finding each other for one moment in time.

We go in together. The bar is half full, a melancholy song playing from the jukebox. I see a row of men in work boots at the bar. A group of women crowded around a booth. Plenty of tables for one that fit this place, with its atmosphere of smoke and grit and cheap booze.

It's definitely not the King's Court.

After tucking me in one of the booths, Sebastien goes to the bar. He comes back with a beer for himself, a chilled whiskey glass that must be my Manhattan. He sets them both down before sliding into the booth.

Not across from me. *Next* to me.

Shifting so that he's looking at me, he watches me for a long moment, then says, "This doesn't seem like your scene. I thought so the night we met. I haven't changed my mind yet."

Not my scene? Well, maybe he's right, but of the two of us, I'm not the Order golden boy covering up his privilege with a leather jacket and a daring smirk. In fact, I want to show him so badly that this *could* be my type of place—and maybe it might've been if I met Sebastien before Eric—that I don't grab my Manhattan.

I take his beer, holding the neck of the bottle between two fingers before lifting it to my lips and taking a sip.

He laughs. It's a soft, amused sort of chuckle as he reaches for my glass, downing half my Manhattan in a gulp.

My eyes widen. Okay. Just because they didn't serve it in a cocktail glass doesn't mean you treat it like a shot, but... damn, that was *sexy*.

You know what's even sexier? When he eases the beer from my hold, taking it firmly in his grip, swiping his tongue over the rim where my lips had just been before tipping the bottle back, drinking that, too.

He lets the bottle settle on the tabletop with a *clink*. "Know what? I think I might like your drink better than that cheap shit they serve here."

I push the half-filled glass of whiskey, bitters, and vermouth toward Sebastien. Then, with his eyes on me, I dart out my tongue, tasting him on the bottle. Not the beer. Just *him*. "It's not that bad."

His eyes gleam in the dim light, and I find myself admitting the truth: "This isn't really my scene. Actually, it's only the second time I've been here."

He raises his eyebrows. "Both times with me?"

I nod.

I think he likes that. I'm glad, too, until he asks me the one question I can't bring myself to answer: "So what were you doing here the first time? When we…"

He doesn't finish his sentence. He doesn't *have* to.

What was I doing?

"Trying to prove something to myself," I say, then I sigh. "I think I'm doing the same thing tonight."

"And what's that?"

"I'm not sure."

I dare a peek over at him. His face calls me a liar, but he lets me have it—just like he lets me have his beer *and* his company.

THIRTEEN

BETSY

SEBASTIEN

shouldn't go back to her apartment.

I should've just dropped her off after our one drink together like a normal guy, not a fucking stalker, then go home. I should sleep in my own bed like someone who isn't slowly losing his mind over a woman who still holds herself like she's made of brittle glass, and I'm the one who might finally shatter her completely.

Then again, I'm Sebastien Reynolds. I've never claimed to be normal. I'm no good guy, either. And if this is stalking… well, I guess I'm a goddamn stalker because I'm sitting in the parking lot, my bike straddled between my legs, watching her bedroom light go off in the window over my head.

I wait another half an hour, playing some stupid game on my phone. Annaliese only had one beer plus a sip of the Manhattan, but my wife can't hold her liquor.

I figure she'll be fast asleep by now, and as soon as I'm too anxious to keep on waiting, I engage the kickstand. Leaving my helmet on the handlebar, I take Annaliese's key out of my pocket, whistling under my breath as I walk into the building like I have every right to be there.

I'm her fucking husband. Of course I do.

I shoot a friendly smile at the woman who takes the elevator up with me. She's sixty if she's a day, but the second I smile, she flushes, patting her hair, murmuring a 'good evening' to me. I echo the sentiment, then wink at her in time to step off onto Annaliese's floor.

Using the copy of her key I made, I let myself into the apartment. After tonight… after my wife finally let me in enough to give me hope… I couldn't care less if she catches me sneaking in. I don't expect a repeat of what happened at the Last Prayer just because that's where my stupid ass brought her tonight. But to see her in that t-shirt and short shorts? If she'd given me any sign that she was interested, I would've had her bent over the bathroom sink before she could blink.

Pity that she didn't. That was my fault, too. I thought I was doing the romantic thing, bringing her back to the place we first met. Stupid idiot that I am, it never occurred to me that, by doing so, I was basically reminding her of the fucker she was running from.

Worse than that, I got the vibe that she thought I only brought her there because it was outside of Harmony Heights. It's the furthest thing there is from an Order establishment, and instead of proudly showing Annaliese on my arm, I was selfish enough to want to tuck her in the shadows and the smoke, keeping her all for myself in that dive bar.

One step forward, two steps back. Still, I'm not deterred. I want this woman, and I'll do anything to have her.

Just not tonight.

Annaliese is asleep when I move slowly inside of her bedroom. She lets out soft little snores, pretty brown hair falling loose around her face as she curls up on her pillow like a kitten that's too tired to pretend she isn't exhausted.

It breaks something in me every damn time I find her like that.

Pausing only to kick off my boots, I crawl into bed behind her, gently, carefully, like she's made of something precious. Though I'm being too risky, my fingers ghost over her hair, reveling in just how fucking soft it is.

She exhales. Part contented hum, part sigh.

With my other hand, I rub my aching chest with the heel of it before I lie on my side, pressing my forehead to the back of her neck as my jaw goes undeniably tight.

Tonight was unexpected. It was a pleasure, don't get me wrong. Since our marriage began, I could count the number of times that Annaliese has reached out to me on one hand. For her to call me and wrangle an invitation out with me... fuck, yeah, I cancelled my other plans.

I actually had every intention of going to the Court tonight. Something came up so that Dallas couldn't be there, but he was sending some other loyal members of his council to sit down with me. Alexandre promised to be there, and if he knows what's good for him, he would've been. Stephen, too, and if he knows what's good for *him*, he would've been sober.

I hate the Order of the Owed for so many reasons. The biggest one? Is how the gossips just can't help themselves. In the weeks since I married Annaliese, the whispers have already started. The rumors. Someone—and if I knew who, I'd handle it myself—had mentioned that Annaliese was supposed to be a Used. Instead of being married off to me, they wanted her to be put into service at the Court.

Over my dead body.

Dallas, of course, told the council to fuck off when one of the members mentioned it off-handedly. I'm grateful for how he has my back—and my wife's—but the truth is that Dallas's power is already shaky. Between his father embezzling from the Order before he died and Dallas refusing to get married himself… he has his own shit to deal with. At this point, half the Order wants tradition to hold. The other half is demanding change. All of them want to test him, and I wish them all good fucking luck.

Still. Every time Annaliese's name gets brought up in these rumors, there's a good chance she's in danger. I can't let that happen.

I *won't* let that happen.

Those aren't the only whispers, either. Too many people never expected me to settle down. That I did so quickly… they don't realize that Annaliese has flipped a switch inside of me, triggering the obsessive side of Sebastien Reynolds that I've kept hidden for way too many years now. They think it's a sham, and while I could give a fuck what they think, *Annaliese* thinks it's a sham, too.

No fucking way.

This is real. What we have is real. Tonight was the first step in proving it, and tomorrow? I'll take it a little further.

For now, I just lie beside her, getting a few hours of peaceful sleep. I close my eyes to the sound of her snores, smiling to myself while promising that no one will get to her while I'm still kicking.

I can't stay. I wish I could, but with the early morning sunlight beginning to stream in through the window, I'm thinking a little more clearly. I made a small enough stride toward convincing Annaliese to love me last night. If she finds me here, sleeping beside her… I'll lose it all. Hell, she'll probably try to invoke the termination clause in her contract.

I won't listen, but still. She'll try, and I don't want her to have to do that.

So, instead, I reluctantly slip out of her bed, looking at her one last time before I grab my boots and go.

My wife looks so small curled up under her blanket, a crease between her brows, almost like she's fighting something even in her dreams.

It kills me to have to leave her, but I do. I sneak out again, locking the door behind me before I go, all while taking a page out of one of Annaliese's binders and pulling my plan together.

Last night, she showed me a new side of her. Now? It's only fair that I get to show her mine.

It all begins with a text. A simple text around breakfast, detailing the first stage of my plan without actually giving her a way to refuse. I just told her what we were doing today, a time to be ready by, and then I went out to make sure I had everything I needed to pull it off.

Six hours later, I guide my bike back into the parking lot where it waited for me last night. My saddlebags are full of snacks and four bottles of water. I tucked a small plastic blanket in there, too. I'm wearing an over-the-shoulder bag that's strapped to my back. Inside of it, I have a pretty white helmet that should fit Annaliese.

She's waiting outside, just like I told her to be. Because I gave her the heads up that I wanted to take her out for a motorcycle ride, she's dressed for it: a long-sleeved blouse, a pair of jeans, white sneakers. Her hair is pulled back in a ponytail, and she's wearing a hesitant expression.

"You really want to do this?" she asks.

"Take you for a ride on my bike?" I give the chrome handlebar a loving stroke. "I've been dying to. I figured I'd give you some time to warm up to me, but if you want to get to know the real Sebastien, you have to understand he comes with Betsy."

She lifts her eyebrows. "Betsy?"

I nod. "Yup. Betsy."

"You named your motorcycle?"

"Of course I did. After all, I built her myself, piece by piece. When you're that intimate with a piece of machinery, you've gotta give her a name." I wink at my wife. "Before you, she was my favorite girl."

I live for the twin pink spots I can bring to Annaliese's cheeks. "And you're sure it's safe for the both of us to ride at the same time?"

Patting the back of my seat, I say, "Why don't you hop on and find out? Just make sure you hold me real tight, love. Trust me. I'll keep you safe." I shrug off the bag on my back. "Here. I even thought ahead and got you your own helmet."

Taking the helmet out, I hold it out to her. She takes it, looking at it as if she's afraid it's going to bite her.

I grin. "What's the matter? Scared?"

"Motorcycle deaths make up fifteen percent of all traffic fatalities," she says primly. "I'd be silly not to be concerned."

"Yeah, but none of them were on bikes built by Bas Reynolds," I boast. "Don't you trust me?"

She thins her lips. For a second, I expect her to scoff and say 'no'. It wouldn't be a surprise. Barely anyone in Harmony Heights trusts me. Why would she—

Annaliese slams the helmet down on her head. "I do. Just don't kill me, alright?"

Pulling my visor down so that she can't see the pride on my own face to hear her say that, I scoot forward, leaving enough space for her to climb onto the back of my bike. "Oh, love. I wouldn't dream of it."

JUST LIKE I HOPED, ANNALIESE CLINGS TO ME THE entire time we take the ride out of Harmony Heights, up the nearby mountains. Her arms are wrapped tightly around my waist, chest pressed to my back, thighs bracketing mine as though she was made to be on this motorcycle with me.

I nearly groan every time she squeezes me infinitely tighter whenever I take a turn.

I've gone this way so many times over the years, I could take the path with my eyes closed. Any time I need to escape the pressures of the Order, this is where I flee to. The Reynolds family has a mountain cabin a couple of miles from here that no one but me uses anymore. One day, when I was about sixteen and pissed off about something so stupid, I don't even remember it anymore, I found a waterfall overlook so beautiful, even a boneheaded teenager could appreciate it.

I've never brought anyone here before. Before Annaliese, I only had two long-term relationships. I dated Caroline Wilson for most of high school, but she wasn't an Order girl—not an Offering, and she refused to join as one of the Used—so I knew that we could never last. Not when I had Reynolds for my last name. A low-ranking member could marry whoever the hell they wanted, but when you're at the top of the secret society, it's an Offering if you want to climb up in the ranks.

I didn't give a shit about any of that. I was also only seventeen, and because I knew it couldn't last, I cheated on her with her best friend, Stephanie. And after Stephanie, it was Grace, then Monique, then Allie…

By then, I figured that it wasn't that I wouldn't take

any Offering as a wife, but that I had no plan to get hitched at all. Who wanted to enter a serious relationship with a guy who made it clear there was no commitment in the future? That began a decade of no strings attached relationships, flings, one-night stands, and a tendency to visit the Used in between that.

Except for Julie.

I thought Julie was different. For the first time ever, I thought *maybe*, but in the end, she was the one stringing me along. She might've been the only one I would've brought up to the waterfall, but she absolutely refused to ever ride with me.

Annaliese climbed on my back barely a month into our marriage—and she really thinks I'm going to let her go?

She doesn't complain at all during the ride. However, by the time we reach the waterfall overlook, she's shaking. Once I stop the bike, she slides off of Betsy on wobbly legs.

"Give yourself a second," I tell her, reaching out so that I can steady her with my hand on her hip. "Your legs need to catch up."

Standing still, she removes her helmet, letting it hang at her side as she glares at me. "You think this is funny?"

I should be honest with my wife. I laugh. "A little bit."

Annaliese tosses the helmet at me. Laughing even harder, I catch it as she huffs before moving toward the overlook. I can tell from her body language the moment she's gotten to the edge of the cliff, peering down at the waterfall below us. She inches closer, hands lifting to her face as she cups her chin, and I grin.

I knew she would love it here as much as I do.

While she's distracted by the view, I quickly fiddle with my bike. Practiced fingers loosen one of the connections. It's nothing dangerous, just enough to buy me some time alone with my wife.

Once that's done, I remove the saddlebags from the back of the bike, throwing them over my shoulder. I leave mine and Annaliese's helmets where I placed them on the dirt before joining her by the cliff.

While she stares down at the waterfall, the white rapids, the clean brook, the boulders… while she's lost in the view, I lay out the plastic blanket, the snacks, and the bottles of water I brought for our picnic. Only then do I walk over to her.

She glances up at me, tears glistening in her big brown eyes. "Sebastien… it's beautiful."

I don't even look at the waterfall. Instead, I look down at her, daring to rub my thumb along the height of her cheek, capturing a stray tear as it falls. "Yes. You are."

She blinks before ducking her head, suddenly shy. That's fine. If my wife needs to hear me tell her she's beautiful a hundred times before she believes it, then I'll tell her a hundred-and-one times.

I drop my hand to her shoulder. "Come on. Let's eat."

Happy to take the excuse to break up the sudden sexual tension, she hurries over to the picnic. I see the look of pleasure that flashes across her face as she plops down, mentally patting myself on the back. Fucking finally, I got something right.

We eat together, sharing the sandwiches, the chips, the apples that I sliced up myself. We bullshit, talking about everything and anything—except for our marriage, that is—and I find myself even more pleased that I thought ahead to mess with the bike. If I could, I'd keep Annaliese up here with me forever.

She doesn't seem to mind. In fact, she seems thrilled by the view, but even more impressed that I didn't just throw down a chunk of money to buy my bike and ride it off the lot.

"You actually really built that?" Annaliese looks at Betsy again, then at me. When I nod, she screws up her face in clear confusion. "I don't get it. You're obviously good with tools. So… why don't you do it as, like, a job? I can tell you enjoy it, too."

She's right on both counts. I'm great with tools, and I'm never more at peace with myself than when I have grease under my nails and a big piece of machinery in front of me as I bring it to life.

But as much as I wanted to leave the reality of the Order behind by bringing Annaliese out here, even I have to admit that that's impossible.

"Because in Harmony Heights," I say lightly, "having the Reynolds name means you don't get to dream small. So what if I've always wanted to own and operate a garage of my own? Not when your name is Sebastien Reynolds. Then you get shoved into politics, law, the Order, or something equally pretentious… or you do what I did and just do *nothing*."

She nods quietly. "I understand."

I'm sure she does.

Worse, that puts a damper on the rest of the afternoon. Both of us quiet, lost in thought instead of appreciating the outdoors, we finish eating. I can tell when Annaliese starts to get antsy, ready to head back, and I prepare myself for her reaction when she finds out that... yeah. That's not happening just yet.

Still, I go through the motions. Cleaning up the picnic, I stuff our garbage and the blanket into the saddlebags before snapping them back into place. I hand Annaliese her helmet, then put mine on. I climb onto the bike. Annaliese climbs behind me.

I start the engine.

Nothing happens.

I try again.

Annaliese lifts her visor. "Um... Sebastien? Why isn't your bike turning on?"

Looking over my shoulder at her, I shrug with as much innocence as I can muster. "Not sure. Looks like Betsy's not getting the spark she needs to go."

I don't think I know how to do innocence, and Annaliese obviously agrees. As though she can tell I'm full of shit, she narrows her eyes. "You built it."

"I did," I agree. "I said I built it, piece by piece. I didn't say I was *good* at doing it."

"Oh, you—"

She stares at me.

I stare right back.

She pats her pockets. "I'll call Miranda. She has her

permit. She can come get us. If not, I'm sure one of your friends can pick us up."

If I called any of my bros, they'd drop whatever they were doing to help me. I'd do the same for them, too. But if they knew I was right where I wanted to be… "Sorry. I thought you noticed. There's no service up here."

I don't think she even noticed that, distracted by our picnic date, she never even took out her phone. I'm banking on that because, while the service is spotty up on the mountain, if she walks around, she'll get a strong enough signal to make a call.

She leaves her phone in her pocket, and I have to swallow my triumphant grin.

Instead, I cluck my tongue. "What's the matter, love?"

"What's the matter?" she echoes. "Your bike is dead. We're probably a good hour, hour and a half out of town by foot, and it'll be dark sooner than later. No one knows where we are, and it's just me and you stuck together out here."

I remove my helmet, making sure she can see the dare on my face. "Is that a problem? That it's just me and you?"

"What? No—"

I chuckle. "It's okay. Tell me, Annaliese… are you afraid to be alone with your husband?"

FOURTEEN
INTERRUPTED

ANNALIESE

Are you afraid to be alone with your husband?

Am I?

Of course not. I'm not afraid of this man, husband or not. But if I'm being honest with myself… I might be a little wary of being alone with a stunningly attractive man that I can't help but be drawn to.

That's just me, though. We've been married for almost a month, and the mixed signals are driving me fucking crazy. Sometimes I can't help but feel like he's hiding me, but at the same time, we've gone on dates. He's not enforcing the Order's 'sleeping in the same bed' rule, but he visits me enough that I don't think that he has a devoted side piece. Does that mean he isn't visiting the Used? No… and I can't ask him. I just… I *can't.*

This was a magical afternoon. Riding his bike after

he basically told me that that was what we were doing today was freeing, and I'd be lying if I said that I didn't enjoy spending time with him… but it's fake. It's *fake*. I'm only fooling myself when I think 'what if'.

What if I could really love Sebastien Reynolds? What if he could love me?

What if this marriage could be real…

I shake my head. "I'm not afraid of you, Sebastien."

"That's good to hear. But," he adds, waving his hand in the few inches that exist between my chest and his while we're both sitting on his dead motorcycle, "you are afraid of this. Of *us*."

Shit.

I hate that he's right. I hate even more that he *knows* he's right.

So I tell him the one thing that I cling to whenever the feelings get too real: "It doesn't matter. What we have… this is fake, Sebastien."

Moments ago, he was chuckling, not concerned in the least that the bike he built with his own two hands had crapped out on him. He was amused, while I was frustrated, but a swift change suddenly comes over him. He tosses his helmet to the dirt. His jaw tight, he swings his leg, climbing off of the bike. The kickstand is still down, so I don't do anything but bounce slightly from the momentum of his quick move before he's right in front of me. Gentle yet firm hands lift my helmet from my head.

Sebastien drops it beside his, and in one fluid movement, grips my jaw, tilting my head back, kissing me. He's strong enough to keep me right where he wants me, and I'm helpless to do anything but sit on the back of the bike while Sebastien kisses me deeply.

I go lightheaded. When he finally breaks the kiss, I'm too dazed to react as he lowers his hands to my ass. Next thing I know, he's lifting me up, taking me off of the motorcycle, settling me on my sneakers directly in front of him.

"Fake?" he grates out. He snatches my hand, shoving it against the front of his jeans. "Does this feel fake to you?"

My fingers find the hard, heavy length of him straining against his jeans.

Oh.

I shouldn't be surprised. Especially not when I've already slept with him. I know exactly what it feels like to have his dick inside of me, stretching me out. Of course I make him aroused. Between his extensive sexual history and how we met... honestly? I'd be offended if he wasn't attracted to me after we got married.

But he never touched me again. Not like this. And because he didn't, I couldn't, and now... I ghost my fingers over the denim, wishing there wasn't any of the fabric separating my questing fingers from his erection.

"Tell me, love? Does that feel fake?" he demands. His breath is hot on my ear, his voice shredded. His arm is wrapped around me, making it so that I can't do anything but stroke him through his jeans.

I shake my head.

Sebastien groans, dropping his. He kisses my throat, tongue dragging against my fluttering pulse.

Sucks on a patch of skin under my jaw, thrusting into my hand.

"This is real," he grunts out. "It's always been real. And if you think it's not… that's my fucking fault. I tried to be good. I tried to give you time, get to know me… because, *fuck*. I want to know you. Don't you want to know me?"

He sounds so vulnerable all of a sudden, all I can do is be honest back: "I do… and I really, really want to touch you."

He barks out a laugh. "Oh, love… I want that more than you know."

"Really?"

Disentangling himself from our embrace, he leans back enough to reach for the button on his jeans. He quickly undoes it, then jerks down his zipper. Digging into his jeans, he grabs his cock, freeing it, and I have to bite down hard to keep from moaning.

Cocks aren't pretty. Sorry. I've only had two lovers, but I've seen more than a few, and they're all kinda weird. I much prefer what they do to me, how they make me feel, than what they look like. That's why, when I fucked Sebastien in the bathroom of the Last Prayer, I barely paid attention. I just climbed on his lap, guiding it into me, and riding him in a way that Eric rarely let me. For him, sex meant I needed to be submissive.

With Sebastien, he didn't seem to mind me taking control the first time. And now…

I grab him. He grunts, and I realize that I need a

little help. Releasing him just long enough to lick my palm, I take him in hand again and begin to stroke.

He bucks into my fist. "Yes. *Yes*. You do that… you keep on fucking touching me just like that, love, and I'll tell you whatever you want to know. Ask me anything. Get to know me." With a quick shove, he pushes his jeans down past his ass, then his underwear. He spreads his legs, bracing them in the dirt, giving me full access to his cock as he pants my name. "Annaliese… I want you to want me. Not just because I'm Bas Reynolds. But because I'm your Sebastien."

I'm distracted. I can see his dark blond curls, plus the thick cock jutting out from them. He's shifting his hips a little, forcing me to move with him until I take over the stroking myself, and while the one thing I really want to know is what Sebastien looks like when he comes in my hand, I think about what he said.

He wants to know me. He wants me to know him.

Think, Annaliese. You're organized. There isn't anything you can't accomplish with a binder, a pen, and a checklist. You certainly can give your husband a handjob *and* ask him some questions about himself at the same time.

Right?

"Um. What's your favorite color?"

His eyes were heavy-lidded, more closed than not, but he quirks them open. Yeah, yeah. I know that was a stupid question, but I make up for it by licking my thumb, swirling it around the head of his cock, before returning to jerking him off.

He grunts. "It used to be black. But now I think it's brown. Like your hair… unh. And your *eyes*."

Charmer. I smile, increasing the pace. "You a cat lover or a dog lover? And don't say none because I don't trust anyone who doesn't like animals."

"Cat," he gasps. "But that's because Adrian got into Loni's pants after he rescued a pair from the shelter. If a pussy can get me back in your pussy, love, then give me a cat any day."

My cheeks heat up. To hear him talk so boldly… so *filthily* like that… I dart out my tongue, dabbing the corner of my mouth as the veins in his neck stand out. He's gotta be close. I hope so. I've done every trick that I was ever taught to pleasure a lover, and a few I'm picking up now because Sebastien is the most receptive one I've ever had…

He's gritting his teeth. His eyes are darker than I've ever seen.

"What are you thinking about right this very second?" I ask.

His gaze snaps to mine, hungry and bright. "You want to know?"

I wouldn't have asked if I didn't. "Yes."

"Just how badly I want to bend you over my bike and fuck you until you admit that I'm your husband and you're my wife."

My entire body jolts. His cock slips out of my hand, I'm so stunned by his admission. He winces, and I grab him again, moving my hand faster and faster as if the rhythm of my arm is enough to knock his heated words out of my head.

He can tell he spooked me. I don't think he regrets being so honest, though he is quick to add: "But not today." I'm touching him, but he's touching me now, reaching out, brushing a stray lock of hair out of my face, his breath ragged as he tells me, "Not until you're ready. After all, we have forever."

That's what Sebastien thinks.

"We have until March," I correct weakly.

Rather than tell me that I'm wrong, he lunges forward, biting down on my bottom lip just hard enough to have me gasping. At the same time, I squeeze the head of his cock, and he comes hard, hips jerking, hot come spilling all over my fingers.

Sebastien releases his bite. His hand covers mine, guiding it through the aftershocks as he comes down from his climax.

Only then, once he has, does he shift his hold on me. His fingers circle my wrist, tugging my jizz-covered hand up until all I can smell is his come. Slightly bleachy and almost sweet, he forces me to look at it.

And then he grins. A crooked grin that's all *Sebastien*, with a hint of a wicked, devilish edge as he says with a dare, "You made this mess, love. Now clean it up."

I do. Darting my tongue out, I lap at his come, licking as much of it as I can from my fingers as he watches, lust brightening up his dark eyes.

"Shit, Annaliese." He shudders. "You're such a good fucking girl. Look at you. Do you always do what you're told?"

Honestly?

I lift up my head. "No. Not always," I tell him, and I

give him my own daring look as I smear the rest of his come across the front of his leather jacket.

His lips twitch, expression both amused and approving. "You're still my good girl."

As Sebastien tucks his spent cock back into his jeans, as the erotic high of what we just did together starts to come down... suddenly, I have a different question for him that I have to ask.

"Am I really? Because... I don't know. It seems like I'm being kept as your secret. Like you're hiding me," I add before I can stop myself. "Just like—"

His eyes sharpen. "Just like who, Annaliese?"

I glance away. "Forget it. It doesn't matter. After all, the contract doesn't say—"

He snorts, followed by a laugh that is more bitter than I would've expected. "Right. The contract." He jerks up his zipper with more force than necessary. "The fucking *contract*. The same contract that says if intimacy is desired, it must be consensual, private, and free of obligation."

Holy shit. He got that clause word-for-word.

I wonder why that's the only section that really imprinted on my fake husband? As though, when it comes down to it, the only part of our fake marriage that means anything at all is sex?

And, yes, I told him he could have that if he wanted. All along, he hasn't... so what changed? And why is he looking at me now like *I* did something wrong when I did exactly what he wanted? I jerked him off. I asked him questions. I licked his come—and I did it all out here in the mountains, which is nice and private and *hidden*, isn't it?

I lift my chin, gesturing with my damp hand around the overlook. "Can't get more private than this, Sebastien. And if we're quoting the contract, it also says monogamy isn't required. That discretion is preferred. You want me to get to know you? Here's a question. What's your opinion on monogamy during our marriage?"

Sebastien stalks toward me. "Why are you asking? You looking for a side piece?"

I'm not afraid of my husband. I'm *not*. But the way he's suddenly looming over me…

I back up, darting around him, putting some space between us. Four feet, five, maybe six… I just need to be able to breathe, and the way his eyes are following me, the most predatory look I've ever seen on his features… I need him to stay over there until I can understand what the hell is going on.

"What? No, I—"

Before I can finish what I was saying, I feel my phone buzzing in my back pocket.

What the… He said there was no service, but maybe he just meant that it was crap. That I needed to walk around to find a spot where my phone would work.

I dip my fingers into my pocket.

"Annaliese," he begins. "We need to talk about this."

No, we don't, because I'm already looking at the screen.

RANDA

WHERE ARE YOU?? I NEED YOU!!!

My heart sinks all the way down to my sneakers. Normally, a text like that would just mean my little sister is overreacting. But she's seventeen, so close to being an adult, she can taste it, and the only thing that would have her messaging me like that was if… if…

Eric.

No.

I look over at Sebastien, the sudden panic so over-whelming, I can barely speak. We're stuck here. I could call Miranda, ask her to come get us, but what if she's in trouble? What if she's in danger? What if—

As though he can tell that something is wrong, Sebastien marches toward me. He plucks the phone right from my hand, reading the message my sister sent.

"Everything okay?" he asks me.

I snatch my phone back. "It's my sister. She needs me. And your bike is *broken*."

A slightly abashed expression flutters over Sebastien's face. Digging into his own pocket, he returns to his bike. I don't know what it is that he does, but a second later, he revs the engine, the motorcycle coming back to life.

He steps around me, kneels by the bike.

I blink. "You said it was broken."

My husband has the nerve to look unrepentant. "It was. Now it isn't."

Sebastien did something to it. To keep me with him, to spend this time with me… he messed with his bike.

Or maybe he just got lucky... I don't know. I don't *care*. If he can get me back to Harmony Heights—back to Miranda—then I can forgive him anything.

Still, as he scoops up my helmet, holding it out to me before grabbing his own, I can't help but say, "I thought you said you didn't do a good job on Betsy."

"You're right. I did say that, love." Slapping his motorcycle helmet onto his head, Sebastien swings his leg over his seat before holding his hand out so that he can help me on. "But that's because I did an *excellent* fucking job with my girl."

FIFTEEN
CONNOR HEYWARD

SEBASTIEN

So... that could've gone better.

Jesus Christ.

I can't believe that. As though I've never been with a woman before, all it took was Annaliese working her hand over my cock, stroking me, her soft fingers working their magic on my overheated flesh and, suddenly, I was splurting all over her. There wasn't even enough time to warn her that I was about to come. I bucked into her hand and, with a gasp of surprise—and a little bit of goddamn shame—I just let go.

Hell, I didn't even mean to push her into feeling me up. It's like they say. One thing led to another, and if her phone hadn't buzzed, the spotty service coming through with the worst possible timing, I'm pretty sure that would've led to *another*. As far as I was concerned, that wasn't playtime. Oh, no. That was simply foreplay, and like I've been fantasizing over since I was able to call that woman mine, I would've had her bent over my bike, ass out, cock thrusting in and out of her delightful pussy as soon as I could get it up again.

Despite the serious topic of conversation, part of me was already imagining her heat wrapped around me, the chill of the waterfall caressing my ass cheeks when the buzz broke the spell. Of course she had to answer. I'd have to be a dick to stop her so I didn't. And when panic clouded her face, erasing any of the wonder and the lust and the desire that had been there as she touched me, there was only one thing I could do.

I repaired the bike in a flash, and though she wasn't that pleased to realize that I lied about that, knowing that I could get her back to her sister in no time was enough for her to forgive me... for now. I'm sure I'll have a lot to do to make it up to my wife. And I'll do it, gladly. But I'm also incredibly aware that I'm on thin ice now.

That's why, after I drove her back to Harmony Heights, bringing her straight to the Crawfords' home instead of Annaliese's place, I didn't push my luck. Part of me wanted to play the 'husband' card and let her know that I would stay. She refused to tell me what had spooked her sister enough that she needed to come right home. Even though the message didn't say why Miranda Crawford needed Annaliese, the stricken look in Annaliese's eyes told me that she knew—and maybe if I hadn't broken her trust up on the overlook, she might've told me.

Fuck me. Once again, it's one step forward, two steps back. I showed Annaliese one of my most private places when I needed to escape Harmony Heights and let her know about my dreams of being a mechanic. I even got a handjob from her which left me feeling so high—until I had to admit I deceived her. So I gave my wife a smile when I did it. The hurt look on her face when she realized I lied to her will stay with me for a long, long time.

So I don't push. I squeeze her fingers after Annaliese climbs off my bike, telling her to keep the helmet and call me when she needs a ride home. That she doesn't refuse… doesn't tell me that she won't… I don't fuck up *that* badly.

I wait for her to disappear into the house. My visor's up so I can see better. Once she's gone, I scrub my hand over my face.

I just wanted an excuse to spend time with my wife without any expectations. Was that so bad? While we were together… and then the way she mentioned monogamy after the act?

I swear to fucking God, that word hits like a damn hammer. A part of me—a small, ugly, jealous part— immediately pictured her with someone else. Another man's hands on her. Another man's mouth on her. Her body underneath the fucker that I still haven't been able to identify…

My stomach had twisted, the worst kind of posses- sive rage boiling up inside of me until I suddenly had to remind myself that she wasn't talking about her being loyal to me.

She was talking about *me* being loyal to *her*.

I know my rep. I know how hard it will be to shake

it, but without even meaning to, I've been loyal to the brunette I met that night at the Last Prayer. Now that she's my wife? Now that I've given her my name, my protection, my *everything*?

I want to be worthy of Annaliese. I want to be a better man for her.

I want to be the kind of husband she deserves.

And that's why, after I close my visor again and start up my bike, I leave Annaliese's family home and head on over to Connor and Haven's.

I need advice from someone who clawed his way out of the same darkness I'm afraid might swallow me whole, and there is no one better than to tell me how he and his wife escaped the oubliette than Connor Heyward.

As of this year, only two people are allowed to visit the Heywards without advance notice: me and Loni Heller. It used to be just me. It took all five of us—me, Adrian, Dallas, Des, and Connor—to get her out of that hellhole she was trapped in, but when she finally stopped being catatonic… finally found her voice again… she made it adamantly clear that she wanted nothing to do with three of us.

She hated Adrian for the way he used to treat Loni, and how she was handpicked to be his Offering back when we were kids.

She hated Dallas because he was Adrian's cousin and Jack Collins' only son. Since she absolutely loathed the former King, her hatred trickled down to Dallas.

And Des… well, he was a douche. Despite how tight we were in school, we'd drifted away some in the years that followed, but we figured that we could still call on him when we needed him. And while Desmond St. James helped with breaking Haven out, he was still a douche about it, and then he eventually tried to Claim Loni and, well, Adrian hit the limit of his patience.

Because I never really upset her, Haven was cool with me. And Connor… she was made for him.

Before Loni left Harmony Heights, back when we were all eighteen or so, she was best friends with Haven. They lost touch after Loni disappeared, and when she was dragged back to marry Desmond, she had no idea what had happened to Haven. Adrian—protecting his new wife from the truth—didn't want her to know what her friend had gone through while she was gone. Eventually, she found out, and he had me visit Connor and Haven to see if she would be willing to talk to Loni.

Adrian thought that might help Haven. Connor thought that Adrian should butt out. The two almost came to blows, with good ol' Bas playing peacemaker. And, hell, I must've done something right because, all these months later, Loni and Haven are back to being friends again.

So she has a pass to visit. Adrian? Yeah, he'll still get a door in his face if he tries.

Me? After I knock, Connor opens the door, meeting me there with a finger pressed to his lips.

"She's sleeping," he whispers, and neither one of us

has to ask who he's referring to. "She had a nightmare last night. Couldn't sleep at all. Eventually, I had to give her something to help her go down."

The quiet pain in his rough voice is familiar. So is the steel just beneath it.

I get it. Haven isn't only his wife. She's the woman he damn near tore the world apart to find, and after he did, he's done everything he can to bring her back to him. It's been a year and a half. She's so much better than she was, but there are times when... yeah. It can get bad, and I don't blame Connor for doing what he has to.

He jerks his thumb over his shoulder. "Did you want to come in?"

"If it's okay."

Connor nods. "Yeah. Just keep your voice down."

"You got it."

Haven's gotta be sleeping on the second floor. We ease our way through the front room, going until we reach the small table in the kitchen.

Before I sit down, I reach into my front pocket. It was something else I had stowed in my saddlebag once I realized I wouldn't have to use it. I grabbed it before I walked down the sidewalk that led to Connor and Haven's cozy home. Now I lay the small glass vial on the table, pushing it toward him.

"You didn't need it?"

I shake my head. "Turns out, my wife sleeps like the dead. Thanks for slipping me the sedative at the wedding, but I never had to use it. I can sneak in, spend a few hours next to her, then get out and, as far as I know, she has no clue that I was there."

Except for my cologne lingering in her space, but I do that on purpose. Call it a subliminal message. I want her to get so used to it that, even when I'm not there, she imagines that I am.

Connor shrugs, pocketing the vial. He's been using the same shit on Haven since he first brought her back home to Harmony Heights. In the beginning… she didn't *want* to stay with Connor. Proving that we understand each other in ways that very few others do—Adrian does, and so does Dallas—I completely understand why he decided to drug Haven, keeping her trapped in his house until she finally realized that he was only doing it for her own good.

They're happy *now*. If you even try to suggest that Haven leave Connor, she has a panic attack that eventually leads to her being sedated again. She's as dependent on him as he is her, and while that might seem toxic to outsiders, that's just part of what happens when you're raised to be involved with the Order of the Owed.

I can't drug Annaliese. It would be easier if I could, but that won't get me my wife. I'll have to try something else, and as Connor looks over the table at my sorry face, he can tell that I didn't just stop by to return the sedative.

He jerks his chin at me. "So… how's it going with you and the missus?"

I can't keep back the sigh. "Fuck me, Connor. Let me just tell you… Adrian had it so much better." At his disbelieving look, I nod. "Yeah. At least he knew Loni had feelings for him once upon a time."

"She hated him."

True. "Yeah, but she loved him, too. When he got her back, he just needed to remind her that she loved him."

"Haven hated me," Connor says, thinking he's being helpful.

"Yeah, but she had a good reason to. And you made it up to her. Once you did, she couldn't help but love you. But Annaliese... she's keeping up walls."

"Knock 'em down."

That's easy to say, coming from Connor Heyward. Knocking things down is his specialty.

"It's not as easy as that. I don't want to scare her... shit, Con, I'm not made to love a woman like her."

"Of course not," he says dryly. "None of us are. We were born with silver spoons shoved so far down our throats that we almost choked on them. Shit. We have marked palms that mean we've never had to work for anything *real*."

He taps his palm, drawing attention to the scar in the shape of the Order's sigil.

I run my thumb over mine without thinking.

"That's why you and—" He stops himself. "It never would've worked."

"Yeah," I murmur. "I know."

Connor watches me for a long, assessing moment.

"Bas... listen. If something's worth having," he says quietly, "you do whatever the hell you can to keep it."

He's talking about Haven now. About the woman

asleep upstairs, who still wakes up screaming. About how far he went to get her, and how far he's gone since to *keep* her.

"She'll be okay," I tell him, hoping I'm not lying to one of my oldest, closest friends. "She's been talking to Loni. That helps, right?"

"Yeah." The hard lines of Connor's mouth soften a fraction. "I'm thinking about getting her own kitten to take care of. Maybe two. Adrian said that they do best in pairs."

"So do even the most broken of us," I point out.

Connor's eyes dart to the ceiling, toward the bedroom where Haven is blissfully unaware of everything he does to take care of her.

And he nods. "Yeah... *yeah.*"

Yeah.

SIXTEEN

GOOD

ANNALIESE

wish I could have stayed on that overlook, staring down at the waterfall, watching it crash into the rocks while no one else existed in this world except for Sebastien and me.

Days later, I can't even be mad about his stunt with the motorcycle. It was actually really nice to see his playful side. For the most part, he's either smooth and charming or suddenly quiet, as though there's a part of him that he's trying to shield me from. For him to purposely disable his bike just because he wanted to spend some more time with me... how could I not be flattered?

Maybe if he'd let the deception go on after I received that text from Miranda, I might not have, but the second I needed to go to my sister, he was popping that small piece back into place, fixing the bike as quickly as he was able to break it. He wasn't going to torture me by thinking I couldn't get to my sister when she needed me. I just wiped the last evidence of his arousal for me on his leather jacket, accepted the helmet he handed me, and we were on our way.

I wish I could have stayed, but Miranda needed me, and as soon as Sebastien dropped me off at my parents' house, it only stung a little that he rode off. I knew he had to. This was between my sister and me, and as soon as she saw me, she threw her arms around me in a tight hug before grabbing my hand, dragging me to her room.

Why was she freaking out? Simple. Because my ex had spent over an hour that day upsetting her, purposely driving up and down our street in his fancy silver BMW. Just in case Miranda didn't notice him while she sat at her desk doing her homework, he actually parked along the curb just outside the house, staring up at her window for half the time.

Eric was stalking my sister. Not because she was his next target, but because he knew it would get back to me. Because he knew that I had blocked him, and he had pivoted to getting my attention the only way he could without creating a scene at my apartment.

I'll give him credit. He knew exactly how to get a reaction out of me. Target Miranda and Annaliese will fall in line.

In a way, it worked. Though Sebastien made sure I took my helmet—*my* helmet because he actually bought me one so I could ride with him… at least, he *told* me that he bought it for me specifically—with me before telling me to call him when I was done so that he could bring me back to my apartment on his bike, I spent the night in my childhood bedroom.

Miranda drove me home the next morning after we checked to make sure that Eric hadn't decided to come back. Much calmer now that she could make sure that I was okay, my sister promised she'd keep an eye out. If Eric came back, I would have to interfere, though she told me that she was more concerned that I *would* confront him than that I wouldn't.

But I have to. I'm the big sister, and Eric Ward is my problem.

I thought he gave up. I thought he realized that I blocked him and he got the hint. I've already been married for almost a month. Odds are, he has to have heard the gossip that Sebastien Reynolds took a wife. If he hears that her name is Annaliese, he'd instantly jump to the conclusion that 'her' was *me*. That's how he works. The world revolves around Eric Ward, so if he wanted to own me, he'd assume that another Owed would as well.

Of course, if he *did* know, I don't think he would just terrorize my sister. I'd expect him at my door. Well, good. If he shows up, I'll just flash him the wedding band on my finger. So long as I have the Reynolds name to hide behind, Eric can't threaten me anymore.

If I'm lucky, my ex will move on to another victim by the time my year as Mrs. Sebastien Reynolds is done. And, true, I do have to admit that, as far back as I can remember, he'd been there, lurking, watching me from a distance, keeping an eye on me from the time I was eighteen until I was twenty-two. By twenty-three, we were officially together, and we stayed that way for two years until I accidentally discovered that his wife wasn't anywhere near as close-to-dead as he pretended, but, instead, living a separate life with her own lover.

That's when he admitted that he would never leave Cicely. There would be no marriage for Eric and me because there would be no divorce for Eric and his wife. It wasn't that he was insistent that I become a Used so that I could continue to be his mistress. Oh, no. By fucking me without offering me marriage, I *was* a Used —and he knew it.

I loved Eric, but he lied to me… *betrayed* me in the cruelest way possible… and now I've found myself in a fake marriage, trying my damndest not to fall even harder for the husband I can't have.

And in case I forgot that because Sebastien took me for a ride on his bike, I get slapped in the face with a dose of reality in the days that follow…

Once I let myself into my apartment the next morning, I close my eyes, and, for a split second, I'm back on that narrow path next to the waterfall. His bike is there, his body braced under mine, the hungry sound he made echoing in my ear as I remember how easily he came apart in my hands.

I can smell him. His cologne mingled with something that I now recognize as exhaust from his bike…

His bike. I think back to how proud he was that he built her—he built Betsy—all by himself. Of how he could break the bike, then fix it, as though he can speak to the machinery. I think of how it's obvious to me that he would be the best mechanic in Harmony Heights if his last name wasn't Reynolds.

And I think of the black Amex in my purse, and how he told me to pick a salary for planning Alexandre Reynolds' birthday before doubling it…

It's a thought. A seedling. A mere what-if. For now, I have to focus all of my attention on Alexandre's birthday. It's coming up quickly, and I'm determined to make it the best bash that Harmony Heights has ever seen. The venue… the guest list… the menu… I have to finalize all of it. And then, if my germ of a plan starts coming to fruition… maybe I can run with a secret gift for my husband that he would never expect.

I owe him. For the name he gave me for the next year, and for the ring on my finger that awards me some level of protection. I *owe* an Owed, and I keep that to myself while I throw myself into getting Alexandre's party ready.

It's easy, too, since I haven't heard from Sebastien since the night he left me outside of my parents' house.

That was three days ago. And, to be fair, I haven't reached out to him, either. How can I? When part of me is convinced that he'll demand answers to questions that I just can't face, and the other part thinks that, now that he spent some time with me alone… when he actually let me touch him again… he decided that, yes, keeping this strictly professional during the course of our marriage of convenience is the way to go?

He doesn't call. Doesn't text. Doesn't stop by my apartment, which is really fucking weird because, despite me opening a window during the day to air it out, his scent lingers.

Or maybe that's because I can't stop thinking about him…

It's okay. I should've known better than to think that a handjob would be enough to convince him to take our marriage of convenience and turn it into something real. He's doing me a favor already by just giving me his name. The picnic was sweet, and hearing him talk about his dream of owning a garage made me feel like he was letting down his cocky guard around me, but that simply means that we're getting to know each other better. We're not strangers anymore, like I told him. We're… well, I'm not sure *what* we are, but I can't expect him to treat me like his real wife all the time because I stupidly got used to it.

And then, right when I'd taken the hint that Sebastien wants to put some distance between us, I get a text in the middle of the day.

HUBBY🩶

I hope you're free tonight. I'm taking you out.

We're going to the Court.

My phone nearly slips out of my hand.

The Court? Where everyone will be able to see us?

Where Eric might have spies?

Sure, I was disappointed when he brought me to the Last Prayer like he was hiding me, instead of going to the Order's club. But now…

Do I want to go?

With him?

With my husband?

Before I think better of it, I type a quick response.

It's a date.

It takes me an hour to decide what to wear to the King's Court.

I've noticed that Sebastien seems to really like it when I'm dressed down. Instead of being an Offering, I'm plain old Annaliese, and that seems to catch his attention. I... I'm not sure I *want* his attention. After that motorcycle ride, I don't know *what* I want, and I end up deciding on a mix between something that Eric would've approved of and the basic jeans and tee that I wore when I went riding with my fake husband.

I choose a skirt that swirls around my knees, pairing it with a silky blouse and a pair of heels that elongate my legs. My hair stays loose, too, and I go for a darker lipstick that will fit in at the Court.

After all, this is the first time I'm going as the wife of an Owed.

A little after eight, Sebastien arrives at my apartment to pick me up. His eyes spark, going impossibly dark as he takes in my latest outfit, and I'm pleased enough to see the obvious attraction on his face. It shouldn't matter to me, but it does, and I'm glad to see that I can at least turn him on.

My husband kisses me like he always does. Cupping

my neck, holding me in place so that he can nip at my bottom lip before guiding his tongue into my mouth. He's held me to the 'hello' and 'goodbye' kiss clause that he added to our contract, and I don't realize how much I've missed the taste of him until he's swooped me up in his arms.

I guess I thought that, since he forgot to give me one after I climbed off of his bike, that he'd given up on them. It's nice to see that he hasn't.

Taking my hand, he leads me to the elevator. I'm basically buzzing. I want so badly to ask him where he's been, why it seemed like he fell off the face of the planet, but I can't. If I was his *real* wife, I'd have the right to interrogate him. As his *fake* wife, I keep my mouth shut until he holds open the door to his Porsche, helping me in.

Only then do I try to start a conversation by filling him in on the party details that I've confirmed so far.

Starting his car, he glances at me. "Hey. Listen. I trust you, love. I know you're going to do an amazing job. Just check in with Alexandre, okay? Get his input so that he doesn't whine that we missed something when it's over. You think you can do that for me?"

I already had it in my notes. I'd planned on reaching out to Sebastien's brother once we got a little closer to May and I had most of the details that Sebastien gave me locked down. Alexandre is aware that his brother is hosting a belated thirtieth birthday party for him. At first, I thought it would be a surprise party, but Sebastien laughed, telling me that his brother would sniff out any surprise that involved him. It would just be easier to fill him in on it from the beginning, and that's what he did.

"Yes. Of course."

"Good." He turns off my street, beating the speed limit as he hits the main road. "That was easy. You think there's something else you can do for me?"

"Sure."

"I want you to trust me."

He said something like that the day we rode on his motorcycle together. Then, he wanted to make sure I trusted him when it came to him driving us out of town. Now? It's clear that he means something else entirely.

I should just shake my head, maybe change the subject.

I don't.

"About what?"

"I've been a busy Bas the last couple of days. Order biz for the most part, but there's more to it than that." Instead of looking at the road, he's watching me. "Someone hurt you, Annaliese, and I've been patient. Ask my bros. I'm not a patient guy. I've tried to figure out who he is, but I haven't been able to. You want to tell me?"

I fiddle with my fingers in my lap. Shit. Do I want to tell him? Yes. God yes. I want to warn him about Eric in case my ex decides to blame Sebastien for helping me. I want him to know that I'm over him, in case that's something he's worried about, and I want to tell him that, while Eric did hurt me, I'm okay.

But I can't.

I can't tell him any of that.

To do so would be to admit that I was a stupid, silly, little girl who fell for the wrong man and made way too many mistakes. It would be to put Sebastien in Eric's crosshairs, and while I'm sure that my fake husband wouldn't be afraid of my former lover, *I* am.

That's the truth. I'm afraid of Eric, and I don't want to drag Sebastien into my mess any more than I have.

So, rather than trust him and answer him, I shake my head, still staring ahead. "I can't."

He raps his left hand on his steering wheel. With a sigh, he rips his gaze from my profile. "I know. Still, it was worth a try."

Sebastien goes quiet for a moment. Then, "You're right, you know?" At my questioning look, he adds, "I *was* hiding you. Keeping you all to myself. But not because I'm ashamed to be your husband. I'm proud of my wife, and I want to show her off. So if you're comfortable going to the King's Court tonight, I'd like you to go in with me on my arm."

The Court… this is what I wanted. Even better, Eric won't be there; his spies, yes, but not the man himself. That's why I went there in the first place after he made his threats. As his mistress, I was meant to go to him. He would never skulk around the Court. It's actually the younger Owed who spend their evenings at the gentle-man's club.

Like Sebastien.

And he wants *me* on his arm?

"Okay," I whisper. "I'd like it if you took me."

His smile is slow and wicked and warm as he slides his gaze toward me again.

"Good."

SEVENTEEN
UNDERSTAND

ANNALIESE

have to admit: the King's Court looks different when I'm not here to sell myself.

Last time, I came alone, walking in terrified and desperate, holding my head up high to hide it while praying no one recognized who I was—or how ruined I considered myself to be.

I expected them to grab me, hold me down, and, on Eric's orders, put the Order's sigil on my neck so that everyone in Harmony Heights knew I was one of the Used. Instead, Sebastien found me, and when I proposed to him—only the second man I ever slept with —he actually said *yes*.

And that's why, this time, I'm finally walking into the Court on Sebastien Reynolds' arm and it seems like every single head turns. I'm not even being facetious. So many of the Owed are involved in their own vices, but there are enough who recognize my fake husband and have to wonder about the identity of the woman he's entering the gentleman's club with instead of leaving it.

I cling to him. The music thrums deep in the floorboards, bass vibrating up my high heels, shades of gold—from the candlelit golden sconces decorating the dark wood walls—washing over the dark red booths and the polished bar. It smells like rich alcohol, even richer cologne, and something that screams 'money'.

Sebastien's hand rests warmly on my hip as he leans in, brushing a quick kiss to my temple.

"Breathe, love," he murmurs. "I've got you."

I know, and that's the only reason why I can walk easily with him as we head right for the bar. For a heartbeat, I'm not sure why he's leading me there. Sure, the first night at the Last Prayer, he had hunkered down on one of the stools; that's where I found him, after all. But when he went back, he tucked me inside of a booth. I'd expected the same treatment here, though I'll go wherever he wants me to go.

Then, as he guides me around the bar, pointing at the couple with their heads bowed together in conversation as they sit on the same side of another booth, I understand.

It's Adrian and Loni Heller.

Adrian's leaning back against the prime leather seat like he owns the damn club—and, who knows, maybe he does—with one arm around his wife's shoulders, the other playing with a lock of her strawberry-blonde hair. Like the day I met him at the wedding, he has an unlit cigarette tucked behind his ear, and a soft look in his pale green eyes as he gazes down on her.

Loni's curled up against him, soft in a way I don't think anyone except for her husband ever gets to see.

Sebastien clears his throat right before he guides me to slip into the empty seat opposite the married couple.

Adrian glances up. His features shadow over, like he's pissed to have been interrupted, though the darkness fades away when he recognizes that Sebastien is climbing in to sit next to me.

"Bas. It's you," Adrian greets, flicking his eyes over me with calculating interest before he nods at Sebastien. "Should've known better. You're always early. Perfect. We can go have a chat real quick."

Huh?

Sebastien sighs. "Do we have to do this now? We just arrived."

Adrian snorts. "You've got a brand on your palm and a ring on your finger. You're not a bachelor anymore, and that means you're on the hook. Do it for Dallas. But," he adds, glancing at me, "we won't be long. I'll bring your husband back to you in no time. Until then, my wife will keep you company."

Loni waves. "Hi."

Beneath the table, Sebastien squeezes my knee, then climbs out of the booth.

Adrian leans over, kissing Loni's cheek. "Princess," he murmurs.

"I'm holding you to it, Heller. Hurry back."

He flashes her a grin, and then both of our husbands are gone, stalking across the dance floor to find a quiet corner to talk their Order business out of earshot of the lady folk.

Sure.

Okay.

Whatever.

I adjust my skirt under me, then glance at my new companion. Loni doesn't seem to mind that we've been abandoned. Following her lead, I try not to let it bother me, either.

Instead, I say, "Can I ask you a question?"

She looks surprised. "Sure. Shoot."

I tap my ear. "What's the deal with the cigarette? Every time I've seen your husband, he has one."

Loni's hazel eyes seem to sparkle in the dim, atmospheric light. "Oh, that? Adrian used to be a smoker." A small, private smile tugs on her lips. "He quit for me. He keeps it there as a reminder. Would he rather smoke or kiss me? As long as he doesn't light up, I'll kiss him whenever he wants."

My cheeks warm. "Sebastien insists that I give him a kiss 'hello' and a kiss 'goodbye' whenever I see him."

She doesn't look surprised to hear that. Maybe that's just how their crew is…

"How are things with you and Bas anyway? I'm so glad you're here. He keeps you all to himself, and I've been dying to check in, make sure you're doing okay."

The way Loni says that, it seems like a *good* thing that my husband is hiding me. Instead of remarking on that, though, I find myself asking, "You call him that, too?"

"You mean 'Bas'? Of course. It's his nickname." Loni frowns. "What do *you* call him?"

"Um. His real name. Sebastien."

Her eyebrows lift. "Ah. Someone's special. As I recall, he used to beat the crap out of boys back in school when they called him that. He was always a scrapper."

"What do you mean by that?"

"Adrian says it's because he was always so sensitive about being pretty. Like, he wanted to prove himself, prove he wasn't the Reynolds they wanted him to be, all because his dad was supposed to be King before he stepped down and Jack Collins took over." Loni's nose scrunches up as she mentions the former King. I take it she's not a fan, which is good because, after all the ways Eric threatened me with the close friendship he had with the King, I kinda hate the dead Jack Collins, too. "He used to be in detention more than anyone else in our grade."

"Really?" I ask. "I… I didn't know that."

There's a lot I don't know about my husband, I'm beginning to realize.

"Oh, yeah. It only got worse while I was gone." Loni taps her nose. "He broke that a couple of times." She gestures over her eye. "Heard he got in a knife fight with some cocky Owed and got that scar."

I know exactly what scar she's talking about, too. Maybe that's why I stare at her now. "You know an awful lot about my husband."

"He's one of Adrian's brothers. If he's important to Adrian, that means he's important to me." She leans over the table, a touch conspiratorially. "Besides… of the five Heirs, Bas was probably the smallest asshole."

That's good to hear. Only…. "Five Heirs?"

"Yeah. That's what I used to call their group of five when we were in school together because we all knew they'd lead the Order one day." Loni leans back again. Lifting her hand, she ticks them off on her fingers. "There's Adrian, Dallas, Connor, Bas, and Desmond."

Desmond. I know him—or *of* him. "Desmond St. James, right? I know him. He worked with…" I stop short before I can say Eric's name, replacing it instead with a gulp, and then, "He was killed—"

Loni doesn't notice my near slip. Her hazel eyes going dark, she cuts me off. "At my wedding."

Oh. "I… I thought I heard something about that. He was supposed to get married to an Offering."

Eric told me. About how Jack had thought about demoting an Offering for having sex before marriage before deciding to let her be Claimed, but that I shouldn't get any ideas… he only did so because the St. Jameses paid him to reinstate the Offering so that Desmond could be the one to Claim her.

It didn't work out too well for the son of one of Eric's partners. Someone shot him dead, taking his place, all because of… "Didn't it have something to do with blood?"

Loni looks surprised that I would know that. "Yeah. You're right. Adrian had a blood oath."

"What's that?"

"You don't know?" Loni cocks her head slightly. "I thought you were an Offering."

I was supposed to be.

"We were first generation," I say instead, explaining

myself. "My dad got invited to join the Order when I was in middle school."

Now she nods. "So you didn't go through Offering training." A wistful look crosses her pretty face. "Lucky."

I guess. The way I see it, I went from being an average Harmony Heights citizen to one of *them* at a pivotal time in my life. Miranda was only four. She grew up knowing what was expected of her. Not me. When I hit eighteen, it was no surprise that I wasn't chosen—wasn't Claimed—since no one really knew who I was… and that's when Eric came along, and I never had a chance to be the Offering they wanted me to be.

I don't want to tell her that, though. I just… I'm not ready.

But I am curious.

"So… blood oath?"

"It's something one of the Owed does," Loni says. "Just to make sure that they can Claim their bride before the Claiming ceremony in August. It's really only done when an Owed is afraid that more than one of them might try to Claim the same Offering. It's a promise made in blood, a promise they make to protect you to the death—yours or theirs. If the King seals it, nothing can come between you."

That's good to know. I mean, I'll never have that with Sebastien, but maybe if Eric tries to threaten my sister's standing again, I can tell her about it. Colt loves Randa. I'm sure he'll sign some blood oath thing to make sure that he gets to Claim her this August—

Hang on.

"Loni? Are you okay?"

Her features are suddenly twisted in a look of pure jealousy. She's not peering in my direction, though. Instead, she's glaring at the dance floor.

I follow the direction of her stare.

Adrian is shaking off one of the Used; it's easy to pick them out now, from the heavily made-up faces to the classy yet skimpy dresses they wear. She pouts as he stalks away from her, making a beeline for our table.

"Goddamn Used," he mutters, throwing himself into the booth. "They're on the hunt tonight, their desperation stinking like cheap perfume." He reaches for Loni. "Come here, princess. I need something to get the taste of it out of my mouth."

Now that her husband is back, having gotten rid of the Used targeting him, Loni relaxes. No. She actually giggles, sliding her arms around his neck, the two of them falling into a kiss like they're the only ones in the club.

I look away, uncomfortable at how obviously they love each other, and that's when I realize that Adrian is here.

Sebastien isn't.

I wait until Adrian stops trying to devour his wife before I clear my throat. "Um. Sebastien. What happened to him?"

"He said he needed to take a piss," Adrian tells me, pulling his wife across his lap. "Said he'd be right back."

A flicker of unease skitters down my spine. I don't know why it does, but as though I can't resist the urge to make sure he's okay, I slip out of the booth, climbing to my feet.

Ignoring Loni and Adrian, I take a few steps away from our table, scanning the Court—and that's when I see him.

He's not heading toward us. He's not in the bathroom, either.

And he sure as hell isn't alone.

My husband—*fake* husband, I whisper to myself—is leaning against the bar, a gorgeous woman touching his arm. She has it all. Big smile. Huge tits. Her blonde hair is styled in voluminous curls, and her red dress leaves little to the imagination. She's a knock-out... *and she's touching Sebastien.*

My vision tunnels. At the same time, something inside of me snaps.

Discreet, I think to myself. If he wants to be intimate with anyone else during our marriage of convenience, he's supposed to be *discreet.*

That? Is the complete opposite of discreet.

She must be one of the Used. I can't see her brand from here, but everything about her... she belongs here, and I don't, but that doesn't stop me. As she smiles up at Sebastien, her red-tipped fingers running along the outline of his bicep through his leather jacket, all I can think now is: he's supposed to be *mine.*

My heart stutters. My blood heats up.

I don't remember making any conscious decision to move. I don't even remember walking. I just know that, by the time I reach the bar, she's laughing at something he said to her, leaning closer, and every inch of me exists to get her away from Sebastien.

I start with words.

"Take your hands off my husband," I hear myself say.

My voice is quiet. Doesn't matter.

I know she heard me.

The woman—who, this close, is clearly one of the Used—startles to be interrupted, then recovers with a sneer that does little to mar her perfect beauty. "Oh, sweetheart. He's been mine longer than he's been yours."

That's the worst possible thing she could've said.

I don't think. I don't hesitate.

I simply grab as much of that gorgeous hair as I can and yank her away from Sebastien. Shrieking, she has to come with me, but once I let go of her, she slaps me.

Fine.

I slap her right back.

She launches herself at me, using her perfectly manicured fingers to claw at my face. I grab her hair again and then… well. I'm not really sure what happens except that, for the first time in years, I stop being the perfect Offering as I slap, I punch, I might even bite… I definitely kick. We're on the floor now, and I'm pretty sure I'm on top of her when the noise around me becomes clear. Someone is calling my name. I ignore them.

I can't ignore the large hand that closes around my wrist, lifting me easily off of the target of my jealous rage, before pulling me back against a hard, familiar chest.

"Enough," Sebastien growls.

I swivel my head, looking up at him, and I realize: he's not growling at me. His eyes are dark, a muscle flexing in his cheek as he glares down at the Used on the floor.

"I showed you my wedding band, Hilary. I tried to tell you delicately that I'm off the market. You should've listened. But what you just did… let me tell you. You touch my wife again, and I will put you through the bar. Slowly. And not the way you like."

She stares at him, red lips opening and closing wordlessly like a fish.

He turns to me. "Love… are you okay? Tell me you're okay."

The adrenaline is still rushing through me. My cheek is damp. My head is screaming in agony from where she yanked out my hair. My entire body burns, and it'll only be worse later. For now? I just nod, burying my face in his chest.

And that's when she finds her voice. "Congrats, Bas. You finally found your new Julie."

Sebastien stiffens, but doesn't respond—until she snaps, "Julie was prettier than this bitch, and that didn't save her. Good luck with this one."

I pull away enough to see the barely concealed fury on his face as he continues to glare down at Hilary.

"I already warned you what would happen if you touch her. Hear this: if you say one more word about my wife, I'll have you thrown out of the Order."

Holy shit.

I've never heard him sound so cold.

The Used is spitting mad. "I hope she's worth it. Because, I promise you, none of us will ever welcome you again after the way you let her treat me on our turf."

He goes from cold to fiery in a heartbeat as he uses his full strength to whirl me around with him. I wasn't expecting it. Between one step and another, I'm flying, my back slamming into Sebastien's chest again as he holds me to him, forcing me to look at the woman rising shakily from the floor.

No. He's forcing her to look at *me*.

"Annaliese Reynolds is my wife. She's fucking gorgeous, and that's only on the outside. You think I'll come crawling back to the Court when I get to call this woman mine? For a beer maybe with my brothers, or to take my wife out dancing. But I will never call on one of the Used again. Do you understand me?"

She thins her lips, glaring at him.

"Hilary. I said, do you understand me?"

This is a side of Sebastien I've never seen before. He took my jealousy and my rage and maxed it. No. He *beat* it.

And I… I *love* it.

Possibly as much as I love him.

Uh-oh.

Where the hell did that thought come from? I'm not sure, but when Sebastien dares anyone to stop him from leaving the dance floor… when he dares *me* to stop him from taking me with him… all I do is let him whisk me away, hoping I can escape the sudden realization that slammed into me.

Maybe I escaped that.

I sure didn't escape the need to suddenly claim me that's come over my fake husband.

EIGHTEEN
MINE

SEBASTIEN

One thing I just discovered about myself?

There is nothing that revs my engine more than seeing my wife lose control. Really, she only has herself to blame for setting me off like this…

Okay. So Hilary touched my arm. I barely noticed, except for a twinge of annoyance that she wasn't Annaliese. It meant nothing to me, and I thought for old times' sake I should let her down gently, showing her my wedding ring, letting her know that I was taken.

Her flirty-ness meant nothing to me.

It obviously meant everything to my wife.

I saw the way Annaliese's delicate jaw went hard, her cheeks hollowing as she sucked in a furious breath. A *jealous* breath.

Then Hilary fucked up. She giggled, putting on an act, dragging her fingers up to my shoulder as though my wedding band was the same as any other decoration. Dallas's spade tattoo. Adrian's earrings. Connor's scar.

No, sweetheart. It was a sign that I'm taken, and I'm not like other Owed. The moment I said 'I do' to Annaliese, I followed in Adrian's footsteps, declaring the Used off-limits.

Too bad Hilary didn't get the memo.

Before I could peel her possessive hand off my shoulder, Annaliese moved. I saw the moment her usual ice shattered, revealing a heated fury that made her radiant a split second before she lunged at the other woman and grabbed.

Annaliese didn't warn the other woman. She didn't clear her throat or meekly point out that I'm her husband a second time. Going against all of the protocols in the Order, my wife yanked Hilary's hair, then slapped Hilary so hard, the impact of flesh against flesh cut through the noise in the Court.

I knew better than to think that Hilary wouldn't retaliate again. She did, and I only wish I had been able to interfere faster than I did. That was on me. Watching my wife get into a slap fight with one of the Used… that was a scene out of my wildest fantasies. If Hilary hadn't brought Julie into it, I would've been able to enjoy it more. Of course, all she did was trigger Annaliese's jealous side again, and now I'm currently carrying my wife away from the center of the Court.

What else could I do? Everyone was staring at the two women, but all I had eyes for was *her*. Annaliese Reynolds, elegant and stunningly angry, finally letting some true emotion break through that perfect little mask of hers she constantly wears.

I see her. I see the woman I fell for all those months ago, and the woman I will do abso-fucking-lutely anything to keep.

Because she's jealous. So jealous that she steams with it, and it's not because of my position. Not because of my wealth. It's because, for the first time in so long, someone wants me for me. If this was just a marriage of convenience, or even a regular Offering-Owed arranged marriage, she would turn her head away, leaving me to deal with the Used.

Only she didn't.

Annaliese Crawford—no, Annaliese fucking *Reynolds*—came bearing down on Hilary like a bat out of hell. She told the Used to get her hands off of me, and when she refused, my wife beat the shit out of her.

My wife. The same prim, proper woman who sat on my couch, her binder a shield, her lips pursed as she laid out clause after clause of our marriage of convenience. Instead of playing that part, I saw the jealousy she couldn't quite hide, and the anger that's a perfect match to the dark side of me.

No wonder I've been obsessed with her since the moment we met. Deep down, I must've recognized that she's the other half of my soul. And ain't that some shit? Before Annaliese, I never believed in the concept of soul mates. Adrian did; he was convinced from kindergarten that Loni was his. Even when I was lusting after Julie, thinking about giving up my bachelorhood for her, something always held me back.

And then Annaliese asked me to marry her, and I nearly fucking tripped over myself to say 'I do'.

The way she fights against me as I drag her away from Hilary, as though she's ready to launch herself at the Used again… I would do it again in a heartbeat. Good thing I don't have to. This amazing, elegant, fierce hellcat is *mine*, and if I don't show her that I'm hers, I'm about to fucking explode in my jeans.

Because it's true. She Claimed me in front of Hilary. Hell, in front of the whole Order. Anyone in the Court who witnessed the fight or will hear about it as the gossips do their job and spread it all over Harmony Heights will know that I'm married, and that my wife is a force to be reckoned with.

Is it any wonder that I'm this turned-on?

Carrying her across the floor, I don't stop until I've reached my destination: the bathroom designated for high-ranking members of the Order so that they don't have to 'mingle' with the lower-ranked members.

Less than five minutes ago, I took a leak in one of the open bathrooms. I never cared about the Order hierarchy bullshit. A toilet is a toilet, right? But, considering the first time I fucked Annaliese, it was in a seedy, neon-lit bar bathroom, and the *second* time I'm going to fuck my wife is in *another* bathroom, the least I can do is bring her to the classiest john in the Court.

This bathroom is single-use only. I feel bad for any Owed who might be taking a shit because, no matter what, I'm getting us in there. Luckily, the door's unlocked, and I yank it open, pulling Annaliese into the room with me.

There's a large mirror over the single vanity. Behind us, there's one toilet. It smells like dark rum and burning wood in here, gold touches on the toilet handle, the knobs near the sink, the sconces on the wall glittering beneath the light. Even more importantly, there's a lock on the door.

Releasing Annaliese, letting her pull herself to her full height that's still a good six inches shorter than me even in her heels, I walk over to the door, engaging the lock for as long as I plan on us staying in here.

That catches her attention. "What are you doing? Someone might need the bathroom."

And? "This is the King's Court. The Owed allow the Used to stay here, but this is *ours*. And if I want to show my wife that she's the only woman for me, I'll do it, and the other Owed can take it the fuck up with Dal if they have a problem with it."

Her eyes widen. The light in here is brighter than the golden light out on the floor. Suddenly, I notice a thin smear of blood along her cheekbone, right next to two shallower scratches. Hilary must've got her good with her nails.

Fuck. That shouldn't be as sexy as it is.

Neither should the furious look in her brown eyes as she glares up at me. I step toward her, but proving that she's still in fight-or-flight and my love is all *fight*, she presses her palm against my chest, doing her best to keep me back.

"Sebastien," she snaps, "I'm so not fucking you right now."

My laugh is low, one part disbelieving, the other part

way too amused that Annaliese can see right through me that easily. She knows *exactly* why I brought her here—and why I locked the door behind us.

Oh, yeah. We're definitely fucking tonight, but that's not the *only* reason I hauled her off to the bathroom…

"Really? You think that's why I dragged you in here?"

Her jaw clenches, an obvious 'yes'. "Well, I interrupted whatever you were doing with that Used woman. So since she's not putting out, I guess I'm the next best choice." She gestures around her. "And another bathroom. Like you think I've forgotten last time. Like you think I could *ever* forget."

You and me, both, baby.

I step closer to her, forcing her hand back against her own body. "You're wrong, Annaliese. I didn't want Hilary. Sure, I've been with her… but that was before we got married. They were *all* before we got married. I need you to understand that. You? You're the only woman I want."

She flinches at my confession. And I know that I was right. She was jealous, and while I won't deny that she has reason to be—lord knows that I've imagined killing her nameless ex a thousand times in my own fantasies—she has nothing to be jealous about *now*.

I catch her chin gently. "Look at me, love."

When she doesn't lift her eyes, I tilt her face up until her gaze meets mine.

"You think I even *saw* her out there?" I murmur. "Fuck, no. I only saw you, love. My wife." I wait for a heartbeat to really send home the message. "My jealous, furious wife who nearly scalped another woman because she touched me without permission."

Her throat works, already flushing. "I—"

She flushes, and I focus on the blood on her cheek. I ghost two of my fingers over it. "You're bleeding."

"It's nothing," she mutters. And then, with enough venom that she has my cock twitching, she adds, "I should probably get a rabies shot now."

Maybe. Or maybe I show her just how desperate a man her husband is.

"Come here. Let me clean you."

Annaliese inches closer to the vanity. I move with her before cupping the back of her neck, drawing her up on her tiptoes. Then, without giving her the chance to protest what I'm about to do, I lean in and *lick* the streak of blood from her cheek.

She shoves me away, clapping her hand over that side of her face. "Oh my God, Sebastien… what the hell? That's so *unsanitary*."

"What's wrong? I'm your husband, love. Part of that is wanting to get as much of you inside of me as I can."

And the reverse, too. Hint, hint, wifey.

Pity she doesn't take that hint.

Ah, well. No one can say hat I don't always go for what I want. In fact, half of the trouble I got into growing up was because I had no impulse control. I got better once I hit my mid-twenties, but the echoes of that Bas Reynolds rears his mischievous head as I lick my lips, then laugh under my breath.

"Besides," I grate out, ghosting my lips along the

edge of her jaw, "it's cute that you think that that's the only place my tongue is going tonight."

She gasps the second she understands what I mean. But you know what? She doesn't try to push me away again, and that's all the permission I need to do this.

I grab her by the waist, hoisting her up like she weighs nothing. I pause only long enough to throw her skirts up before setting her on the bathroom counter. The sink rattles, but holds. Her knees fall apart around my hips in sheer reflex.

"S-Sebastien—"

I flash her a grin, wicked and sinful and full of promise. She gasps again and, taking that as my cue, I drop to my knees.

Her fingers immediately dive into my hair, gripping hard. That makes it a little more difficult for me to work her panties off of her, though the way she lifts her hips just enough to help me… yeah. She wants this.

She wants *me*.

From the moment I got her on my lap in the Last Prayer, I was dying to find out just what Annaliese tastes like. I thought it would take longer before I had the chance, but now that it's here… I'm fucking *salivating*.

Go slow, Bas. Be smooth. Despite how she approached me at that other bar, it's obvious that Annaliese is not as experienced as I am. I'd put money down that the fucker sure as hell didn't worship her the way that she deserves.

The way that *I'm* going to worship her…

"You fought for me," I growl, kissing the inside of her thigh. "You *bled* for me. You think I'm letting you walk out of this room without reminding you who you belong to?"

"Sebastien, wait—"

But she's already pulling me closer, tugging my hair, her breath breaking before I even touch her.

She wants me. I want her. But I need her to admit it.

I nip her skin. She gasps, and I peer up at my wife.

"What if I beg?"

"Beg? What do you—"

"You heard me. I've spent months… *months*… wondering what you taste like. Do you know what that does to a man like me? The fucking *wondering*?" I inch a little closer, move a little higher, my lips near her groin. I take a deep breath and whimper. "Please, love. Are you really going to torture your husband like this?"

"I would never—"

Good answer. Making sure she's secure on the edge of the sink, I shift my hold on her so that I can spread her wide open.

And when I finally put my mouth on her…

"Sebastien!"

I smile against her pussy. Yeah. That's what I wanted to hear. Sure, it's not 'husband', but as long as she knows who's currently going down on her… yeah. I can handle her losing herself enough to shout my name to the rafters like that.

"Sebastien… oh *God*—"

"God can't help you, love," I murmur, speaking against her clit, hoping the reverberations of my voice help rev her even higher. "You're being kissed by a devil, and you're owned by an outcast. But that's the best thing about fucking the bad boy, baby. He knows how to make a good girl feel *amazing*."

Big talk, but I sure as fuck back it up.

Then again, her nails scrape my scalp, and I almost lose *my* fucking mind. Her taste... she tastes so good, I could spend the rest of eternity between these thighs. Only my aching cock, screaming, begging, pleading for its turn keeps me from dragging my worship of the most beautiful creature I've ever known into another lifetime.

We have one. A long one, a *forever*... and it starts with *this*.

I wait for my wife to come. When she finally does, when she *breaks*, I hurriedly get to my feet, catching her before she can slump forward.

I flip her around before she has any idea what I'm doing, guiding her hands to the sink and bending her gently over the counter. Her breath fogs the mirror.

Caging her beneath me, I have my arms braced on either side of her, my chest pressed to her back, pinning her beneath me.

Fuck. Her body fits against mine perfectly, like she was made for this.

Made for *me*.

"Look at yourself," I whisper against her ear. "Look at what you do to me."

She glances up. Together, we both watch our reflections. The hungry, determined look on my face. The dazed, well-pleasured expression on hers. Her cheeks are pink. Mine are hollowed.

I'm *starving*, and all I do is feed on how beautiful my wife looks in the aftermath of an orgasm.

I look closer. That… that's not hesitation on her face. That's pure want, even as she reminds me in a breathless, husky voice, "You said that you'll wait until I'm ready."

Oh. I *know*.

Reaching down, I dip my pointer finger inside of her. When I pull it back out, it's shiny with her arousal and my saliva. I hold it up so that she can see it in the reflective glass. "Yeah, I think you're more than ready."

She doesn't argue with me after that. Just like our first time together, she just gropes behind her, searching for my cock so that she can feed it inside her waiting pussy.

Uh-uh, love. Let your husband take care of you this time.

I squeeze her fingers, then shove them away. She whimpers, back to bracing herself on the vanity, and I grab my cock. She's so slick, I miss the first time I try. Feeling like an unpracticed teen, I mutter a curse under my breath, telling myself to focus. I want her to want me as much as I do her, and if I fuck this up—

Yes! My cock lodges inside of her heat. She groans to feel me stretching her out. Knowing damn well that it better have been more than four months for her like it has been for me, I press into her… going slow, making her take every inch… pushing until I can't give her any more.

She moans my name. "Sebastien…"

For her, I want to be Sebastien. I'll always be Bas Reynolds, but when Annaliese insists on using my full name, I feel like she's christening me anew every single fucking time. She gives new meaning to the name I've tried to shed over the years. Instead of clenching when I hear the syllables, I have to do everything I can *not* to run to the bathroom and jerk off.

That's how I've managed all these months. At first, I just wasn't interested in casual sex anymore. After we were married, all I wanted was to be with my wife.

And now I finally am.

"You belong to me," I pant, nuzzling her neck, grunting softly as I drag my cock halfway out before shoving myself back in, making her bump up against the vanity. She doesn't complain. In fact, she squeals so I do it again… again… and *again.* "You understand me, Annaliese? You're mine, and that means I belong to you, too."

Her knees buckle.

That's okay, I hold her up so that she doesn't go anywhere except on my cock.

"The next time one of those women touches me without your permission?" I hiss darkly against her throat. "I'll do worse to her than you did. And you'll smile as you watch because you… you're just as broken as I am, Annaliese Reynolds. And that's why we found our way to each other. Because, fuck it, we were *meant* to."

She gasps as I quicken my pace, railing her as she clings to the porcelain sink for dear life. "*Sebastien*—"

I'm not done. "But I don't think I'll have to, love." I kiss her shoulder. Then, feeling inspired, I bite her. It's not hard. Nowhere near enough to break skin like Hilary did during their fight, but the urge came over me and… well, when it comes to Annaliese, I'm done with resisting those sort of urges. "Once the whole Order knows how vicious and possessive my wife is, they won't want to risk it."

Though that would be a bit of a shame. Seeing Annaliese fight for me… I don't think I've ever felt more chosen in my whole goddamn life.

And when she shrieks out my name, a second bite more than enough to have her coming all over my cock, I know I made the perfect choice in choosing *her*.

ONCE SHE'S ABLE TO WALK ON TREMBLING LEGS AGAIN, we leave the Court together, not even bothering to say goodbye to Adrian and Loni. That's fine. Now that my bro and I checked in on how Dallas is doing, odds are Adrian and his wife already headed out once they realized that I went off *somewhere* with mine.

Annaliese… I offered to carry her on the way out. She glared at me, muttering something about how everyone is probably already talking about her. Between the fight and how quickly I whisked her away to the bathroom before locking the door, keeping it locked for so damn long… they all have to know that I fucked her in there, too.

Damn right. Turnabout is fair play, love. You want to stake your claim, telling all of the Used that I belong to you? Well, just in case that fucker who hurt you was having an evening cocktail, I want him to have no doubt in his mind that Annaliese belongs to *me*.

I made that perfectly clear. With my jizz running down her thighs, another pair of her panties tucked securely in my pocket to add to the pair that I've used to rub one out to ever since that night in the Last Prayer, even Annaliese herself can't deny that she's mine.

As far as I'm concerned, this changes things. And that's why, once I dropped her off, taking my goodbye kiss as my due, I drove my Harley-Davidson Low Rider S back to my place. I parked it in the attached garage, putting mine and Annaliese's helmets on the matching hooks on the garage wall. Then, hopping into the Porsche because I'll need more space, I drove right back to Annaliese's apartment.

The light in her window is on. Usually, I wait until she's asleep before I let myself in with her key. Tonight, though, I'm actually glad that I made it back before Annaliese settled down.

I would've rather not have to wake her up to pack if I didn't have to.

Less than three minutes after I park, I'm at her door. I turn the knob, nodding in approval to find it locked. Annaliese has a bad habit of forgetting to lock up sometimes; a product of living in a middle-class neighborhood in Harmony Heights, I guess. Good thing I spend most of the night here otherwise I'd be worried about what might happen to her while I was trying to give her *some* space.

Of course, that means that, when I let myself in, walking into her living room, she doesn't understand how I did it.

She's so fucking cute. The way she jumps despite the

fact that I had her bent over in front of me an hour ago… I smirk. "Hello, wife." I beckon her closer with my fingers. "Come here. I want my 'hello' kiss."

I knew I was probably pushing my luck, but I had to try. That's why, when she just blinks at me in stunned surprise, I let it pass.

Finally, she finds her voice and asks incredulously, "Sebastien? What are you doing here? How did you get in?"

I lean against the doorframe, a slow, dangerous smile tugging at my mouth. "Oh, love," I laugh, twirling the keyring on my finger, making sure she sees it. "I've been letting myself in for ages."

"I—*what?*"

It seems pretty obvious to me. "What? You know what the Order says. An Owed gets to spend at least one night a week in bed with his wife. Call me an over-achiever because I've been sleeping with my wife every night since we got married."

Her cheeks blaze red. "You… no. Tonight was the first time—"

"That I fucked you as your husband?" I guess before nodding in agreement. "Yeah. Of course. I'm no perv. I said I would wait until you were ready. Tonight you were. Every other night…. Sorry." I'm not sorry. "I haven't had a good night's sleep since we met"—mainly because I was obsessively thinking about the one that got away—"and, turns out, the only way I can sleep is beside you."

She folds her hands in front of her. "Is that why you're here? So we can… *sleep?*"

If only, love.

I rise up from my lean, walking the rest of the way into her living room. I only stop when there's about a foot or so between us.

I brush my thumb over her cheek. "Like I said, I told you that I would wait until you were ready. Well, I waited. I waited until you accepted what this is."

Her expression is so adorably puzzled. "What… what is it?"

"Real." I cup her jaw. "And my wife?" My voice drops to a possessive growl. "She lives with *me*."

Her breath catches. "Sebastien…"

"Pack a bag," I tell her, making it undeniably a command. "Take what you need for tonight. We'll get the rest tomorrow."

I stroke her cheek with my knuckles, soft in a way I don't know how to be with anyone except *her*. "But starting right now? I'm taking you home."

I wait for a beat, seeing if she'll argue. Seeing if she'll instantly deny doing any such thing.

Seeing if she's going to bring up that fucking binder.

And when she doesn't?

I grin.

"*Our* home."

NINETEEN
ANNA

ANNALIESE

t's May 1st. Can you believe it?

I guess that makes sense. At first, I couldn't get over how I attacked the Used like that. Then there was that encounter in the bathroom which, if you can believe it, was even hotter than the *first* one.

I definitely can't forget the way my husband brought me back to my apartment only to show up again barely an hour later, a copy of my key in his hand, a smirk on his face, and the admission that he made a copy directly after we were married—and that he's been letting himself into my place to sleep next to me because, and I quote, he hadn't 'had a good night's sleep since we met, and the only way [he] can sleep is beside [me]'.

Part of me wanted to call bullshit. The other part? Thought: *fuck*, that's so damn romantic. To need to be close to me so badly that he broke into my apartment, telling any neighbor who saw him that he was my husband—which, technically, *true*—and always leaving before I woke up.

He was the perfect gentleman, too. He said he never touched me while I was asleep, and I believe him. I would've noticed if he had a bit of a somno kink, fucking me while I was knocked out. But, no… I had no idea he was there, though I can definitely say that I finally understand why I couldn't get the smell of Sebastien's yummy cologne out of my nose.

Because he was there. He was *always* there.

And now he is—because I'm living with him.

By the time I leave Sebastien's house—*our* house—and arrive at the party venue an hour before the first guests are scheduled to arrive, my binder is already open to the color-coded 'final sweep' tab, and I'm too busy double-checking the dinner menu to actually remember how to breathe properly.

And that's ridiculous. Absolutely ridiculous. I planned this party down to the last detail. When I was working with Mom, we ran events ten times more complicated than a birthday party, even if the guest of honor is a high-ranking Order member.

But that's the thing. This party is for my, well, my *brother-in-law*, and if that wasn't bad enough, Sebastien hired me to do this. He had the faith that I could take his black Amex, my phone, and my laptop, and give Alexandre a party to remember.

So his birthday was back in September. For obvious reasons, he refused to admit that he turned thirty. Ever since Sebastien took a wife, though, his older brother has made it obvious that he has no intention of following the life path that had been set out for him long before he was born.

Good for him. Seriously, if I could've escaped the Order before everything got so damn complicated, I might have. Of course, then I never would've met Sebastien so… no. Maybe I wouldn't have.

I didn't just meet Sebastien, either. I *married* him. And while I can try to convince myself that my nerves have everything to do with seeing this party go off without a hitch, the truth of the matter is a lot more selfish than that. This is my Order debut as Sebastien's wife. Almost two months of marriage, and I'll finally introduce myself as his wife to more than just my family and his.

To be fair, I'm actually surprised it hasn't happened already. Or maybe it did. The… altercation at the Court spread like wildfire. Seriously. It even reached Harmony Heights High because Miranda made a point to call me and teasingly say, "Everyone's talking, Annie. Word is Bas Reynolds is officially off the market—and you don't want to mess with his wife."

She already knew that. My sister was at our wedding, but I've been so careful to keep my marital status hidden because of Eric. After he repeatedly drove by my parents' home, freaking her out, I knew I made the right choice. I'm sure he did it on purpose. He probably stalked my place, too, and I didn't even notice. Now he can go right ahead because I've been living with Sebastien for the last two weeks.

Did I appreciate the heavy-handed way he decided that, as his wife, I would live with him? Not at all. I didn't refuse him right away. After the way I acted at the Court and how he fucked me for it, telling me with both his words and his body that I'm his... yeah. I finally went home with him.

I haven't left yet.

Adrian Heller made some phone calls. While I curled up in Sebastien's bed in a room he insisted I think of as ours now that we're happily engaging in the intimacy clauses of our contract, Sebastien's close friend arranged to have everything I owned moved from my apartment to Sebastien's home.

He had a point. Our contract will continue for another ten months. And while I put in a section about separate residences, no one said we *had* to live apart. Why pay rent for my apartment when I could live with my husband for free?

I couldn't argue with that. He paid me way more than I ever would've charged for planning Alexandre's birthday—another reason why this has to be the best one ever—and it would be smart to squirrel some of that away. Plus, it would be a load off of my parents. They helped me with my rent while I was in the apartment. If I need to move out of Sebastien's place at the end of the year and find a new one for me, I should be able to stay afloat for a while even after the big purchase I just made.

For now, I'm just enjoying the time spent with Sebastien. In his home, in his arms, in his bed... I'm enjoying the time that I have with my husband while I can.

I just really, really wish he wasn't my *fake* husband.

THE PARTY IS ALREADY IN FULL SWING. SOFT LIGHTING, A dozen different white flowers pouring from crystal vases, a string quartet perched near the open bar… it's everything Alexandre asked for when I sat down with Sebastien's brother to find out his vision for this event. I think I pulled it off, too. It's modern elegance with just enough ostentatiousness to remind everyone that this party is for a member of the Reynolds family.

The room is crowded, too. Everyone who's anyone in Harmony Heights is here, carrying their flutes of champagne, mingling with each other based on their status in the Order. I've smiled at so many of them, it feels like my face might crack, but just as the waiters started to wind around the tables, serving dinner, I began to get a little nervous.

Everyone who's anyone in Harmony Heights is here… but what about Eric? I don't know why it's hitting me now that he could have decided to attend the party. Alexandre didn't do invitations. It was an open guest list, with the expectation that those who should come would.

I was too busy before to wonder about who's here. Now that we're halfway through it and everything is going very well, I'm just waiting for something to go wrong.

Suddenly, warm fingers brush the small of my back, heating me up through the silky light blue dress I picked for the occasion. My heart jumps, though it beats triple-time when I glance behind me and see my husband.

Sebastien.

He's been checking on me all night. I'd bet he knows everyone here, and there are plenty who whisk him away to chat, but he always finds his way back to me. Like now. He's close enough that I feel the heat of his body through the silky material as he closes the small gap between us.

"You alright?" he asks.

I nod. "I'm fine. I just… there's a lot to do."

Sebastien leans down, lips brushing my cheek. It's not quite a kiss, but I'm suddenly aware that the gesture was enough to have several heads swiveling our way.

"Relax," he says softly, ignoring them. "I have full faith in my wife and her binders."

He's teasing me.

I can't help myself. I grin, laying my hand on the front of his leather jacket. So it's out of place with the men in their suits, the women in their gowns… but, I'll tell you, he's the most striking, attractive man at the whole party—and he's with me.

"Thank you," I tell him.

"Don't mention it, love."

For the next few minutes, Sebastien stays parked at my side. His pose is casual. Confident. One arm hangs loosely around my waist, the other resting in the front pocket of his jeans. There's no denying it's a possessive hold, or that he's preening to show me off to anyone looking our way.

And the strangest thing is… just having him near, I finally begin to relax.

Next to Sebastien, I'm happy. *Safe*. I feel loved—but I shouldn't.

This is only a marriage of convenience.

Still, that knowledge doesn't do a damn thing to stop my pulse from jumping every single time he glances at me.

I wish he could stay by my side the whole night. When Sebastien is near… I don't think about Eric. It's like Eric doesn't exist, and that's foolish of me. I can't monopolize my husband's time. There are so many people who come by to talk to him, but when Dallas Collins stalks over to him—dressed in a dark suit that doesn't make the King any less dangerous than he appears to be—I'm secretly glad that Sebastien follows him away so that they can bow their heads together, having a whispered conversation on the other side of the ballroom.

Sebastien tells me that I shouldn't be afraid of the King. That's easier said than done. In Harmony Heights, there is no one else who has the ultimate power to ruin my life or my sister's. Everything we want hangs on one man's whim, and while Sebastien assures me that Dallas is better than his father was at leading the Order, old habits die hard. I spent years with Eric's voice in my ear, whispering that he was the only one who could protect me from Jack Collins.

Jack Collins is dead. It doesn't matter. If Dallas decides to demote Miranda, everything I've done since I left Eric would've been for nothing.

Well… maybe not for nothing. But still. I'm getting better at not flinching when Dallas comes near, and though I'd rather have Sebastien next to me while I watch over the party, I just put on my 'business' face and mentally run through the checklist in my binder while he's occupied.

And that's when I hear someone call my name.

"Anna!"

At least, I *think* it's my name. No one calls me 'Anna'. I'm Annaliese, or if you're my baby sister, 'Annie'. Sebastien calls me 'love', and though I keep thinking he'll stop, he hasn't yet. But 'Anna'? I'm not sure if that's me.

It is.

I turn to see Alexandre heading my way, a drink in hand, plus two stunning women in matching satin dresses trailing at his heels. A quick peek at their necks reveals that they're both wearing the Order's brand, marking them as Used. His dates, I'm assuming.

Alexandre's grin is bright and wicked as he bears down on me, kissing my cheek as though we've known each other all our lives instead of the both of us having met... three times? "This is perfect. You outdid yourself."

I smile politely. "Happy birthday. Belated, but still."

He laughs, brushing that part off. "It was worth the wait, I assure you. Right, girls?"

Alexandre is laughing, I'm smiling a prim smile, but the two Used... oh, they look *pissed.*

Worse, they size me up with open disdain. I guess I should've expected that. Neither one is the woman that I ended up in a slap fight with at the King's Court, but the

Order's club is as ripe for gossip as Miranda's school. They would've all heard about it.

Good. Maybe then the rest of the Used will know better than to flirt with *my* husband.

Fake husband.

My smile wavers.

Whatever.

"Anyway, Anna, I just wanted to stop by and thank you. Maman is having a wonderful time. Dad wants to hire you for every family event for the next decade. With a discount, of course, since you're family."

I'm 'family' now. I won't be in a year, but there's no way in hell I'm admitting that with those two shooting daggers at me with their gazes.

So, instead, I murmur, "Of course. I'd be happy to."

Alexandre is Sebastien's older brother by fourteen months. They have the same pretty features, dark blond hair, brown eyes… and, yet, watching him schmooze, all I can think is that I got the sexier brother.

I don't know if it was the way I answered him or if he could see my judgment on my face, but Alexandre decides to cut the conversation short. "I'm glad. Oh. Sorry. Looks like we have a line forming to thank our gracious hostess. So now I'll bid you adieu… come on, girls… and you can come over here and say 'hello' to our Anna."

I try to rearrange my features into a pleasant grin, prepared to greet another of Alexandre's guests. "Hello—"

"Anna, is it? Since when?"

My heart fucking drops. So does my stomach. That voice… that fucking *voice.*

I know it intimately. Just like I know those icy blue eyes.

Eric.

It's Eric.

And he's *here.*

My ex looks immaculate. Of course he does. Tailored suit, model smile, the picture of Order perfection.

But those eyes… in those eyes, I see promise. I see fury. I see lust.

I see *trouble.*

I gulp, trying to hide it. "Annaliese. You know that."

"Oh, sweetheart. I do. But you've obviously changed so much since you left me… I just wanted to make sure that wasn't something else."

I don't know what he's talking about—and then he backs me up against the wall, cornering me before I can make my excuses and make my escape. His eyes flash, his deceptively broad build suddenly looming as he lashes out, grabbing my wrist.

"Eric—"

He lifts my hand, thumb tapping the underside of my Order wedding band. "I know you're joking. Tell me this is a joke. You're not married. You *can't* be."

I jerk my hand out of his hold. "What are you doing here?"

"It's the event of the year, according to my sources. So *scandalous.* An Owed celebrating his thirtieth birthday without a ring on his finger instead of being ashamed that he's alone… when I heard that a premier event planner would be hosting it, I knew I had to come."

A premier event planner… that's how I used to teasingly refer to myself when I was working with Mom. It was my dream. It took creativity and organizational skills, and I was so good at it when Mom finally let me join her team. But then I met Eric, and he wanted me to join him at his firm and… and…

He came here for me. Shit. That's what he's saying. He couldn't care less about it being Alexandre's birthday celebration. Oh, no. He finally had the chance to corner me—and that's exactly what he's done.

The rest of the room disappears. It's just me and Eric's blue eyes and the gold wedding ring weighing heavily on my finger.

He's glaring at it. "Take it off."

"What? No!"

"I'm not asking, Annaliese. I'm telling you. You're not married. You can't be. Now. Take. It. Off."

I shake my head. "You should leave, Eric, before—"

"Before what?" he snaps. "Before your husband decides to come over here? Let him. Whatever sniveling Order member you fucked to give you that… why, yes. I think I *do* want to meet him."

Oh, no.

No.

I thought my husband would be safe. That, no matter who I married, Eric would get the hint that he was off-limits. This isn't a one-night stand, even if Sebastien *was* my one-night stand. I'm married, and the only two who know for sure that this is a marriage of convenience are the two who signed the marital agreement that evening in Sebastien's living room.

Alexandre thinks it's real. So do my folks, and Sebastien's. I'm pretty sure Sebastien's friends—brothers—know better, but they'll keep his secrets.

Just like I'll keep mine.

"That's not a good idea," I say weakly. "You should go."

"Only if you come with me," Eric counters.

What? "I can't."

"Of course you can. I'm done playing these games, sweetheart. You will unblock my number. You will get into my car. You will come home with me, and if you're lucky, I might buy you a diamond to replace that cheap-ass band on your finger." He leans in, so close I can smell the booze on his breath. "Take it off, sweetheart. Let's see if your finger's green."

I fist my hand. I love my ring. It's like a shield, and there's no way in hell I'm removing it until the year is up.

I'm just about to tell him that, too, when a very familiar male voice cuts in through the thrum-thrum-thrumming of my pulse, the thudding of my anxious heart, and the din of the crowd suddenly slamming back into me.

"Excuse me. I'd like a moment with my wife."

Sebastien.

TWENTY
PERMANENT

SEBASTIEN

finally found the fucker.

Now, did I expect that it would happen during Alexandre's party? Nah. We just left the invitation open to whoever wanted to show up. Because Alexandre may hate the expectations that being a high-ranking member of the Order... the first son of a founding family... has thrust on him, but the Order *is* his life. He uses it to get perks, to get women, and to progress in his career. To celebrate his thirtieth belatedly, I hired my wife to throw a party that's for Alex *and* the Order. So long as you're affiliated with the Owed in some way, you have an in. It was easier than getting a list of exactly who my brother wanted at his birthday bash.

And while all of that is true, I won't deny that I had an ulterior motive. It's been nearly two months since Annaliese asked me to marry her. It's bothered the shit out of me that, no matter how close we've gotten—and, okay, forcing her to come live with me helped with that —she refuses to talk about the Order member who 'ruined' her. This is an Order party. Maybe the fucker would show up.

I get it. I do. When she had questions in her eyes after Hilary mentioned Julie in front of her, I shut that down. I couldn't bring myself to tell Annaliese about her, so I didn't. Making her tell me about her past... if I want to keep her right where I have her, I needed her to tell me herself.

But now I don't have to.

Because I know *exactly* who hurt her.

Eric Ward. A lawyer who works at the same firm that Des used to before Adrian took care of him, he's one of the old guard. A friend of Jack Collins, and a smarmy prick who thinks he's too good for the Used. I've heard about him. He used to go down to the Court, but he was too rough, too mean, and he got the idea in his head that they should go to him just like the girls did the former King. That was a couple of years back. He stopped visiting the Court, and since all of Harmony Heights knows that Eric's wife, Cicely, has been in a long-term relationship with the gym teacher at the high school, rumors ran that he found a live-in mistress of his own.

As I watch the way he looms over *my wife*, possession in his stance, lust in his eyes... I know exactly who that mistress was.

I don't care that we have an audience. I don't care that Alex's party is going on around us. I just see the way that he's cornered Annaliese, as though he has the *right*, and all I can think about is getting that fucker away from her.

Dallas needed to talk to me about… I don't fucking know. Some bullshit. The last time I looked over here, Annaliese was talking to my brother. Alex is an ass, but I know better than to think he'd ever hit on my wife. I told him he needed to go over there and thank Annaliese for all her hard work, and that was probably what he was doing.

But the next time I looked up? She was being talked down to by a middle-aged lawyer who was just itching to get my boot up his ass.

I cross the room quickly, not paying attention to anyone I bump into, just in time to hear him say, "—done playing these games, sweetheart. You will unblock my number. You will get into my car. You will come home with me, and if you're lucky, I might buy you a diamond to replace that cheap-ass band on your finger." He leans in, so close I want to grab him by the back of his jacket, yank him off of her. "Take it off, sweetheart. Let's see if your finger's green."

Oh, you *fucker*.

If anyone is buying Annaliese a ring, it's me. And he knows damn well that the Order rings are solid gold. Impractical but pretty, like so much of the Order of the Owed, but I'll replace that, too, if Annaliese wants something else.

There isn't anything I won't do for her—including saving her from this creep.

I sidle up behind him, working hard to pull a charming, easy-going smile to my face. I'd rather not beat the shit out of Ward in front of Annaliese if I don't have to. Playing the same old part, once again becoming cocky Bas Reynolds, I tap Ward on the shoulder.

"Excuse me. I'd like a moment with my wife."

The older lawyer turns around, ready to tell me to fuck off. Trust me. I've had more than enough people hunch their shoulders, sneer their faces, and give me the same order in a derisive manner. Something in my own expression seems to bring it out in them, but by the time he looks up at me, the words die on his lips.

Yeah, asshole. I'm a good four inches taller than you. Suck it.

His jaw works. I widen my grin.

And then he spits out, "Wife?"

Oh. That's what caught his attention. He had no idea that Annaliese is *my* wife. Not really surprising. I do my best to stay out of the Order, Annaliese kept our wedding small, and she sure as hell wasn't about to send a 'I got hitched' memo out to the prick who hurt her.

I nod, then, because I'm an asshole, too, I hold up my left hand, making sure he can't miss the matching wedding band on my finger.

"Reynolds. You must be joking. It's not bad enough you ruined one life. Now you're taking Ms. Crawford down with you?"

What a fucking bastard. Of course he had to throw Julie in my face… but to make it seem like *I'm* the one who ruined Annaliese by marrying her?

Because damn right, dickhead, I *did* marry her, and I

remind him with a smug, "Mrs. Reynolds." I tap my ring again. "She took my last name. Didn't you, love?"

Annaliese looks from me to Eric and back. She has a 'deer in headlights' expression. I nod at her, letting her know I have this.

Eric glares at me, blowing air out through his nose. "The Claiming ceremony is in August. And, forgive me, I was under the impression that Ms. Crawford had her Offering status revoked."

Annaliese flushes.

I want to throttle this asshole.

Keep it cool, Bas. You definitely got this. "A special dispensation from the King. I wanted to marry her. She said 'yes'." Well, *I* said 'yes', but he doesn't need to know that. "The King gave us permission. Even attended the wedding."

Ward moves toward me. I could dodge him, but I choose not to. I need Annaliese to know that I'll stand up for her, and that includes standing up to this bully.

He jabs me in the chest, speaking through gritted teeth. "Your name won't protect you, Reynolds. Just because you finally fell in line—"

I slap his hand. "Fell in line? What does that mean?"

"Alexandre stepped down. Everyone knows it." Ward jerks his hand, gesturing around him. "That loser is thirty, no Offering in sight, and no hope he'll choose a bride in August. But you... you must have finally realized that the only way to survive in this town is to play along with Order politics. Take an Offering..."

He snaps his head back, searching for Annaliese. She

hasn't moved an inch, and it takes everything I have not to shove him away from her as he bears down on my wife again. "Only you weren't one of those, were you, Annaliese? You were demoted."

Ward spins back on me. "Did she tell you about me? That you married my sloppy seconds? How does that make you feel, boy?" He's spitting now, so damn angry, it's making him reckless. "That when you fuck her, you know she's comparing you to me? That she probably wishes I was the one on top of her—"

That's enough. I fist my hand, ready to punch him to get him to stop talking about my wife like that, but before I can, Annaliese finally finds her voice. "Eric, *please*."

It's the way she uses his name. Even I can hear the history in her plea, and so can he. He thinks he won, too. She didn't call for me. She called for *him*, and his expression is triumphant before he turns to look at Annaliese again. "Anything for you, sweetheart. You've made your point. Come back to me. You don't want a pretty boy. You want a man."

He turns to look at Annaliese, but while he's back to running his mouth, she moves around him. Next thing I know, she's clutching my arm, giving her head a royal shake. She's *Annaliese* again, the prim, perfect, once-Offering as she looks down her nose at Ward.

"You're right. And I have one," she announces, squeezing me to her.

She squeezes my arm, but that's not all. As Annaliese claims *me*, she squeezes my motherfucking heart.

I look Ward up and down myself. "You heard the lady. I think you should go."

"Why, you—"

I *tsk*. "Listen to me… you want to start something? Fine. Whole damn Order knows I pull up. But if you fuck up Annaliese's hard work… you fuck up my brother's party… you'll really see what this pretty boy can do."

Ward snorts. He backs down, he's not happy about it, and he snorts. "I Claimed her first—"

"Bullshit."

"Excuse me?"

I laugh under my breath. He looks so scandalized all of a sudden. "Don't play those games with *me*. You're right. I'm not made to go along with the sanctimonious Order crap. I can dance around this all night if that's what you want, but why should I bother when I'd rather spend it with my wife?" He glares, and I let him see how dead fucking serious I am now. "So let me make this clear. I married her. I fuck her, and when I have her bent over in front of me, she sure as hell pants my name, asshole. Not yours. So you have a past with her. All of Harmony Heights knows about what I've done. I don't give a shit. All I care about is my future with this woman." I duck my hand out of her hold, throwing my arm over Annaliese's shoulder, tucking her into me. "And she's *mine*."

Ward works his jaw. For a second, he's speechless, until he sneers. "You think your shit don't stink 'cause you're a Reynolds. When we get rid of Collins, I'll do my best to make sure you won't be the next King."

Yeah, right. "Good luck. Dallas isn't going anywhere."

"If you say so."

Prick. I know what he's doing. He can't get to Annaliese. I made that perfectly clear. She's mine, and I'll claim her as much as it takes to get it through his thick skull. But Dallas… he's going after one of my brothers, the dick.

He can *try*.

"And I don't want to be King even if he gave up the title," I tell the lawyer before giving her a possessive squeeze. "All I want is Annaliese."

"I won't let you—"

Yeah. I'm done with this. "Do you have a blood oath?"

Annaliese's head snaps over to me, a curious expression on her face as she searches mine. Huh. I wonder if she has any clue what that means in the Order. A blood oath… I made sure to have one the second I knew I would be marrying her. Sure, I didn't tell *her* that, but the way she's looking at me…

Ward scoffs.

I've had enough.

Releasing Annaliese, I surge forward, poking him in his suit, digging my finger into his chest. "Did you swear an oath in blood or not?"

"I have a wife—"

"Yeah," I snap, "and so do I. Now you listen to me, Ward. You'll leave her the fuck alone or else I'm calling in my blood oath. You know what happened to Desmond St. James. He worked in your law office, didn't he? Where is he now? Something to think about, okay? Because I'll do worse if you hurt this woman again." Looking away from the lawyer, I turn to Annaliese. "Love? Come with me. I think we need a little fresh air."

And he needs to get the fuck out of my sight before I murder him in the middle of the venue.

Annaliese nods, sliding her arm around the back of my leather jacket; even at Alex's party, I'm wearing my standard uniform of short-sleeved shirt, jeans, and road jacket. My wife didn't mind. In fact, she told me how handsome I looked before we left for the party, and now I wonder how often she said the same thing to *Ward*—

No. Not going there, Bas. Focus on Annaliese. She's tucked against my side as I lead her out into the night. It's May. Warmer than it has been, yet she's trembling.

I rub her shoulder. Don't think about that prick. Focus on your *wife*. "Breathe. Can you do that? Just breathe."

Annaliese stops. Once again, she glances up at me. "You threatened to kill Eric."

"Oh, no. I don't make threats, love." I drop a kiss to the top of her hair. "I don't bluff, either. You say the word, I'll gut him like a fish. No one would ever stop me. Hell, Dallas and Connor would each hold an arm while Adrian advised me on the best spot to cut him with my knife." I chuckle. I can't help it. This is serious, but… they're my brothers. They *would* do it, and I… "I'll do it, too. The blood oath means that I reserve the right to protect you from any harm. If he hurt you—"

She cuts me off with a stroke to my chest, though when I look down into her face, her expression is hard to read all of a sudden. "Sebastien… you did it? You really did it? You signed a blood oath? For a fake marriage?"

I grit my teeth. Maybe if we'd had this discussion at a different time, and not right after Eric Ward put the thought of my Annaliese fucking him into my head… but he did, and I'm struggling not to lose it, and now she's trying to pull the same ol' 'marriage of convenience' crap.

I cup her jaw, leaning over her. It's important to me that she sees the absolute honesty in my eyes as I say, "Oh, love… when will you finally get it through your pretty head? It's *never* been fake."

Like clockwork, my wife—my *wife*—starts to argue, but I… I just can't do it anymore.

I step away from her. That shuts her up, and she only gets more confused when I start to remove my leather jacket. I *never* take it off. She's never seen me without it except for when we're lying in bed together, and I've been careful to wear long-sleeve shirts at night.

It's finally time she understands why.

I didn't mean for it to be a secret. In the long line of ways I've screwed-up, getting an impulsive tattoo—the only one I have—doesn't rank anywhere near the top. It's just… I was playing for keeps. Playing for forever. If she knew that I considered her mine from the start, she would've kept her distance. She told me she wasn't interested in love… and what did I do?

I show her my arm. I show her the four letters tattooed on the edge of my left forearm, done up in a simple script that means everything to me.

Beneath the outdoor lamp in the parking lot,

Annaliese squints and reads, "'Love'?" She glances up at me. "Is that why you call me that? Did you call…" She swallows the question, shaking her head. "How many other women have been your love, Sebastien?"

I know what she meant to ask. I also think I know why she changed it at the last minute. It doesn't matter.

"Only you," I swear. "Sure, I have a habit of using pet names with people… you're proof of that. The night we met, I nicknamed you 'love', and I've used it ever since. And *that* is why I got this tat. Because you're the only one I've ever called 'love'. You're the only one who'll ever be my wife."

Annaliese swallows. "It's… it's temporary. Right?"

Fury flashes through me. I work to tamp it down. "Temporary? Fuck, no. And you know why? Because *nothing* about us has *ever* been temporary."

She nibbles on her bottom lip. My cock twitches. "I don't understand…"

I need her to. Five minutes ago, it wasn't that important, but now? I *need* her to understand.

I reach into my back pocket, pull out my phone. While she watches, I open it, then find my photos. Scroll… scroll… scroll… *there.*

Turning the phone around, I show her a picture. It's my freshly inked tat, the clear saniderm wrap stretched over the letters. There's no denying it's real. You can see the red skin beneath it, plus the ink is so much darker than the healed-over tattoo.

She blinks, stunned. "It's *real.*"

"Look at the date," I tell her.

Annaliese gasps. "You got it the morning after we had our wedding?"

"Like I told you. I never thought I'd get married. I wanted to commemorate it."

"But that's *permanent.*"

I use the tip of my pointer finger to tilt her head up. "Yeah, love. And so are we."

TWENTY-ONE

THE MOUNTAIN CABIN

ANNALIESE

don't want to return to the party. If I had my choice, I'd just go home. Walk, Uber, drive… whatever it took, I'd be gone. But this was my debut as Sebastien's wife. It was my fault that it didn't occur to me that Eric would show up at Alexandre's party. In my brain, Eric was my past, Sebastien my present, and safety my future. They weren't supposed to interact.

And, oh, did they…

I hate that Eric affected me the same way as always. He made me feel like a silly little girl who was being scolded, and I… I let him. I had no intention of leaving with him, but if Sebastien hadn't rescued me when he did, Eric would probably still be doing his best to convince me to come along.

That's how he won me in the first place. Between wearing me down with the constant refrain that I couldn't do any better than a powerful, wealthy lawyer, then pointing out how lucky I was that he chose *me* to be his… and then slipping in some flattery that twenty-three-year-old Annaliese was helpless to fight back against… in the end, going along with it was so much easier than fighting. Falling in love with him was so much easier.

I don't love him anymore. If I had any doubt about that, whether or not positive feelings lingered, and that I would have regrets the next time I saw him… yeah, no. I was already so pissed and frustrated that he would try to upset my sister. But after the way he showed up at Alexandre's party to confront me? I might've quailed a bit under the weight of those icy blue eyes, falling back into the old habit where he talks at me and I just stand there and take it, but the whole time… *the whole time…* all I kept thinking about was how I wanted him to just leave me the fuck alone.

And then Sebastien suddenly appeared. He saved me, and he threatened Eric, and he admitted that he went to the King and got a *blood oath.*

Loni told me about those. In the Order, it's another level to a Claiming. If an Owed signs a blood oath, he's swearing to take care of the woman he's Claiming —to the death. If the King seals it, he's giving the member permission to do whatever it takes to protect his wife.

Would Sebastien really do that for a *fake* wife? Because if anything happened to me… if he fails in his duty… the vicious Order says that the Owed will spill their blood again. That's how serious a blood oath is. Through Miranda, Deirdre confirmed it. A blood oath says that my life is worth his. If I lose my life because he failed to protect me, he forfeits his.

And if anyone hurts me, he can kill *them*.

It's rare. Loni made me think it was common enough because she has one with her husband, but it only takes five minutes around Adrian and Loni Heller to pick up on just how obsessed that man is with his wife. No… *devoted*. That's what Sebastien said. Adrian was devoted to Loni.

Is Sebastien devoted to me?

I don't do fake…

He has a tattoo. As I reluctantly take the arm he offers me—covered with his leather jacket again, though the image of what's underneath it is burned into my memory—to lead us both back into the venue, I keep thinking about the word inked on his skin. *Love.* He got a tattoo the morning after our wedding. He got it for *me*.

Who does that if they plan on walking away after the year they agreed to?

I don't know, but the same question beats a constant refrain against my skull as we rejoin the party.

Eric is gone. I'm not all that surprised. Deep down, he's a coward. He can bully me all he wants because, well, he always has. But once Sebastien interfered? Once my husband threatened *him*? Of course he fled.

Does that mean that I think this is over? That he'd take the hint and finally give up on me, moving on? Maybe. I'm not sure. I'd love to think so, but I don't have the mental capacity to think about it at this moment. Not when Sebastien has switched his hold on me so that I'm tucked under his arm, wheeled around the party as we make our goodbyes to the guests two hours before the scheduled end of the party.

We drove over to the venue together in Sebastien's Porsche. I allow him to lead me out to the car, but once I'm sitting in the passenger seat and he's sliding in next to me, I turn to him.

"He knows we're married now."

Sebastien's expression is flat. That's not usual. No matter what, there's always a hint of charm. It's his own shield against the world. I realize how much I've gotten to know him in the last two months or so because whenever that easy smile is gone... I know that the real Sebastien is peeking through.

Only now? I have no idea what he's thinking. And when he says, "Is that a problem?" in a carefully controlled voice, I can tell it's not good.

"What? Of course not. It was only a matter of time. But Eric..." I shake my head, trying to hide my fear, instead showing my husband my disgust. "He's dangerous."

Sebastien reaches out, laying his hand possessively on my thigh. "So am I, love."

I suck in a breath. "Sebastien..."

He rubs my knee. "Not to you. I hope you understand that. Never to you. I'm a dick, Annaliese, but I'm your dick. You don't have to be afraid of me."

I have *never* been afraid of Sebastien Reynolds. I don't think there's anything he could ever do that would cause him to inspire fear in me. "I know," I tell him. "And I'm not. Afraid *for* you, maybe—"

"Ward doesn't scare me."

He should. He has fifteen years on Sebastien, and while my husband has purposely avoided the Order as much as he can, Eric is firmly enmeshed in it. I'd like to think that Sebastien's close friendship with the King will help him, but if Eric starts targeting Sebastien now because of me… I'll never forgive myself.

I choose my words carefully. "He has connections and no morals. You're a good guy, Sebastien—"

He snorts.

I continue anyway. "You *are*. He's… not. He told me if I ever chose another guy, he would…" At the last minute, I change what I was going to say. "…it would be bad. And he didn't just threaten to demote me. He threatened to take Miranda's future away from her. I can't let him do that."

"So we don't," is Sebastien's easy answer.

I wish it *was* that easy. "He wields his influence in the Order like a weapon."

I need Sebastien to understand that. Because of his high rank… because he's purposely made it so that he doesn't care… he has the privilege to flip off the Order and not let it affect him. But for someone like me? I'd have to leave Harmony Heights, start over, escape if the Order turned on me—and that's assuming that I could. That they would let me.

And that's when he lifts his hand, cupping my jaw, turning my face so that I'm not looking at the floor of the car, but him instead. "So? Know what? The Order rules my life. It rules yours. Why do we let it? I say we stop."

I blink up at him. I would've thought that the Order

didn't touch him at all… but maybe I was wrong. Remembering his dream of being a mechanic, of owning his own garage… yeah. I was *way* wrong.

"Okay," I say breathlessly.

It's not his usual easy grin. Nope. When his lips quirk upward, it's an honest smile that makes his face even more beautiful.

"Let's leave," he says slowly, rubbing his thumb along the edge of my jaw. "Just get out of town for a few days."

What? "Leave?"

"Yeah. You finished Alexandre's event. And I guarantee your phone is going to explode with other Order families begging for your services after this." He lowers his hand, wrapping his palm around the side of my throat as he leans in. "You deserve a break. And I want some time alone with my wife now that this job is done."

The word 'wife' sends a shiver up my spine.

"What do you think, love? We can go home, pack a few bags, leave tonight… just you and me?"

What do I think?

I lay my hand over his and nod. "Let's go."

It's so hard to believe it, but less than two hours later, Sebastien is pulling up in front of a large cabin—complete with an attached garage—that's hidden in the spring-green mountains. During the day, sunlight would pour over the valley like spilled gold. At ten o'clock at night, it's dark yet still undeniably beautiful, the moon shining down on it instead.

The path is rocky. Just like the waterfall, tucked away on these same mountains, the Reynolds family cabin is concealed from passersby. You have to maneuver your vehicle through closely grown trees, down a barely-there path, and if you don't know exactly where you're going, you could either get lost or end up way too close to the mountain's edge.

Sebastien, of course, knows the way intimately. On our drive up, he explains that, while this is technically his family's mountain home, he's taken it over himself. This is where he goes when he needs to get out of Harmony Heights.

This is where he goes when he needs to get away.

I find out why almost right after we park outside.

Sebastien told me to dress comfortably before we left the house. Because I have this need to wear his clothes as my pajamas lately, I traded the dress I wore to the party for one of his long-sleeved button-down shirts and some leggings. He's dressed the same, but the way he moves lightly on his feet as he hurries to open my side of the car, he already seems to be in a much better mood.

Grabbing the two duffel bags that we packed for our few days' stay, he jerks his head at the second building, the one attached to the cabin. It's smaller than the main structure, and I get the idea that it's similar to the attached garage back at Sebastien's house, until he says with a touch of pride, "That's my workshop."

I give him a questioning look.

He shrugs. "I could never have a garage of my own

in Harmony Heights, so I turned this spare garage into one. This is where I build my bikes. When the pressures become too much… I ride up here, throw myself into the work, and only come back down to Harmony Heights when I've got my head on straight."

I think about it for a moment. "So… sometimes, when it's like you've fallen off the face of the planet, this is where you are?"

Not banging other women, but working on his bikes?

I don't add that part. I don't *have* to.

Sebastien's grin takes on a wicked edge. "Did you miss me, love?"

I fight hard to force back my flush. "I know this is only a marriage of convenience. I don't have any right to be jealous or to wonder where you are when you're not around."

He shakes his head. "One of these days, Annaliese, you'll figure it out. Until then, I'll make this clear: next time I need to disappear? You'll be right there with me. I've never brought anyone up to this cabin to see my workshop before… but you? I hope you like the mountain air. We'll be spending a lot of time up here."

Leaving me with that, Sebastien carries our bags inside, and for a moment, it feels unreal. Like that afternoon by the waterfall, it's just us. No Order. No judging eyes. No threats or danger or Used shooting me nasty looks because they want my husband…

I exhale, then trail behind him into the cabin garage. He flicks a switch, revealing a half-assembled motorcycle.

"See? This is where I come to work. To breathe."

I run my fingers along the cool metal of the bike. "You… built this?"

I knew he built his main bike, Betsy. He told me all about that. But to see one in this state really hammers that message home.

He shrugs, but there's pride hidden in the gesture. "Working on it. To be honest, when I 'fell off the face of the planet', like you said, it's because I needed some distance. I stayed away from you because I was so damn desperate to have you. I really needed to get my head on straight. Didn't want to push you."

He glances at me, voice dropping. "But the time for pretending is over. After tonight… I hope you see that, too."

I'm not sure what he means. If it's because of Eric or how we ran away together… it doesn't matter. Heat pools low in my stomach regardless.

I clear my throat, purposely changing the subject before I melt. "Do you still want to be a mechanic?"

He sees through my switch immediately. Of course he does. Sebastien is a whole lot more intuitive than he wants the outside world to believe, but he's kind enough to let me have the dodge.

"For now," he murmurs, brushing his fingers over my arm, "I want to be your husband."

My breath catches. He grins, then says, "Come on, love. Let's head into the main cabin. I think it's time we have a little chat."

Uh-oh. Chat?

For a second, I want to turn and bolt. Running seems like a fucking amazing idea, but where would I go? Sebastien has the keys, and I have no idea where I am. Besides, he's right. There are so many things we've been keeping from each other, and no matter what *this* is, it's time we get it all out in the open.

So I follow him through his workshop, into the kitchen of the cabin, before he guides me to a cozy living room. There are two large couches, a small table between them, and a dim fireplace to the side. I could just see myself enjoying this space. Curled up with a book on one of the couches, the flames flickering around me, setting the ambiance… but that's not tonight.

Tonight is about something different, and I brace myself for it as Sebastien sets down our luggage before dropping down on one of the couches. He gestures at me, and I perch down on the other. My knees lock together, fingers twisted as I wait for Sebastien to speak.

And when he does, I try not to shudder.

"Okay. I think it's time. So why don't you tell me about Eric."

My throat closes. "Sebastien—"

"And if you do, I'll tell you about Julie."

That stops me cold.

He doesn't look away when he says her name. Doesn't flinch. Doesn't soften it, either.

Julie. Since I've been involved with Sebastien, I've heard whispers. Rumors. I couldn't bring myself to ask Miranda to see what they could be referring to. I guess, in a way, I didn't want to get confirmation on what I already expected.

But then even Eric threw her in his face tonight. *It's not bad enough you ruined one life…*

"Who was she?" I asked.

"Her name was Julie. Julie Madden." He sighs, leaning back in his seat. "It was four years ago. I was even more determined then not to have anything to do with the Order, and when I met Julie, she didn't seem to have any connections. And I… I didn't look too hard. Shit, I didn't *want* to look that hard. She was so sweet. So loving. She made me feel like I wasn't the big screw-up that everyone thought I was."

I can't help myself. "You're not—"

"And you wonder why I love you? No one ever stands up for me, Annaliese. No one except my bros, and they know that I'm a screw-up and accept me anyway. I worked hard at it. I need you to understand. They wanted me to be the black sheep, and I played the part. But when I met Julie… I thought… maybe. Maybe there was someone who loved me for me, chose *me*, not because I was a Reynolds, but because I was Bas. I was Sebastien."

Something tells me that that wasn't the case. I stay quiet, though I have to bite my tongue not to remind him that to me, he *is* Sebastien.

It's okay. He already knows it.

His eyes are warm as he looks at me, even as he lets out a hollow laugh. "Turns out I was way wrong. Not only did Julie target me specifically for my last name, but she'd already had a fling with Alexandre before he cast her aside. I tried so hard to shield her from the Order, to keep her out of that life, even he didn't know I was falling for his ex-lover. But that wasn't even the worst part. Julie was gunning for us because she was already married to an Owed in Jack's inner circle. Another arranged marriage. She hated him, but he refused to let her leave him, so she thought someone with my rank… my *pedigree*," he spits out, "would be able to save her. Only I didn't. I couldn't."

Oh, no. "What happened to her?"

"She jumped," is his wry response. "Isn't that what always happens in the Order? It finally came out. We were caught together, and her husband found out. Oh, they say that she jumped to save face after cheating on her husband, but I think you've been involved with the Order long enough to know that… our women? They don't jump. They get *pushed*."

I've heard that before. Rumors ran that the wife of the former King had a similar 'accident'. It's easier to call it suicide than what it really is: murder. And Sebastien lost his Julie to the same fate.

"It was my fault. If I hadn't loved her… or if I loved her enough to save her despite her admitting she never cared about me… she wouldn't have fallen." His expression is back to being flat. "After that, I stuck to one-night stands and the Used. I couldn't risk falling in love again… until you."

My heart jumps. That's the second time he's said something like that tonight. The first time, I purposely ignored it. But now? On the heels of his confession?

I decide that, before he can convince himself he cares for me, he needs to hear *mine*.

He wants to know about Eric? I tell him.

I tell him everything. All of the years I spent with him, and the manipulation… the threats… how I was so sure I loved him, but I was nothing more than a toy to the man who ruled my life for so long…

Sebastien doesn't interrupt. He just lets me talk, listening as my voice starts out shaky, becomes firm throughout my story, before finally growing weak again as I tell him, "So that's that. And I understand if that's enough to make you want to end the contract. I didn't… I *couldn't* tell you about him until now. But I put in that termination clause, about how we could end our marriage of convenience if either of us hid anything important. I understand you better now that I know about Julie, but I also understand if Eric—"

Sebastien snorts. Actually snorts. "You can't be serious, Annaliese. I can't end it. Even if I wanted to, it's just not possible."

I don't understand. "Why not?"

"Because there is no contract."

<h1 style="text-align:center">TWENTY-TWO
RUN</h1>

ANNALIESE

stare at him. "Um. What? Of course there is. We both signed it…"

Sebastien gets to his feet. I pause, letting my words trail to a close as he ducks behind the couch, going through his luggage. When he's standing again, he's holding a black velvet box about the size of my phone.

"A couple of days into our marriage, I knew that this was it for me. *You* were it for me. So I took your binder, grabbed mine, and I burned those fuckers in that fireplace." He uses his shoulder to gesture behind him at the dead grate. "I scooped up the ashes, brought them to this jeweler I found online. And he used the ashes to make this."

Moving over to me, he pops open the lid on the box. My eyes go wide when I see the gold chain nestled on another black velvet bed, but it's the small, heart-shaped pendant that really catches my attention. At first, you'd think it was a glittering diamond, but as he lowers it in front of me, letting me peer closely at it, I see the hint of black specks that might just be the melted plastic and burnt paper that used to be our marriage contracts.

My heart slams into my ribs.

I rerun what he said. *A couple of days into our marriage…* So he got a tattoo and then burned our contract? From the beginning?

"Sebastien—"

Before I know it, he's lifting the necklace out of the jewelry box. He lets it fall to the floor, freeing his hands to undo the clasp and settle it around my throat. I can't even stop him, and I don't know if I would've if I could. I just sit still as he puts the necklace on me.

"There," he says softly, lips brushing my ear, "now you know all of my truths. Julie broke my fucking heart, Annaliese. But you, love? You put it back together without even realizing you were doing it. And now you have mine."

Remember that oppressive feeling like I needed to bolt from earlier? It comes back tenfold.

I wait until he's given me a little space before I jump to my feet.

Suddenly, I can't breathe. The weight of the necklace he gave me is nothing, but the meaning? It's too, too much.

"Sebastien, I—" I swallow. "I just… I need a moment. Okay?"

He stiffens. "Annaliese?"

I take a step away from him. Another. The cabin door is right over there. I just have to reach it.

"Mountain air," I gasp. "I need some air."

His jaw tightens. His eyes darken.

And then he reaches out, lashing my wrist with his hand, as he says one word that has me freezing more than his sudden grab does—

"*Wait.*"

Damn it. The emotion he poured into that single syllable? How can I resist him?

I shudder out a breath. "Okay."

Sebastien lets go of me. It's his turn to wait, checking to see if I'm going to continue to dash out the door, but when I stay where I am, he lets out a relieved breath of his own, chasing it with a hollow laugh.

"Be honest, love. How bad did I fuck up here?"

"What? I… I don't know what you mean."

He arches an eyebrow. "I just told you I loved you and made it clear that there will be no leaving me forever. I gave you jewelry that proves it. And you look like you're about to do a runner. So, yeah… I fucked up. The question is how bad did I fuck up, and is there any way I can fix it without sending you running out the door? Because you can try. I mean, I'll *chase* you, but you can try."

I dart out my tongue, dabbing my bottom lip. "It's not like that."

"It's not? Okay. Fine. I'll bite. Is this about Julie? Because I promise you that I would've *never* hurt her. You're safe with me, Annaliese."

"I know." If there's one thing I *do* know, it's that.

"And I'm glad you told me about her. I'm sorry, too. Sorry that you lost her. Sorry that I kept Eric hidden from you—"

"I'm not."

I blink up at him.

He gives me a crooked grin. "Okay. I wasn't quick enough. Yeah, I wish you would've trusted me enough to tell me about that prick. If I knew, I would've handled him long before now." Sebastien huffs, shaking his head, never losing that grin. "Adrian's gonna flip his shit when he finds out who the fucker was."

I must have made a confused face because he goes on to explain: "The fucker. That's what I called him. I knew that there was some guy who hurt you… the reason why you felt like you had to marry *anyone*. I've been trying to figure out how that fucker was since the night we got engaged. Even had my bros on the hunt. I just never thought it would be a man like Eric Ward which just proves that I'm a fucking idiot. You deserve the best, Annaliese. A man like Ward could give you the best."

"He could," I agree softly, "but he couldn't give me the one thing I wanted."

"Yeah? And what was that?"

"I just wanted to get married."

Something sparks in his dark eyes. "You're my wife."

I nod.

"I couldn't marry Julie. Fuck, I don't know if I would've if I could. She was using me the same way that fucker was using you. But who knows? Maybe we were supposed to get our hearts broken so that, when two broken people like us found each other, we could be whole again." Sebastien jerks his head. "Shit. That was sappy. It sounded better in my head—"

"No," I say, cutting him off. "I… I think I get it. And maybe… maybe you're right."

"You think so?"

I shrug. "I mean, yeah. So we met in a really weird way. Got married before we ever really knew each other. I'm not going back to Eric. You can't go back to Julie. So if you want to see what happens, where this goes… I know you burned the contracts," I say, rubbing my thumb over the pendant he put on me, "but I have copies. And it says we can negotiate—"

"No."

Sebastien's harsh 'no' is so unexpected, I take a step back, moving closer to the door. "What?"

"You heard me, Annaliese. You're still trying to put walls up between us. Still trying to give yourself a way out."

"It's not me—" I begin.

His jaw flexes. "If you're going to tell me that you're trying to give me an out, let me save you the trouble. I'm not going anywhere. I told you from the beginning. If I married you, I was playing for keeps. There is no year-term. No contract. There is no 'renegotiating' because this? This is 'til death do you part. And I don't mean like how the Order does it, where you live your life and I live mine. I love you. You understand me? And I'm done with pretending that I'll let you get away from me."

A nervous twinge has me jerking in place. "Sebastien, I don't know—"

He's not done.

"Love isn't gentle for people like me, Annaliese. It's sharp. It cuts. And I'll bleed for you every time. Because you? You're my wife, and you have been since the first time you let me in. It just took us both a minute to catch up, but if you think I'm letting you go, you better grab a knife. 'Cause the only way my heart will stop beating for you is if you carve it out of my fucking chest."

"Sebastien—"

He moves closer to me, digging in his pocket as he closes the slight gap I put between us. When only a few feet separate my husband and me, he yanks his hand out, showing me the folded pocket knife he was carrying with him.

"Connor gave us… the five of us… these when we graduated middle school." He twirls it. "I want you to have it."

Middle school… he's had to have owned that for at least fifteen years. And he wants to give it to me?

I hold up my hand, warding him. "That's okay. You keep it."

"I insist." Sebastien moves into me, pressing the cool metal against my palm, folding my fingers over it. "Now you have the tool you need to stop me loving you." With his now-free hand, he tilts my chin up, forcing me to look at him. "Carve out my heart. Slit my throat… because, I'm telling you, that's the only way you'll get me to stop."

"Sebastien…"

He looks down at me, waiting for me to finish speaking.

But how?

The weight of the pocket knife he gave me is almost as bad as the necklace. Suddenly, the room is spinning. Suddenly, I really need that air. That space.

"I'll be back," I blurt out.

He furrows his brow. "Love?"

No. Not 'love'. Not now.

I flash him a thin-lipped smile, then turn. The door is unlocked. I don't even bother to grab a light jacket. Just me, one of Sebastien's oversized button-down shirts that he lets me use as pajamas because he rarely wears them, my comfy leggings, and my sneakers... phone? Nope. I even place the pocket knife down on the stand by the door before I grope for the knob, turning it roughly, then bolting out the front door.

I have to. I have to run, even if I don't understand why.

I need to *go*.

Suddenly, the woods are too quiet. The cabin is too small. And Sebastien... he's too *everything*. Sexy and kind, possessive and perplexing. Demanding and so broken if only because he believes he is... but who can blame him? When the Order's bad boy finally tried to settle down, he chose an unavailable woman and has to live with the regret that he inadvertently caused her death. Then, by the time I came along, he agreed to a year—only to decide to ask for forever.

If I was him, I'd never fall in love again. I was led on by Eric, and I *did* vow to keep my heart out of this 'relationship'. I tried. I swear, I did. This was supposed to be a fake marriage—but somewhere along the lines, it stopped being fake to me.

And Sebastien? If I can believe him, it was *never* fake.

Oh, he said that before. I never believed him. Tonight, though? There's something different about him. And I don't just mean because he opened up to me. I opened up to him, too, and I feel like a huge weight's been lifted off my shoulders. I thought... I thought that, if he found out about Eric, he would invoke the termination clause in the marriage agreement.

Only he didn't. Instead, he gave me a piece of jewelry made from the *ashes* of said agreement.

The same piece of jewelry that is bouncing up and down, hitting my chin, hitting my chest as I race through the trees.

Branches whip at my arms as I sprint through them, my breath catching, my heart thundering against my ribcage.

I know it's stupid. Running... I know that I can't outrun Sebastien. I can't outrun his feelings or mine. Even more importantly, if I keep it up, a tiny part of me is convinced that he'll follow like he said.

I wasn't kidding, though. I just need space. A minute where I can make sense of all of this. I feel like I've been running since Alexandre's party earlier tonight when Eric found me and Sebastien threatened him. Sure, my legs weren't moving like they are now, but I've barely taken a deep breath until this moment.

Shit. That's not even a deep breath. That's gasping

as I struggle to get in enough air. Running, Annaliese? Really? I don't know what I was thinking.

Well, no. I can answer that. Because the truth is that I totally wasn't thinking, was I?

I just took off, and as I hear leaves crunching behind me... slow and steady footfalls... the sound of someone stalking my loud steps... I know that Sebastien *did* come after me. He's not even trying to hide it. It's like he wants me to hear how easily he's been able to catch up to me, and just in case I start freaking out that it's a stranger on his family's mountain land, he calls out for me.

"Annaliese."

It's my name, deep and rough and too, too close.

Where is he? I spare a few precious seconds to look behind me. I don't see him, but that doesn't mean he isn't there.

"I know you can hear me, love. That's fine. Keep running if that's what you need."

I nearly trip over my sneakers. Because that? That wasn't permission from my husband.

That was a *challenge*.

He must be closer than I first guessed. I choke on my gasping breath, tripping again because my brain wants me to go faster than my feet. Shaking it off, I duck around another tree before cursing to see that I've reached the edge of the damn mountain.

There are still woods all around me, but right ahead? That's a cliff, and if I keep running, I'll take the same sort of swan dive that his Julie did.

What now? There's nowhere left to run. I'm not

even sure *why* I bolted in the first place. It's not like I really can outrun my sins *or* my husband. I gave it a good try, though, my mistakes and my insecurities and my goddamn fantasies for what could've been dogging my every step.

All of that, plus Sebastien because all I hear is the drumbeat of his boots against the dirt before, suddenly, he's *there.*

A hand closes around my wrist.

It's not rough. Not punishing. It's a gentle grab with a more forceful tug, snagging me, pulling me back. I take a half-turn, not sure how to react, before he decides for me. My captor spins me fully, my free hand going up in time to slam my palm against Sebastien's slightly heaving chest.

He reaches around me, laying his hand on the small of my back. I'm trapped, and I have nowhere to look but up at him.

His hair is slightly mussed from the run. Beneath the moonlight, his eyes are bright with excitement and something hungry.

"Got you," he murmurs, a hint of a smile ghosting his lips.

Like he's happy he caught me. Like he's thrilled I ran in the first place.

Like he'd do this again and again, and no matter what, he'll always be there to catch me…

And he does. Have me, I mean. And maybe I didn't really mean to run. With everything happening… with this thing between us getting way too real… I bolted, believing that I would only piss my fake husband off by fleeing. But that expression is the farthest thing from 'pissed', and all I can think about is how he chased me. I ran, he followed, and now I'm caught.

Literally.

Never losing that grin, his face shadowing over, Sebastien moves. His hold on my wrist tightens, his body pushing against mine, and I'm helpless to do anything other than trip over my feet as he backs me up until my spine hits the solid bark of one of these too many trees.

The shock of contact snaps another breath out of me, then his name. "Sebastien—"

"No."

His tone is light, almost playful, as he edges impossibly closer, crowding my space until there's nowhere for either of us to go except into each other.

His cologne goes to my head. I was already dizzy, from panic and fear and the anxiousness I hid for too long, but the essence of Sebastien overwhelms all my other senses. I see him, breathe him, *need* him… but I can't have him. He's not mine. Not really.

And I've been fooling myself that I can keep this thing we have strictly professional. I'd break every damn clause in the contract if I could. I wish I was stronger. I wish I'd met Sebastien before another man ruined me. I wish—

"Annaliese. *Love.* Look at me. Look at your husband."

My hands fall to my sides. My eyes snap back to his face.

And, knowing that he has my complete, undivided attention, his grin widens into a small, delicious smirk.

Shit. My breathing stutters, heat spiking low in my belly in a way I can't ignore—or hide. He has to know.

He *has* to.

Sebastien releases my wrist. I don't even think of trying to buck against him so I can make my escape. He knows that, too. Still smirking, his hand slides up my side, slow and absolutely deliberate, before he wraps his fingers purposely around my throat.

It's a soft hold. More question than warning, though I can't pretend I don't see what this really is.

A *claiming*. Not an Order Claiming, but something different. Something more meaningful. Sebastien is pinning me in place beneath him, keeping me right where he wants me.

My knees nearly give out, but I'm not worried. If they do? He'll catch me before I fall. I believe that with everything I am, even though I shouldn't. Then again, this is Sebastien Reynolds. He is the definition of *should*n't, but God help me, I want to so fucking badly.

His thumb rests against the pulse hammering frantically beneath my skin.

"I caught you, love," Sebastien says quietly, eyes locked on mine. "And now you're mine."

I am, aren't I?

Then again, haven't I been since that night in the Last Prayer?

TWENTY-THREE

AND I'LL FOLLOW

SEBASTIEN

My wife's pulse hits my thumb like a drumbeat. It's fast, panicked, *alive*, and I can't tell if it's because of Annaliese's mad dash through the trees—or because I have her under me like this, knee lodged between her thighs, my hand a collar for her pretty, pretty throat.

My pulse is thudding, too, but I know why. As I peer down into her wide brown eyes, all I can think is: she ran away from me, but she didn't get that far.

That's okay. Let her run. I'd chase this woman to the end of the world, and it's about time she figured that out.

"What are you running from?" I rasp, leaning in until our chests touch.

Her thighs close around me. She gasps, eyes fluttering shut for a second, her throat flexing under my fingers. But then she pops them open again as she whispers, "I don't know."

"Yeah, love," I answer, my body bowing over Annaliese until only a few inches separate my forehead from hers, "you do."

I let my thumb stroke the edge of her jaw. She shivers under my caress.

"You're scared of what this is," I say. "Scared of wanting something again. Scared it's gonna blow up in your face like last time. But, let me tell you something, Mrs. Reynolds: it can't. It *won't*. Because I'm not *him*."

Her breath catches. Out here in the darkness, in the quiet, in the woods, I hear it. It's a small, broken sound that Annaliese tries to swallow, but it's no use.

Besides, she's not running from me. Not really. She's running from the bastard that hurt her, and she's running from the promise of forever I offered her when I placed that pendant around her neck.

From the moment she proposed a marriage of convenience, spelling out her expectations in that marital agreement that I took pure fucking delight in burning, I could tell that she'd been hurt. She was wounded. I didn't know if she could ever love again, but I crave her affection like Adrian used to fiend for a hit of nicotine.

I'm addicted to Annaliese Reynolds, and there's no amount of rehab in this damn world that will get me to stop wanting her.

I'd hoped I could go slowly. I could, well, court her… woo her… take her on dates, show her my sweet side. Even when I was fucking up, making bad decisions, or dealing with the aftermath of being blamed for Julie's death, I never quite lost that part of me. Oh, I hid it. I covered it up with a cocky attitude, fighting anyone who got too close unless they were one of my brothers.

And then I looked into Annaliese's brown eyes as she sat down one stool away from me at the Last Prayer. She was lost, but determined, and by the time I had a taste before she fucking walked away, I knew that I'd never forget her. I *didn't*. Three months later, I was still obsessing over a one-night stand, and when I had the second chance to keep her—to *Claim* her as only one of the Owed can—I jumped at it.

Fuck it. I'm nothing if not an opportunistic bastard, and I prove that I am more than ever while keeping her pinned beneath me.

Turning into her, I press my body to hers. Just like that afternoon by the waterfall, I don't let her escape the proof of how much I want her. How much I've always wanted her.

Shifting my hips, I dig my erection into the soft side of her belly, near her hip.

She gasps, hands flying out to clutch my t-shirt.

I smirk. Beneath me, my wife is wearing one of my dress shirts. Considering I'm so much wider, so much broader than Annaliese, it hangs on her frame. As I move my knee, making her ride my thigh, the shirt rises, falling, rustling in time to her frantic breathing as I stimulate her pussy.

She's not scared, though. I asked her once. Is she afraid of her husband... and when she told me she wasn't, I believed her. I'd be a piss-poor husband if I frightened my own wife. All I want her to know is how serious I am. How much I hunger for her… how much I *want* her… how much I fucking *worship* her.

"Do you understand me, love? I'm not the man who hurt you. I'm not the man who threw you away. I'm stupid, but I'm not *that* stupid. I have you. I told you back at the cabin the only way you can get rid of me. Where's the knife, Annaliese?" I squeeze her side. "Did you bring it? Or are you all alone with me, completely defenseless?"

I would never hurt her. She has to know that. If she didn't, I would have much bigger problems than I already have. I'm teasing her, both with my words and the way I keep dragging the denim of my jeans along the thin material of her leggings.

Her mouth trembles. Her fingers tighten in my shirt.

I press her deeper into the tree with my body so that neither of us can go anywhere. I'm still not trying to frighten her. Nope. I'm anchoring her there, keeping her from running, keeping her from pretending that I've reached my limit. I want her. I caught her.

Now I'm going to take her.

I give my wife one chance to stop me.

"Say something," I beg, the seductive edge obvious in my voice.

"I don't know what you want me to say," she gasps.

"You could say 'stop'. You could tell me to let you go. You could tell me that you don't want me… I just want honesty, love. That's all I'll ever want."

Besides her. I will always want this woman, and I'm sick and tired of pretending that I don't.

Marriage of convenience?

Fake marriage?

Never—and now she knows it.

Annaliese looks up at me. Her eyes are big, wide doe eyes, as she says softly, "If you want honesty, Sebastien, then I can't say any of that."

Fuck it. That's all the permission I need.

Dropping my head, I release my hold on her throat at the same moment that I crush my mouth to hers. Instead, I brace my palms on either side of her face, the bark scratching at my skin, the taste of her mouth enough to make me ignore the scrapes as I dig my fingertips into it.

Her hands fly up, gripping my shoulders, nails digging into my skin. Without my leather jacket, I feel it as it cuts into my flesh; feel it, and revel in it. Especially when my wife arches into me, kissing me back like she finally gave herself permission to want me, too.

This is different. Since the night at the Court when she showed me her jealous side, having that slap fight with Hilary, I've been fucking Annaliese regularly. She just needed to know that I wasn't sleeping with the Used on the side. Once I promised her that I wasn't… once she realized that she trusted me enough to believe me when I told her that I didn't want to be with anyone but my wife… she's been sleeping in my bed, curling up next to me, and if part of me has a hard time getting past the idea that she's only doing it to satisfy a clause in that goddamn contract, I ignore it because at least I'm burying my cock inside of my wife every chance I get.

Including now.

Only… this *is* different. Because when I fuck Annaliese—when she *lets* me—it'll be with the understanding that the contract is gone. It never existed, sure, but she's wearing the remnants of it around her neck. I want to fuck her because I love her, and not because a perk of being her husband is getting my hands on that sexy little body whenever she'll let me.

Dragging my hands over her shoulders, down her side, I pause when I reach her hips. Shoving my hands behind her back, cushioning her, I pull her harder against me. Then back to kissing her, her surprised gasp swallowed by my lips.

I pull away only when breathing stops being optional. When I'm lightheaded and so fucking horny, I'm prepared to fuck through the tree to get to her.

But, first, I glance down at her.

Her face is flushed, eyes glazed, lips swollen from my kiss.

"Sebastien…" she breathes. "Babe."

My cock twitches to hear her finally give me a pet name of her own. "Yes?"

She swallows. "I shouldn't want this."

Lifting my right hand, I brush her hair out of her face, trailing my knuckles along her cheek. "But you do, don't you?"

Her eyes close. And quietly, so very quietly, she says: "I always have."

I smile down at my wife. It's slow. It's dangerous.

It's *hungry*.

"Good."

Letting go of her, relying on her aroused yet boneless state to keep her right where she is, I crouch down. A hand on each side of her leggings and, whoops, there they go. I get them around her ankles before I lift up her right foot, slipping off her shoe. Settling it back on the grass, I grab her left foot, getting rid of that sneaker. Doing the same thing again, I take off her leggings. Another grab, and her panties are off, tossed into the darkness behind me.

I stay low. Curving my hand around the back of her calf, I stroke her silky soft flesh, smiling to myself as she shivers. Oh, love. I'll give you something to shiver about. In one quick motion, I lift her leg up, settling it over my shoulders, baring her pussy to me.

I bury my face in it, nuzzling her curls, dipping my tongue in between her folds, warming her up with my mouth.

She gasps, falling forward enough to cling to me, fingers threading through my hair as I lap at her cunt.

"God, Annaliese…" I breathe against her. "You don't have any idea what you do to me."

Her answer is a keening cry as she goes up on the tiptoes of her other foot, rocking her pussy against my mouth. I guess the small gap I put between us to speak wasn't good enough for my wife. I blow a warm breath out, enjoying the way her cry sharpens, how her fingers tighten in my hair, tugging, *yanking*, urging me back where I was.

"Please," she gasps. "I need…"

I nuzzle her clit. She chokes. I smile. "I know exactly what you need, love. You just let your husband give it to you."

She doesn't answer me.

Hm.

I don't think I like that.

One hand is clutching the underneath of her thigh. My other hand moves in front of me. I lift my hand, slapping the top of her mound with enough force to have her squealing. I wasn't going for pain. Nope. That was all about giving her a jolt of pure pleasure before I demand, "Who am I?"

Annaliese digs her heel into my back. "Seb— Sebastien."

Wrong answer, wife.

I slap her again, then take one finger, dipping it inside of her. She's so hot, so *slick*, I know that she's ready for me. Her pussy sucks at the digit, trying to swallow me whole, and I oblige by working a second finger in there.

I fingerfuck Annaliese as slowly as I can. The way she's squirming… the way she's untangled her fingers from my hair, throwing her hands up over her head as she clutches at the tree… my cock wants to take the place of my fingers desperately.

Down, Bas. Not yet.

I use my thumb to pluck at her clit. I've gotten to know her body intimately over the last couple of weeks. I can play it like it's a fucking violin, and the way she's panting for me is music to my ears.

But, my love, we can do a little better than that.

I increase the pace, prepared to let her come on my hand if that's what it takes. But though I have every intention of fucking her—and it's just such a boost to my ego that under her breath, she keeps on panting 'fuck me' over and over again—not until I get the right answer to this question.

"Let's try this again. Who the fuck am I, Mrs. Reynolds?"

She's close. I can tell. I know her so damn well, it won't take much more to have her exploding. I jam my fingers in her, and she squeals. "My husband!"

That's my girl.

"Am I fake?"

"What?"

It's the way she doesn't immediately have an answer to that question… See, I was prepared to let her come on my hand, but you know what? I just changed my mind.

I pull my fingers out of her, stopping all stimulation. Instead, I lick my fingers clean of Annaliese's sweet juices, smiling around the one in my mouth as she takes her leg back. She's shaky, glaring down at me as I stay crouched in the dirt.

I give her my most innocent grin. "Something wrong, love?"

"You stopped," she accuses me.

"I did."

"You don't… you don't want to do this?" Her anger fades, replaced with confusion. "Oh. Okay. Um. If you could just hand me my leggings, then—"

Fuck me. Once again, I'm screwing up. This is a biggie, too. Letting Annaliese think that I'm rejecting her instead of teasing her… Shit. This has Ward all over it. The second Dallas gives me the go sign, that lawyer is a dead man. Not only because he thinks he can target my brother, but for all the little ways he took something beautiful and left her beautifully broken.

I have to remember that. I can't treat her like any other lover. She's *not* any other lover. She's Annaliese. She's *my wife*, and if I need to remind her a hundred times instead of my own insecurities leading me to have her tell me again and again that I'm hers...

"I am your husband. Your *real* husband. You're my wife. That's it. That's all. I know it. You know it. And now we can consummate this fucking marriage for real." I jerk open the button on my jeans. Yank on the zipper. Grab my cock rougher than I should.

I don't care. I fucked up, letting her think I didn't want her.

I will *always* want her.

I stalk toward her. Stumbling away, eyes lit up in excitement, her back hits the tree again.

Scraping the shit out of my knuckles, I shove my hands behind her again. This time, I find bare skin under my dress shirt. Taking an ass cheek in each palm, I lift her up, urging her to wrap her legs around me.

Our eyes meet.

"How much do you want me? Tell me," I demand.

"So much."

I release a hand, using it to grip my cock at the base. "Say it again, Annaliese."

"I. Want. You."

It's not 'I love you'. I know I'll have to wait a little longer for that. It's only been two months after all, and she's been hurt before. That's fine. I have her now. I'll have her forever.

I find the entrance to her pussy, shoving hard, filling her with one quick thrust.

She gasps. I bury my face against her neck, scraping my teeth along the curve where it meets her shoulder. Then, voice muffled from where I'm sucking at the same spot, I tell her, "You're mine. Say *that*."

I am insecure. I'm broken. I'm the black sheep, and the one who was never worth shit. The one time I thought I had someone who was mine, I was wrong. I need this woman. I need her to belong to me more than I need to breathe.

If she betrayed me, I would never survive it.

If she left me, I would follow right behind her.

If she runs, I'll chase—and when I catch her again, she can expect a repeat performance of *this*.

I pull out just enough that, when I slam into her again, she feels it all the way through her body.

Her fingers clutch my shoulders, holding tight as she bounces on my dick. "I'm yours."

Finally.

Every last restraint burns away. There's no more teasing. No more taking it slow. Depending on her mood, Annaliese likes to be pampered, her body worshipped for hours. At other times, she likes it rough and fast, and if a part of me gets super fucking turned on seeing my prim, proper wife come apart as I fuck her like a goddamn animal... well, it's nice to let myself go, too.

And that's exactly what sex beneath the moonlight,

with the woods surrounding us our only audience, calls for.

Using all of my strength to hold her at the same time as I really begin to fuck her, I move her away from the tree so that I don't mess up her back any more than I already have. She's taking every inch of me like she was born to, crying my name to the wilderness, holding me so tightly, even if I tried to deny her her orgasm again, she'd take a chunk out of my shoulders before she ever let me go.

Her head is thrown back, hair trailing down past her shoulders. When I pick up mine from the hickeys I purposely left on her skin, I see her eyes are closed.

Hell, no.

"Look at me while I take you," I rasp, forehead pressed to hers. "I want to see your face when you realize just how fucking real you and me have always been."

Her nails dig even deeper into my skin. I wouldn't be surprised if my t-shirt is covered in blood by the time we're done, and, fuck, that thought shouldn't be as hot as it is, especially when she snaps her eyes open.

I nip her bottom lip.

She gasps. "*Sebastien.*"

I thrust again. Harder. *Faster.* I know how close she was when we started, and while I consider it a failure if I don't wring at least two orgasms out of my wife whenever she gives me the great pleasure of touching her, I can tell that I won't last much longer, either.

That's okay. We have tonight—and every fucking night that follows.

"You can run from me," I whisper against her lips, voice shaking with how hard I'm holding on, eager to keep from coming inside of her until she starts climaxing around me first. "You can run all you want, love. But understand this: I will always fucking come after you."

Her legs tighten around my hips, pulling me deeper as she gasps, "Don't stop, babe… *please—*"

"Never again," I growl, kissing her hard, swallowing her moans. "You hear me? *Never.*"

As though that was all she needed to hear from me, Annaliese's body clenches around me as she shatters in my arms. She lets out a soft grunt, an almost sigh, and I can't help it.

I follow right behind her, giving her all I've got.

We hold each other through the rest of it until she's curled up against my chest, head lying on my shoulder. Her arms are wrapped around me. My legs are shaky as hell, but somehow I manage to keep on standing as she presses a whisper-soft kiss against the corner of my mouth.

"Thank you," she says softly, her deliciously husky voice even more ragged and raw than usual. "For coming after me."

I clutch her to me, making another promise. Another vow.

"You can run," I answer. "But you will never get away from me."

This is it, love.

'Til death do us part.

ANNALIESE

We stay up at the mountain for three days, every minute of it a fucking dream.

I didn't realize how much I needed this. How much I needed *him*. For those three days, it was just us, just me and Sebastien. No Order politics. No planning. No worrying about Eric or where Sebastien was. I knew exactly where my husband was: in bed with me, reminding me again and again that I'm his.

I'm so afraid that, when we return to Harmony Heights, everything will change again. In a way, I'm not wrong—but not like I was scared of. For the first time in two months, being married to him feels easy. It feels *real*.

Of course it does. According to Sebastien, it *is* real.

I slip from time to time. Old habits are hard to break, but when Sebastien lovingly gooses my side whenever I slip up, calling this 'fake', referring to it as a 'marriage of convenience', I'm slowly beginning to accept that he's right.

Think about it. There isn't a contract anymore; I have the remains of it hanging on my necklace. All there is is a properly filed marriage license, my wedding band, and a blood oath. In all ways, I'm his wife, and I'm so damn glad that—as his wife—I finally have the chance to give him something to show him how much I care.

I already had it set into motion before Alexandre's party. After going up to the mountain and seeing Sebastien's workshop firsthand, I'm even more determined to show him my surprise.

It was easier than I thought it would be. All I had to do was find one for sale, negotiate a down payment I could afford, and pay to change the name on the sign out front. A week after we're back in Harmony Heights, I get a phone call that the title's been changed and the electrician finished installing the light-up sign on the front of the building. Because I want to show it to my husband before he rides by it and sees it himself, I insist on the two of us taking a drive downtown after dinner.

There isn't anything that I can ask him that he won't give me. Is he curious? Of course he is. But when I direct him to park on a street two blocks away, he just smiles at me, then does it.

Now we're walking hand-in-hand down Main Street when I tug him toward the building on the corner. Squeezing his fingers, I keep on pulling him until we reach the garage bay door. It's evening, the red lights gleaming over our heads.

I tilt my face. "Look."

Humoring me, Sebastien does—and then he drops his gaze to look down at me again.

"Annaliese?"

I can barely hide my excitement. "Do you like it?" Please, please, please like it…

His lips part. He works his jaw. For a moment, he's silent, and then he croaks out: "It says Reynolds Garage."

I untangle our fingers, clutching the upper arm of his leather jacket instead. "It's yours!"

"Mine?"

"I bought it for you," I tell him.

He turns. His eyes—*Jesus*—his eyes are wide, stunned, bright with something I can't quite name. "You… bought it. For me?"

"A down payment," I amend quickly, suddenly feeling shy. Does he like it? I still can't tell. "With the paycheck you gave me from Alexandre's party. I—"

He shakes his head slowly, like he can't process the words. "You bought me a *garage*."

"You said it's what you wanted. It was your dream. But you thought the Order couldn't let you have it." My throat tightens as I echo what he told me before we went to the mountain. "'The Order rules my life. It rules yours. Why do we let it?' I'm not. And neither are you. You're an awesome mechanic, Sebastien. Fuck what they think. You deserve this." I trail my hand down his sleeve. "And, this way, you don't have to go all the way up to the mountains to work on your bike. You can work here, and I'll always know where you are."

There. Another confession. Now that he wants me to be his wife, I'll show him what being *my* husband means.

I'm jealous. I'm possessive. I hate not knowing where he is, or who he's with, and if I thought I could get away with tracking him, I would… but even if I can't, I can do *this*.

I can try to make him happy. After all, that's what he's done for me since the beginning…

I wait for him to answer me. To say something. To say *anything*.

And that's when, suddenly, he turns on me, grabbing both sides of my face with his hands.

"Love," he breathes. "*Annaliese*. What have you done to me?"

I laugh, breath shaky. "Hopefully something good."

Ducking his head, my husband kisses me. Hard. I can taste the hunger, the desire, the absolute *need* in the stroke of his tongue against mine.

When he pulls away, he presses his forehead against mine. "No one's ever given me such a thoughtful gift before. Not like they saw me. Shit… you *see* me."

Maybe I do. But… "You gave me everything I wanted, Sebastien. I thought it was only fair that I did the same for you."

"You did that, though," he whispers. "Because, from the moment you walked into the Last Prayer and sat down on the stool next to my helmet, all I've wanted was *you*."

A soft, helpless sound leaves me as I whisper his name. "Sebastien…" I swallow, fisting my hands in his shirt. "Babe. You have that, too."

And when I initiate the next kiss on my own, I hope he can believe me.

I'VE NEVER SEEN SEBASTIEN SO CONTENT.

Like Deirdre Dawes told Miranda more than two months ago, my husband is inherently sweet. He's a *good* man. He never thought he was, and so many of the things he's done in his life before he met me were because he didn't believe he could *be* a good guy. But the foundation was always there. I saw it when we first met, otherwise I never would've slipped my hand into his leather glove, no matter how fucking gorgeous he is.

He has his dark side, too. It's hot and it's sexy, and it makes me melt every damn time. I'm helpless to love him. And I know. I swore up and down that this would be a marriage of convenience, that, next March, we would go our separate ways… but the idea of saying goodbye to Sebastien has *my* dark side coming out.

So that's that. We're a perfect match, and every time I reach up, rubbing my thumb over the pendant made from the ashes of our marriage agreement… whenever I nuzzle the tattoo on his arm that he got to commemorate our wedding… I wonder how I ever thought that I'd be able to keep things strictly professional between us. Even before we started having sex regularly, I honestly believed I could play the part of an Order wife, lying flat on my back, letting my 'husband' fuck me, then let him roll off of me to find some Used to keep him company next.

Hilary Morgan helped me learn that lesson. I'm as possessive of Sebastien as he is of me, and while he promised he'd cut off the fingers of the next woman who touched him without his permission, I'm the one he gave his pocket knife to. So that pleasure will be all *mine*.

But watching him work in the garage—grease on his hands, rock music humming from the speakers, a motorcycle engine on the stand—it's like seeing the weight fall off him piece by piece. The cabin workshop helped, but building his shop her in town where everyone can watch him do mechanical magic? I don't think I could've given him a more thoughtful gift with his own money.

He already has plenty of 'customers'. Nosy Order members who pretend they want a tune-up, but who just want to gawk at the Reynolds screw-up working for a living. He doesn't care, and if he doesn't, I don't.

Not when his mother came barreling into the garage last week while I was hanging out with him, hugging him so hard that the wrench he was holding fell out of his hand. Ambre Reynolds kissed both of his cheeks, then mine, before beaming at her son.

"This is what you were meant for, Sebastien. I'm so proud of you."

His father followed behind his wife. While she dabbed her proud eyes with a handkerchief, Guy shook my hand and told me, "Thank you, Annaliese. My son couldn't have chosen better."

I cried in the manager's office for ten minutes, so happy that his parents approve of me—and *him*. I'm not being hidden anymore. I'm another member of

Sebastien's family, and after all those years with Eric… it's all I wanted. It doesn't matter how our relationship began. We're together now… we're *happy* now… and it's even better that Eric has finally decided to back off. For all of his threats about what he would do to the man who replaced him in my life, as soon as he confronted me only to have Sebastien confront him, he's all but disappeared.

Well. *No.* Eric has disappeared from my life. He hasn't stopped plotting against the King just like he threatened that night at Alexandre's party. In fact, he keeps trying to gather enough of the old guard together to push Dallas out of office completely. They're trying to use a clause in the Order of the Owed manifest that says that the King isn't exempt from the 'get married by thirty' rule. If Dallas Collins doesn't have a wife by next November, they'll push to have him replaced.

Sebastien's name has come up. He laughed, saying he'd rather slit his own throat than subject me to being the wife of the King, let alone take the position from his 'bro'. Especially since Dallas has taken the attempted coup to heart. He doesn't want to be King, but he doesn't want the old guard screwing things up again, either. So he's picking an Offering out now—his own marriage of convenience—and my husband has somehow earned himself a seat on Dallas's council, alongside Adrian and a few other Owed.

Alexandre is helping. So is their father; with Guy throwing his support behind Dallas, most of the Owed are staying out of the politics. Sebastien is stubbornly doing what he has to because he wants to keep me safe. Sure, he's loyal to his friends, but he hates that Eric is the one working behind the scenes to overthrow Dallas.

He wants to gut him. I thought he was kidding.

He wasn't.

And that's how I discovered that, since he joined the council, he's also taken over Dallas's role as enforcer. The second Eric does more than just run his mouth about betraying Dallas, he has the King's permission to take the sleazy lawyer out of the picture. For now, everything Eric and his compatriots are doing is technically legal, following the law, but the second it isn't…

I'm not sure how I feel about that. On the one hand, I never want to see Eric again. On the other, the idea of Sebastien being the one to eliminate him… my husband is a good man with a dark side. I'd hate to see it become even darker because of me.

The worst part is that I first thought Sebastien was kidding when he offered to take care of Eric for me. I'd laughed, told him I didn't need protecting.

My husband didn't laugh back. Instead, he kissed my temple before murmuring, "You have no idea how many men I would kill to keep what I have. I'm not letting anyone near you ever again."

But Eric is leaving me alone. He stopped harassing Miranda, too, and we only have a little more than eight weeks until the Claiming ceremony when Colton will have his hand branded by fire, the mark of the Owed ruining his palm, before he tells everyone gathered that he intends to take Miranda Crawford as his wife.

In fact, Sebastien told me that Eric actually dared to

show up to a council meeting with Cicely on his arm. They were presenting themselves as a unified front, and I really believed it was over. That Eric's cruelty might be focused on Dallas, but it's not me he's after anymore.

Too bad I was *wrong*.

TWENTY-FIVE
UNLOCKED

ANNALIESE

Sebastien got called into an emergency meeting at the Fortress tonight. It was Adrian who sent him a text, telling him he was needed to sit in on a discussion with him, Dallas, and Connor Heyward. The fact that Connor would be there made it impossible for Sebastien to refuse, choosing dinner with me over heading out to see his friends for Order business.

He offered to let me go with him. Connor's delicate wife, Haven, was just dropped off at Adrian's house so that she could stay with Loni and the Hellers' cats. I was invited to go hang with them, the third member in our Order trio until Dallas finally chooses his Offering—though, if it is a marriage of convenience and not a love match, there's a good chance Connor won't let Dallas's new wife anywhere near his—but I declined. I was happy to just stay home myself, get a little work done, maybe watch some TV while I wait for Sebastien to come home.

About half an hour after he left, he sent me a text:

HUBBY🤍

I don't think I'll be coming home soon.
Lock the door, love. I brought my keys.

Oh, Sebastien. After he proved how easy it was for him to break into my apartment, he has this fear that someone will do the same here. I tell him he's being silly. No one in Harmony Heights is dumb enough to go up against Sebastien Reynolds. Sure, my husband is loaded, but they're taunting a leather-wearing devil if they think they can rob him.

But if it makes him feel better, I'll do it. So I text him back that I'm on it before tossing my phone to the couch. I'm in the living room. Besides the bedroom, it's my favorite one in the house. Not only because it has a huge television and a comfy ass couch, but because this is the room where Sebastien and I first signed our contracts.

Humming to myself as I pad toward the front door, I freeze when I swear I hear something. It's a soft creek, followed by a pair of footsteps as though someone has just let themselves into the house.

Cold dread shivers up my spine.

"Hello?" It has to be my husband. Maybe the text was delayed because service in the Fortress can be shit sometimes, and he sent that before he turned around and came home for something. "Sebastien? Is that you?"

No answer.

I roll my eyes, chiding myself. It's nothing. I imagined it. Sebastien put the idea in my head when he told me to lock the door. There's no one here—

I step into the foyer and freeze.

Because that's Eric Ward standing there, the door closed behind him.

Oh, no… *oh, no*. It can't be. The salt-and-pepper hair… the shrewd and cold blue eyes… the suit that I've seen him wear a hundred times. This *scene* has played out a hundred times. Jonathan warning me that the master was home, and how he expected me to be standing in the front room, hair perfect, dress perfect, makeup perfect, ready to do whatever it was he expected of his mistress.

Only I'm not his mistress. I'm Sebastien Reynold's wife.

And I'm in fucking trouble.

"What are you… how… how did you get in here?"

Eric looks insulted by the question. Duh. I know exactly how he got into my home, and his answer confirms it: "Silly girl. You didn't lock the door."

He crosses his arms over his chest. His cruel gaze sweeps over me, lips curving in distaste when he takes in my appearance. My bare legs, the oversized shirt that I stole from Sebastien's closet after we had a before-dinner quickie, my sex-fluffed hair wild and down since I had no plans of leaving the house.

Something ugly sparks in his eyes.

My stomach revolts. Something ugly. Something hate-filled.

And Eric is looking at *me* like that.

I take a step back. I don't know exactly where I'm going, but *away* seems like a pretty good idea even as I whisper, "You shouldn't be here."

He raises a brow. "Why not? It used to be our routine. Me coming home to you or the both of us leaving the office together." His lips twitch, then curve into a mocking smile. "Now you're playing house with the Reynolds boy."

My fingers curl at my sides. *Boy*. Sebastien is twenty-nine. In the hierarchy of the Order, his name puts him on top of Eric. He's my *husband…*

I swallow, wrapping my arms under my boobs, hugging myself. "Eric. You need to leave. Please."

He steps closer. "No. I don't think I will."

I back up. "Sebastien will come home soon—"

"*Good.*" He says the single syllable just the way that my husband does. But then Eric smiles, sharp and deranged, and I have to bite back my moan of fright. "I want him to see you choose me. And if you don't… I told you, sweetheart. I told you what would happen if you chose anyone else. Annul your marriage. Claim fraud. I don't care. You're coming home with me or else…"

My stomach drops to my feet as his threat trails off. I don't have my phone. I don't have *anything*. It's just me and Eric, and the insane gleam in his eyes.

"But why?" I choke out. "You have Cicely!"

"Why? Because I miss you." Eric steps closer, clearly stalking me. "I *love* you."

I stare at him. Love me? Not the fuck he doesn't.

"You're incapable of love," I whisper. "You just want to own me."

His smile widens. Another step. "I *do* own you."

I flinch.

"You've had your fun," he tells me, voice tightening. "But it's over. I didn't put five years into molding you, shaping you, creating the perfect mistress just to see you with another man. Not my Annaliese."

I'm an idiot. As he moved closer, I stopped matching him step for step. Suddenly, he's right there, within arm's reach. It's too late to do anything but stand my ground, which is what I do as I tell him plainly, "But I'm not yours. I belong to Sebastien."

I love *Sebastien.*

Oh, Eric doesn't like hearing that. His face twists into an expression of fury, and I'm so stunned that he dropped his mask that I don't protect myself as he slaps me. It's open-handed, flat across my left cheek. The sound cracks through the entire foyer as my head snaps sideways. Even worse, the momentum knocks me to my knees as my cheek burns.

Before I can even let out a soft cry of pain and fear, Eric lunges down. His arms wrap around me, lifting me easily up off of the floor. I want to struggle out of his sudden hug, but my ear is ringing. He clapped that, too, in his strike, and I'm too dazed to do anything but let him drag me down the hall.

Down the hall and toward the stairs that lead up to the second floor where our bedroom is.

The way he's groping me, the way he's dragging

me… I suddenly know exactly what Eric means when he says that he'll show Sebastien I chose him. If my husband comes home, finding me and my former lover in bed together… if Eric has me under him in mine and Sebastien's marriage bed, no matter how he got me there… I don't know if Sebastien can forgive me that. After all, we've only been married for two and a half months. I'd like to think that Sebastien would realize that I would never go back to Eric, but then I remember how the first time I fucked him, I did so to forget about Eric.

What if Sebastien believes that I haven't?

No. I can't let him do this. I struggle, yelling 'stop', yelling 'no', but all Eric does is continue to manhandle me, maneuvering me up the stairs. Of course he figures out easily which room is the master bedroom. I don't even want to think how, but no matter how I try to go boneless so that he can't continue to carry me into the room, Eric is too strong. Too determined.

And I'm scared out of my fucking wits. Scared and angry. Scared and *furious*.

"Get the fuck off me!"

He spares a hand to pop me in the mouth again. I see stars. It was a lucky hit, shoving my nose up, making my eyes water even as he snaps, "My Annaliese doesn't curse. So maybe… maybe you're not mine anymore."

That's what I've been trying to tell him. "Get out," I repeat. "Before Sebastien comes home—"

"Oh, no. You don't get to send me away." He drops me. I hit the floor hard, but before I can crawl out of his way, his hands are around my throat. "You don't get to leave me."

I twist beneath his weight, panic clawing at my lungs. "Let… let go—"

He snarls, and I choke. He squeezes, and I start to buck underneath him.

"Eric…" I gasp out, clawing at whatever part of his wrist I can find. "I can't… what are you… *please…*"

"It's okay, sweetheart," he says, his voice suddenly so tender, I'm even more terrified than I was. "And when you stop breathing, you'll take your final swan dive."

What?

His grip tightens. Stars spark at the edge of my vision, the black creeping in as my airway continues to close.

Eric leans in, smiling like a man delivering a love confession. "You realized you couldn't spend your life with Reynolds. And I wouldn't have you back. So you killed yourself. Like Reese Collins. Like Sebastien's Julie."

No.

No.

His voice drops to a dangerous whisper. "In the Order, the only way out is death. Your boy threatened me with it. Well, who says it has to be mine?"

Something snaps inside me. Fight or die, Annaliese. Fight or give Eric the pleasure of disposing of you like so many other Order women.

Fight or—

Before I lose consciousness, I slam my knee upward with every ounce of desperation I have left. He wasn't expecting it. He must've thought I was already gone, but he underestimated me like he always does. *Good.* All I needed was one hit, and I get it as my knee collides hard between his legs. I aimed for his cock. After all, it's caused me more grief than it ever did pleasure.

Eric folds with a strangled sound, grip loosening enough that I can finally crawl out from under him. He's already fighting to get to his feet. I back up, looking at the window, knowing that if I can't get out of this, I'll be *tossed* out of it, my body left for Sebastien to find.

No. I finally got my happy-ever-after. I won't let Eric Ward fuck it up for me.

With the same rage flooding through me as the night I attacked that Used, all I want to do is hurt Eric. Because it *is* Eric, I want to hurt him badly. Spinning around, I dash over to the dresser.

The pocket knife that Sebastien gave me is in the place of honor on top of it. Without even thinking twice, I grab it. My hands are shaky. I don't drop it, though it takes more effort than it should to flip it open. But I do. I fucking do. I get the knife open just in time for Eric to grab my arm, whirling me around to face him.

His icy blue eyes are as murderous as I feel. "You worthless little—"

I stab him. In his neck. In his throat. In his cheek. I keep shoving the blade into whatever part of him I can find as he howls, trying to cover the stab wounds as I make them. Blood spurts hot across my hand. I ignore it. I ignore *him*. I just keep stabbing with Sebastien's knife, and when Eric drops to the floor, I climb on top of him and jab the knife over and over again into his chest.

Screaming, sobbing, shaking… I don't stop until he stops fighting back.

Until he stops moving.

Until the howls in my head go silent.

Until everything inside me finally breaks…

Finally, I drop the knife. My knees give out at last, and I collapse next to Eric's corpse, curling up into the fetal position, sobbing so hard my ribs ache. The tears don't last. The gasps replace them until all that's left are my pitiful cries as I stay on the floor.

And that's when I hear my husband's voice calling my name, and I can't even bring myself to answer him.

TWENTY-SIX

I LOVE YOU

SEBASTIEN

knew something was wrong the second I pulled into the driveway.

Dallas was crashing out. The pressure to find the perfect Offering was getting to him. Adrian has been doing background checks on a few who might suit him, but Dallas has a reason why he can't marry each one. He refuses to step down as King, either, which I get. To do that would mean that his old man was right. That Dallas wasn't cut out to lead the Order. He'll Claim an Offering at random before he ever lets Jack Collins into his head like that.

The problem is his mom. Therese Collins. After losing Lucy the way he did, he's convinced that anyone who is tied to him will suffer their fates. Even if it's just a marriage in name only—like mine was supposed to be before I set Annaliese straight—it doesn't matter. Dallas kills in the name of the Order, but he refuses to be responsible for another woman losing her life... no matter how she does... because she got involved with him.

His mother was murdered by his father so that the old King could have his fun with the Used without allowing Reese Collins to do the same. Lucy... she's lost to him, something the three of us know. Because Adrian, Connor, and I have now settled down, finding the woman that's perfect for us, we understand that Dallas had his and lost her.

But the old guard keep pushing, and August is approaching. Dallas just has to be married by his thirtieth birthday; unlike the other members, he doesn't have to take part of the Claiming ceremony in August mainly because, as King, he's the one presiding over it. Still. We've already come so far, made so many good changes with Dallas in charge. Plus, I don't want to be King. If I wasn't married, I wouldn't have to worry about my name being thrown into the ring for succession. However, I am, so I have a vested interest in keeping Dallas in the top office besides him being one of my best bros.

So when he called a meeting of his inner circle—with me, Adrian, and Connor—I knew I had to go. I offered to bring my wife to Adrian's house so that she could spend time with Haven and Loni, but I wasn't surprised when she declined. I'd just fucked her brains out when Dallas's message came through, and as hard as it was to leave my wife behind when she looked like she was ready for round two before we ate dinner, I went.

She should've been fine. I warned her to lock the

door because I'd be gone longer than I thought, and she seems to think that danger is for other people. Sometimes her naiveté is charming; at others, I want to roll her up in bubble wrap to keep her safe.

But then I pulled up into the drive, parking my bike next to a silver BMW that didn't belong. Someone had left the car behind Annaliese's coupe. While my Porsche is in the attached garage, my wife prefers to leave her car out in the driveway. I never argued. If it made her happy, then it made her happy, and I got into the habit of leaving my bike next to her car.

That's Annaliese's. Whose is that?

I know. I'm a goddamn mechanic. I know exactly how much a car like that costs, and it's out of the Crawfords' comfortable middle-class budget. Besides, Miranda is using a beater before she gets her license, so it's definitely not Annaliese's sister. It's not my brother or my parents.

But someone *is* here, and I think I know—and if I'm right? Tossing my helmet to the asphalt to get rid of some extra weight, I hop off my bike and book it toward the front door.

I grab the knob. Jerk it. Shove the door open.

Because it's unlocked. Annaliese texted me back an hour ago, telling me that she would lock it, but there's a car out front, and the door isn't locked.

I storm into the house. "Annaliese?"

No answer. Jogging now, I check every room on the ground floor. The television is on. Annaliese's blanket is on the couch, her phone next to it. At one point tonight, she was curled up, watching TV, but she's not now.

Where is she?

I head to the stairs. Taking them two at a time, I burst out into the hall before marching into the bedroom.

My stomach had already plummeted the second I realized the door was open. Now? I nearly hurl, and it has nothing to do with the blood splashed everywhere or the state of the dead body on the carpet.

For a quick second, I recognize the tortured death mask that once was Eric Ward. He's on his back, so many holes in him, he's like fucking Swiss cheese. His eyes are open, blood spattered everywhere. My blood-coated pocket knife is next to his ear, the weapon of his destruction.

No. I'm wrong. The weapon of his destruction is the bloody brunette beauty curled up on her side, two feet from the dead man.

My heart lodges in my throat. In a rough voice, I call my wife's name. "Annaliese."

She doesn't turn.

I shake. *Tremble.* The idea that he might've hurt her so badly that she didn't survive him after she killed him… bile seeps past the lump in my throat. I swallow it back, then bolt over to her side.

"Annaliese!" I drop down, gathering her up in my arms when I see that her eyes are open. Wide. Staring… but she's not dead. She's breathing roughly, moaning under her breath, body shaking as bad as mine… but she's *not dead.* "Oh, love… what did he do to you?"

Later, I'll tell myself it was the soft way I uttered her nickname that brought her back to me. She blinks, once, twice, then jolts. Next thing I know, she's clutching me, pulling me to her, climbing into my lap, her hands on my face.

Tears streak hers. Her neck… *fuck*. Her neck is ringed with red, purple bruises already blooming.

What did this fucker do? Strangle her?

As she gazes up at me in obvious panic, my wife tries to speak, words tumbling out in broken pieces as she says, "Eric… he broke in… he grabbed me… he tried to, said he would… he would—"

I hold her close. "It's okay." She's digging her fingers into my jaw, but I refuse to look away from her pleading brown eyes. She's scared, but she's also worried about how I'll react.

She doesn't have to be.

Lifting her up in my arms, I push myself to my feet, then set her on the edge of our bed. I don't look at Eric again. I've seen all I need to, and if I focus on that prick instead of my wife, I'll probably freak her out with the things I'll do to desecrate that monster.

Fuck Eric Ward. Annaliese needs me. She needs her husband.

"You're safe," I tell her, voice low, trying to ground her, ripping her out of her panic. "You're safe now, love. I'm here."

Her breath hitches. "I didn't know what else to do. He was going to open the window… I didn't—"

"I know," I say. "I know exactly what happened. And you didn't do a fucking thing wrong."

It's all in the bruises around her neck. In how Eric Ward drove to my house—*our* house—and let himself in; I one hundred percent believe that Annaliese wouldn't have. In how he's in our bedroom, my wife half-dressed, her fear so thick, it nearly covers up the coppery stink of blood.

She protected herself. It doesn't matter what from. She doesn't need to tell me, doesn't need to explain herself. Hearing her say 'window' like that... I know exactly what Eric's plan was.

And my amazing fucking wife stopped him.

Crouching down in front of her, I brush my thumb over her cheek, wiping away some of the blood that I really hope isn't hers. It's on her face, my old t-shirt, her injured neck, her hands...

I take one, pressing a kiss to the top of it. "Listen to me. Why don't you go and wash your hands off, love? Then, when I get back, we'll sleep in one of the guest rooms. Or, fuck it, a hotel. Wherever you want to go... we'll go."

She blinks up at me, still frightened. "When you get back... where are you going, Sebastien?"

I stand up, giving her one of my charming smiles. "To get a shovel."

Her lips part, but no sound comes out. She just folds in on herself, then nods. "Okay. I... I need a shower. I want to wash him off of me."

"Don't come out until I'm back. Yeah?"

She nods again, and because I can tell that Annaliese needs it, I kiss her, blood and all.

Then I jog downstairs, nearly kicking myself to see that my dumb ass left the front door wide open. I shove it closed, making a mental note to search Ward for his keys so that I can get rid of his car, then head to the attached garage. I grab a shovel, snorting to see that it isn't even dusty. I've helped Dallas bury worse things than this when he's called me up and asked.

When I come back upstairs, Annaliese is still sitting on the bed, staring at her hands like they belong to someone else.

I drop the shovel to the floor, moving purposely toward her. "I got you, love."

Slipping my hands beneath her arms, I lift her gently. She's shaking so hard I feel it down to my bones. I murmur soft assurances to my wife as I carry her into the bathroom.

I undress her slowly. There's no lust, no need, just reverence for this woman I adore, and unadulterated fury at the marks on her skin. Her cheek is bruising. Her neck is swollen. There's a series of scratches on her hip, and her jagged, broken nails a memento of how hard she fought to save her own life.

Eric Ward is lucky he's dead. I finally understand how satisfied Adrian was to gun Desmond down, and how he'd do it again in a heartbeat. If I could resurrect Ward myself, then send him back to Hell, I would.

But I didn't. My fierce little event planner did, and I'll spend the rest of my goddamn life making it up to her that she had to.

If I'd been here—

I shake my head. No. I can't think like that. I wasn't here, but Annaliese is okay, and next time? I *will* be here.

For now, I focus on getting her clean. Still holding tightly to her, I spare a hand to turn on the shower spray.

Once it's at the perfect temp for her, I help Annaliese climb in.

Her breath stutters. "I'm sorry—"

"Don't." My voice cracks like a whip before I make myself gentle it. "Don't ever apologize for surviving. You hear me?"

She sniffles, then nods, and all I can do is join her in the shower, leather jacket, boots, and all. She needs me, and I'm here now, and if all I can do is rinse the blood off of her, then get rid of the mess in our room… that's exactly what I'll do.

No. That's not *all* I can do.

"I'm sorry," I whisper, using the washcloth I grabbed to start washing away the blood. "I should've saved you."

She shakes her head weakly. "Babe… you did. It wasn't even just the knife… if I didn't have you to think of… he wanted you to come home and find me on the back lawn just like Julie. I couldn't do that to you. I couldn't let you lose someone else."

My heart fucking breaks to hear that. Another lump lodges in my throat, and I turn my attention to my wife. I cup her cheek, kiss her forehead… her wet hair… the bruises on her throat. And then I push the washcloth into her hand.

"Stay here. Let the water run. Scrub if you can. I'll come back for you."

She nods, and though it's so damn difficult to walk away from her, I absolutely refuse to let her return to the bedroom and see Eric Ward still lying there.

So I grab a towel, swiping it over my face. Shucking

my jacket, my shirt, my pants, I get naked in the bedroom, then quickly put on a change of dry clothes. Ruffling through his suit pants, I take out his phone, his wallet, and his keys. The phone will be destroyed. The keys will help me disappear his car. The wallet will end up in a dump somewhere.

Returning to my wet pants, I yank out my own phone. Grateful it's waterproof, I tap a quick message to Dallas.

> Need clean-up. My place. EW. Calling in my blood oath.

Barely a minute later, Dallas sends me a thumb's up, and I smile.

It's good being bros with the King. I don't even have to explain why I need clean-up. I probably didn't even have to remind Dallas that I have a blood oath. Eric deserved to die, and if I say so, Dallas will agree.

From his days as an enforcer, he has connections when it comes to clean-up. I'll shuffle Annaliese out of our room once her shower is done, leaving Dallas's crew to take care of the blood in here. As for Eric…

I drag his heavy ass corpse over to the window he planned to toss my wife out of. Throwing open the glass, I punch the screen out. Once it's clear, I heft him up, then drop him down to the ground below. I toss the shovel after him. Once I have Annaliese settled down, I'll bury the fucker.

It's the least I can do.

Annaliese is sitting on the shower floor when I return, arms wrapped around her knees, water still pouring over her. Her brown eyes have gone back to glassy, her lips trembling, though I'm not sure if it's because the water's cold now, or because she's still processing her first murder.

She's alive, though, and that's all that matters.

For the second time tonight, I climb into the shower. Dropping low, I go to my knees, then fall back on my ass. I pull her into my lap, my recent change of clothes already soaked.

She buries her face in my chest, fingers twisting in my shirt like she's anchoring herself to me.

I cup her head, holding her close.

"This really was a marriage of inconvenience, wasn't it?" she murmurs against my pec, voice small, broken, but just as prim as it was when she walked into my living room, binder in her hand, determined to get me to agree to a year.

I huff out a dark laugh, stroking her wet hair. "What do you mean?"

"Well, you just had to dispose of a body for me."

"Oh, love…" Pulling away from her, I tip her chin up, forcing her to meet my eyes. "You know damn well that wasn't my first."

She blinks. I can see it in her expression. She didn't *know*… she guessed, of course, and now she has confirmation. I wait to see if her body language changes. If fear will return to her eyes the same way that Eric Ward left it there earlier.

I hold my breath, then add, "And I'd dispose of a hundred bodies if I had to for you."

A weak, incredulous sound escapes her throat. My heart jumps. I know that sound. It's not because she's frightened. It's more like she doesn't believe I could love her enough to actually do that.

"I'm serious," I insist. "You've met Adrian. That man knows where all the bodies are in Harmony Heights, figuratively *and* literally. And Dallas… before he was King, he was an enforcer. He's responsible for his fair share."

Her brows lift slowly. Hesitantly. "And you?"

"I hated being called in for Order jobs," I admit. "But when one of my brothers needs backup, I'll answer the phone every damn time."

She swallows.

"And you," I add softly, "could've called me. I hope you know that there isn't anything I won't do for you, Annaliese."

She looks down into our laps. With a jerk, I think she just realized that she's completely naked and I… I'm not. With a quick shake of her head, sending water droplets everywhere, she tells me, "I didn't know what to do when he let himself in… or after I stabbed him and stabbed him and just… I couldn't fucking *stop*."

"No binder for first-degree murder?" I tease gently.

"That was self-defense," she whispers as the shower spray falls around us.

"Exactly." I smile, feeling a fierce wave of pride. "You know it. I know it. So don't even think about it. He's not worth a second of your pity."

Her head snaps up. A hint of fury—real and bright—shines through her expression. At the same time, relief shudders through me because *yes*.

That's my girl. My *wife*. She's not broken. No ruined. Okay, maybe she's in shock, but she'll be fine.

Because she's *mine*.

I bury my hands in the soaked strands, angling her head up so that I can kiss her. We get water in our mouths at the same time, but I couldn't care less. Annaliese is responding. She's kissing me back. She's climbing even further into my lap, clinging to me before she pulls back enough so that she can whisper against my lips:

"He wanted me to choose him. To annul our marriage, claim fraud or some shit. I told him to get the fuck off of me when he grabbed my arm." A whisper of a laugh. "He didn't like that I cursed at him. He liked it even less that I told him that I belonged to you."

I shut my eyes, jaw clenching. It doesn't matter. I can still see the ring around her neck. "That's why he… yeah. I figured it was something like that."

Her hands slide up my chest, tentative but sure. "I didn't even get the chance to tell him that I love you."

My heart fucking *stops*. A second later, my eyes pop open.

Her smile could have me killing a *thousand* men for her.

"What did you say?"

She scoots closer to me, legs wrapping around my waist as she looks me dead in the face. "That I love you."

It's my turn to drop my head as I bury my face in her tits. "Fucking *finally*."

And when she lowers her hands, reaching for my button to help me get out of my wet jeans so that she can prove to me just how much she loves me, I let her do that, too.

I'll let her do *anything*.

EPILOGUE

TWO MONTHS LATER

ANNALIESE

The bonfire crackles, flames licking at the stone wall surrounding the base before rising up, billowing in the August breeze. It carries the stink of burned skin with it. You'd think that, after more than a half an hour of watching new members get branded-in and some of the Used choosing the fire in front of the crowd, I'd have grown nose-blind to it.

Nope. It had only gotten worse to the point that Sebastien waited until Colton Claimed Miranda—my baby sister accepting his Claim—before he laced his fingers with mine, tugging on my hand, and leading me away from the crowd gathered around to watch the Claiming ceremony.

They're only eighteen. Miranda already told me that she and Colt are planning a long engagement. He wants to attend the Order University, and as his new fiancée, she's going to be attending the same school, free of charge. They'll plan their wedding after they graduate, well before Colt turns thirty.

Or, rather, *I'll* plan it. My type-A personality nudged me to nag Miranda for a season at least. I've blocked off the autumn five years from now so that I don't accidentally book another party. Oh, no. I'll give Miranda and Colton the wedding they deserve.

Just like I planned the best wedding for my husband and me.

I liked the intimacy of us getting married in St. Catherine's with only our family there to see us exchange vows in front of Father Francis. The reception at Sebastien's favorite café was perfect, even if that bitchy waitress purposely spilled the glass of red wine all over my dress.

Because she did. Sebastien totally confirmed it, and after that, we haven't gone back yet.

And, true, I might've thought it was a fake marriage then, but I know better now. I still wouldn't change a thing about our union, though I notice Sebastien watching me curiously out of the side of his eye as he guides me away from the assembled crowd.

"What?" I ask.

"Just wondering something."

"Yeah? What's that?"

One hand is wrapped around my shoulders. It's August in Harmony Heights, and that means it's really, really hot. Kind of swampy really. I know how much my husband likes it when I dress down—as though I'm shaking off the last remnants of Eric's training—but I chose to wear a thin-strapped, lightweight sundress to my sister's Claiming ceremony. I paired it with a pair of high-heeled sandals, bringing me a little closer in height to Sebastien. Instead of being tucked under his arm, I'm snuggled up against him, resting my head on the edge of his shoulder.

He's not wearing his road jacket. It's near. He left it in the car, but he pointed out that, if I'm dressing up for the occasion, he might as well do the same to support his sister-in-law. I nearly started to drool when he revealed the crisp light pink polo he has on over his dark denim jeans. He managed to match his shirt to my dress perfectly, and if I can't wait to peel it off of him and bury my face in his chest… that's okay.

He is my husband, after all.

I smile up at him.

Sebastien nearly misses a step before righting himself, squeezing me closer to him. "Fuck me, love. One smile from you and I nearly fell flat on my face. I gotta be more careful."

I wrap my arm around his lower back. "It's okay. I've got you."

He drops a kiss to the top of my head. "I know. And that's what has me thinking… do you regret not getting to go through this?"

"Through what?"

"The whole Claiming bullshit. I could go in front of Dallas and the others and tell 'em that you're mine. Claim you for real. Let all of Harmony Heights know that you're the Offering for me."

He's already done that. In a million small ways since I was panicked and desperate enough to walk around the Court, asking whoever would listen if they would marry me, Sebastien Reynolds has proven that he *chose* me. That he *loves* me.

"I'm your wife."

"You are," he agrees readily.

"And didn't you tell…" I hesitate. It's been two months, and I still stumble a little whenever I think of the prick that I wasted so many years with. "…*Eric* that you have a blood oath?"

"I bled all over that fucking piece of paper." He turns his hand over so that we both can look at his brand—his brand, and the thin pink scar that bisects part of it. "I was a little eager," he admits with a low chuckle. "Cut myself more than I meant to, but I Claimed you in front of Dallas that day. It was sealed by the King. You were considered mine in the eyes of the Order from that moment on."

That's what I thought. "We had our wedding. We've been married since the end of March. Five months now, babe… I don't think I can be any more Claimed than that."

"I was hoping you'd say that." He gives me another squeeze. "Hey. Come with me to the car? I have something in my jacket pocket I want to give you."

When I first married Sebastien, prepared to keep him at a distance, determined to do whatever it took to refrain from falling for him, I would've refused. I didn't want his gifts. I stubbornly ignored any clue that he might've had his own motives for agreeing so easily to my 'marriage of convenience' idea.

I blamed it on sex, on how I tried to use him to forget Eric only to realize that Sebastien Reynolds is unforgettable. I blamed it on some need of his to play hero to a woman in trouble. I blamed it on anything and everything except the very clear reality that I was drawn to him, he was drawn to me, and in the almost year since I spotted him alone in the Last Prayer, I've understood that he's the only one for me.

Eric tried to mold me into the perfect mistress. He thought that that was all I was good for. The perfect makeup, the perfect hair, the perfect outfits… he turned Annaliese Crawford into his private plaything. For too long, I let him, and by the time I met Sebastien that first time, I didn't even know who I was anymore.

I have my husband to thank for helping me regain my sense of self. Sometimes I want to wear sundresses. Sometimes I'll trade them for a t-shirt and cut-offs. Maybe one day I'll twist my hair up in a chignon. Another, I'll throw my hair into a messy bun, sticking a pencil in it so that it's within reach while I'm planning another event.

He encourages me to work while also reminding me that, if I don't want to, I don't have to. He has more than enough money to support us both, but like how I did everything I could to turn Reynolds Garage into a reality, my husband is my biggest cheerleader when it comes to building up my own business.

I'm the premier event planner in Harmony Heights these days. The title used to belong to Mom, but with both of her daughters either engaged or married into the Order, she and Dad have taken a step back from the secret society.

I asked Sebastien if he wanted to do the same. As my husband is fond of saying: fuck the Order. With Eric dead and Miranda Claimed, I'd be happy to never have anything to do with the Order of the Owed ever again.

But Sebastien… as long as his closest friends are running the show, he'll be involved. I get that. His loyalty to them is one of the things that made me realize that there's so much more to him than his pretty face, charming yet cocky attitude, and the dark side he can't quite hide.

If he loves you, you're golden.

If you cross him, you're dead.

If you marry him, you better be prepared for forever because that's all he can offer—and I'm the luckiest woman in Harmony Heights because he chose to marry *me*.

I wear the remains of the contract I once drafted in the pendant hanging off the chain he placed around my neck. Even if either of us was still trying to follow any of its points, there's only one that Sebastien cares about: the termination of the year term to our marriage of convenience.

This agreement does not constitute a lifelong marital expecta-tion unless mutually renegotiated…

If you ask my husband, we 'mutually renegotiated' our marriage the night up in the mountains, when he told me he loved me, when he gave me that necklace, and when he fucked me up against a tree after chasing me for the first time.

Yes. The *first* time. I unlocked a kink in my husband that even Sebastien didn't know he had, and I realized that running from Sebastien, knowing that he'll forever chase me… it does it for me, too.

He knew we were made for more than a year. Me? When the first thing he said after discovering that I'd stabbed Eric to death was to tell me to wash my hands while he went and grabbed a shovel—after he made sure that I was okay—I knew that I'd be a fool to ever let him go.

So I haven't. I won't. And if he wants to give me a gift, I'll thank him the best way I know how: by trading my sandals for running shoes and begging for a five-minute head start before I take off into the woods behind our house.

That'll be later, though. For now? I walk with Sebastien over to his Porsche. He positions me outside the passenger door, then goes around to his side. His jacket is pooled on the driver's seat. After letting himself into the car, he grabs something from the inside of his jacket before closing the door.

I can't see what it is. The reason for that is simple. When Sebastien joins me, his hand is fisted around a small black jewelry box.

He hands it to me. "For you."

I take it. "What is it?"

"Open it, love." Sebastien's eyes sparkle, the same mischievous look I fell in love with twisting his features.

I do. Popping open the lid, I see a thin ring. The

outside is gold, like the ring I'm currently wearing. The inner part shines like diamonds.

"It's a ring."

"Every Offering who gets given to an Owed wears the stock standard band. But my wife? She deserves a wedding band as unique as she is."

"It's beautiful."

"It's ashes."

That's how he had my pendant made. But wait—

"How? I thought you used the ashes from the contracts to make my necklace." They don't look the same. There are small black specks that stand out on the pendant. In the light of the setting sun, the ring glimmers and gleams. "Are you sure this is part of the set?"

"It's not those kind of ashes, love. The jeweler I commissioned to make the ring is a pro when it comes to cremation rings."

Cremation…

Oh.

Oh.

"I thought you…" I lower my voice. "…*buried* him."

Sebastien cups the back of my neck, trailing his fingers along the side of it. "I did. But I know better than anyone that no secrets stay hidden in Harmony Heights. Bodies don't stay buried. Dallas is the King today, but there are plenty of pricks just itching to knock the crown off his head. Leaving him to rot in the ground seemed good enough to me, but Adrian—"

I should've known. Adrian Heller, I've learned, is the brains of the Order these days. "He thought it would be better to get rid of the body entirely?"

He nods. "Nicky Mathers runs the funeral home. He has connections everywhere in the biz, including a crematorium. For the right price, he'll toss a body in the furnace, no questions asked. I asked for enough of Ward's remains to have this made for you."

My husband had a wedding ring made for me with the ashes of my former lover. "Um. Why?"

His lips curve into a ruthless smile. "It's a reminder."

"Of what?"

"Of what will happen to anyone who thinks they can come between me and my wife. Every time you see it sparkle, just know that there isn't anything you can do that will get me to stop loving you. Kill a guy? I'll bury him. Run away? You fucking know I'll be at your heels. Try to leave? Good luck, love, because I still have the tracker app on your phone. You picked me, Annaliese. Now you're stuck with me. You could've had any man in the Order begging at your feet"—and to prove it, my husband lowers himself down to his knees, his palms a possessive brand on my hips as he tethers me to him—"but this is where I belong and I ain't going anywhere."

Sebastien Reynolds is the most fascinating man I've ever met. On the outside, he's pretty and charming, the sort of guy you'll fling your panties at if he so much as smiles your way. Not even the small imperfections to his beautiful face warn you what's really under his skin. They should. A man who had his nose broken twice in the same year, leading to an adorable, crooked slant in the slope, or a man who just dodged getting his eye taken out in a knife fight, the inch-long scar over it a reminder of how reckless he can be... a man who hides

his dark side with a wink and a dimple in his cheek…
he's beautifully broken, another casualty of the Order
of the Owed, but he's *mine*.

I slip the ring on my finger, adding it to the ring he
gave me during our wedding.

Letting the empty jewelry box fall to the asphalt of
the parking lot, I cup Sebastien's jaw. One firm tug and I
get him to unfold his big body, rising up to his feet again
before I go up on my tiptoes, demanding he kiss me.

He does. Clutching me to him, his fingers threading
through my hair as he arches my back so that he can kiss
me deeper, I surrender to my husband's hunger,
enjoying every stroke of his tongue, every nibble on my
bottom lip.

By the time he finally pulls away, I want to shove
him into the driver's seat and tell him to take me home.
I'm sure the Claiming ceremony is over by now.
Miranda will be going out with Colton to celebrate, and
I won't mind spending some quality time with my
husband.

Sebastien takes my left hand, kissing my palm. I'm
thinking he knows exactly what *I'm* thinking when the
lusty look on his pretty face switches to one of curious
concern in a heartbeat.

"Dallas?" he calls out.

I glance over my shoulder. I know that Dallas Collins
is one of Sebastien's long-time friends. He's still the
King, the head of the Order, and I'm still a little wary
when he's around. Sebastien promises that Dallas is
nothing like his father. I want to believe that. Years of
brainwashing courtesy of Eric means that I'm trying,

but it might take me a little longer to think of him as 'Dallas' and not the most powerful man in Harmony Heights.

Not Sebastien. He jokes with the King, goes out for drinks with him, invited him to our wedding, and makes comments that would have any other Owed being booted from the Order.

Now, though? As Dallas comes stalking away from the crowd, the King leaving the ceremony without any sort of entourage or hangers-on, even I can tell that something… something's not right.

He had to attend. That's part of the job, I guess. Looking like he'd rather be anywhere else, he presided over the ceremony. It must be over now if he's heading for his nondescript black coupe, but the way his eyes look wild, his phone clutched tightly in his hand… I wouldn't be surprised if he got a call and needed to run.

It's possible. It's also not my business, and I move closer to Sebastien, letting Dallas pass us by without a word.

I do.

My husband doesn't.

Wrapping his arm around me as though he can't resist having his hands on me at any given moment, he raises his voice. "Dal? Hey, Dallas? You okay?"

Dallas Collins stops short, head snapping our way.

I gulp.

Sebastien's fingers dig into my side. "Bro? You good?"

"Uh. Yeah." Liar. Because of his friendship with Sebastien, I've gotten to know Dallas a bit, and even I can tell he's full of it. As though he can sense me looking at him, he spares me a quick glance. "Hey, Annaliese. Tell your sister congratulations from me. Bas? Look, I've gotta go. I..." He runs his fingers through his hair. A muscle jerks in his cheek. "Fuck. Where's Adrian? I need to talk to Adrian."

"I don't know," says Sebastien. "I didn't think he would come to the ceremony. Maybe he's at home with Loni."

"Yeah. Sounds about right. I'll have to try him there. Thanks."

"No problem. You need anything, you can come to me. You know that, Dal. Right?"

He nods absently. "Course I do. It's just... it's fine." Rubbing his thumb along the black spade tattoo on the side of his neck, Dallas mutters, "It better fucking be."

Then, with a quick nod, he keeps on going, heading for his car.

I look up at my husband. "What's that about?"

Sebastien frowns, eyes following Dallas as he makes it to his car, jerking the door open and slipping inside. "I'm not sure. But it's okay. I'll call Adrian later and find out."

"You're a good friend, babe," I tell him, patting his chest.

Turning away from Dallas, he peers down at me. "What about 'husband'?"

I lay my hand over his heart. "The fucking best."

He laughs. "Shit. I'm such a bad influence on you, love. You never cursed until you met me."

"Not quite. I never cursed where one of the Owed

could hear me and judge me," I point out. "But then I finally met one who was the least judgmental asshole I've ever met in my life. Plus, he curses like a sailor. It's shocking." I snuggle into him again. "I like it."

"I'm still an asshole, though."

That's what he thinks. I disagree, but while I'm working on unraveling years of brainwashing of my own, Sebastien is doing the same. Good thing we have each other to escape the complete hold the Order has on us…

"Yeah, but you're *my* asshole."

"That's all I've ever wanted to be."

"An asshole?" I tease.

"No, love. *Yours*."

I turn around, moving my arms so that I can throw them around his neck. "For a year?"

His eyes flash even though he knows I'm teasing. "Forever."

I grin. "Just checking, babe. Just checking."

was there, or what I was doing, but it doesn't matter. My husband swears that he won't leave my side during my recovery.

That we can start over as we both heal.

He wants a second chance at having a wife. I won't say no to Dallas being my husband…

I just wish I *remembered* him.

DALLAS

Lucy Wright.

My biggest regret.

I would've given up anything for her, even my future as the head of the Order of the Owed. But when she rejected my proposal to protect me, I let her walk away. She married another Owed because my father insisted on it and I… I couldn't stop her. After that, it was easy for her to leave Harmony Heights.

To leave *me*.

Five years later, I'm finally about to move on myself. I have an Offering all lined up ahead of my thirtieth birthday, plus a wedding to plan—and that's when I get the call.

Lucy has been hurt. There's been an accident.

She needs me.

Only… she doesn't remember me. She doesn't remember *anything*. The accident left her with a hole in her memory, and I'm ruthless enough to fill it.

Because Lucy? She's my wife now, no wedding required.

* *Husband Who* is a dual-POV dark romance that finished **The Order of the Owed** trilogy, though there is one more book to tie-in to the series… and if you keep reading/clicking/scrolling, you'll get a sneak peek at it.

KEEP IN TOUCH

Stay tuned for what's coming up next! Follow me at any of these places—or sign up for my newsletter—for news, promotions, upcoming releases, and more:

CarinHart.com
Carin's Newsletter
Carin's Signed Book Store

facebook.com/carinhartbooks
amazon.com/author/carinhart
instagram.com/carinhartbooks

ALSO BY CARIN HART

Deal with the Devil series

No One Has To Know *standalone

Silhouette *standalone

He Sees You *standalone

The Wish List *standalone

The Devil's Bargain

The Devil's Bride *newsletter exclusive

The Devil's Playground

Dragonfly

Dance with the Devil

Ride with the Devil

Reed Twins

Close to Midnight

Really Should Stay

The Order of the Owed

Oubliette

Bloody Wedding

Inconvenient Marriage

Husband Who